PAST PRAISE FOR KATI

D1506401

For *Fields of Fig and Olive*

"A promising debut collection...Place and character are vividly evoked and the distinct flavor of a different culture well caught . . . "
—*Kirkus Reviews*

"It is difficult to heap enough praise on this author for her astonishingly vivid depictions of landscape and her ability to evoke spirit of place."
—*Seattle Times*

"The stories offer insights into the cloistered world of Arab women . . . how women find means of expressing themselves in severely circumscribed settings."
—*Los Angeles Times Book Review*

"In her Middle East world, sexual roles are sternly defined and jealously protected. But you don't have to be antediluvian to love the exotic settings and the humanity of the people in the 14 stories by Abdul-Baki. She has been blessed with the ability to make foreignness familiar."
—*Chicago Sun-Times*

"An excellent 'translator' of Middle East sensibilities, particularly those of women. Her politics are feminist, her theme is human ethics, and her writing is finely honed."
—*Ms. Magazine*

"This collection is truly a breakthrough in the world of Middle Eastern literature . . . written in English by someone who has a foot planted . . . in both the West and the Middle East."
—*Rocky Mountain News*

"She challenges Western ways of thinking about the nature and behavior of Arab women and men and causes us to question some of our assumptions about the intricate relationships of families and lovers."

—The Trenton *Times*

"Abdul-Baki's skillful and realistic presentation of characters, along with her masterly use of flashback and other narrative techniques, contributes to making her collection one of the most successful of its kind."

—World Literature Today

"She does what every Arab leader would like to do—humanize the people of Arab descent, something long overdue in American literature."

—Former U.S. Senator James G. Abouresk

_____

For *Tower of Dreams*

"She is a skilled craftsman . . . The spirit of place and landscape are palpable...she shines in her ability to penetrate the psyche of young Arab women."

—*Seattle Times*

_____

For *Ghost Songs*

"A tranquil and beautiful novel . . . it gradually heats up into a thorough and tense examination of culture mores—both Arabic and American—without ever becoming judgmental."

—Philadelphia City Paper

"She presents Arab culture . . . in narratives of exquisite technique, deep insights, and beautiful English . . . it bids fair to establish her as an Arab-American fiction writer worthy of wide recognition."

—World Literature Today

A

Marriage

in

Four

Seasons

A Marriage in Four Seasons

A Novel

KATHRYN K. ABDUL-BAKI

She Writes Press, a BookSparks imprint
A Division of SparkPointStudio, LLC.

Copyright © 2018 Kathryn K. Abdul-Baki

All rights reserved. No part of this publication may be reproduced, distributed, or transmitted in any form or by any means, including photocopying, recording, digital scanning, or other electronic or mechanical methods, without the prior written permission of the publisher, except in the case of brief quotations embodied in critical reviews and certain other noncommercial uses permitted by copyright law. For permission requests, please address She Writes Press.

Published 2018

Printed in the United States of America

ISBN: 978-1-63152-427-1 pbk
ISBN:. 978-1-63152-428-8 ebk
Library of Congress Control Number: 2018947282

For information, address:
She Writes Press
1569 Solano Ave #546
Berkeley, CA 94707

She Writes Press is a division of SparkPoint Studio, LLC.

All company and/or product names may be trade names, logos, trademarks, and/or registered trademarks and are the property of their respective owners.

This is a work of fiction. names, characters, places, and incidents either are the product of the author's imagination or are used fictitiously. Any resemblance to actual persons, living or dead, is entirely coincidental.

For Ahmad, with love,

who has always gallantly changed

our hotel room.

Prologue

Joy stumbled over the vacuum cleaner as she ran to the kitchen to find her phone. She had been vacuuming the living room when the pain shot through her, first in her back and then her abdomen, spearing her insides. Then the water started to spill onto the rug, a steady, ominous trickle.

She grabbed the phone and called Richard's cell number. His voicemail picked up.

"My water just broke," she said. "I think I'm in labor. Please call back. Hurry!"

The nurse in the doctor's office told her to call 911, her voice almost scolding Joy as if she should know better than to expect the doctor to be available for an emergency during lunch hour. Joy grabbed a kitchen towel and clenched it between her legs to halt the stream, then sat down and took deep breaths, as she had been shown in the birthing course. She put both of her hands on her round, taut stomach and held it tight, trying to stop whatever was going on from continuing. She felt something was about to rupture any second, and she had to hold it in.

This couldn't be happening now. They still had three months to go, and seven more classes before she'd be ready. She hadn't even packed her hospital bag. She had stayed home today, giving her students a study period instead of going into Manhattan because she had barely slept the night before. She should have known better than to start vacuuming.

Fingers trembling, she punched in 911.

A Marriage in Four Seasons

"I'm in labor," she blurted to the woman on the other end of the line, her voice shaking. "Please come get me. What? I'm Joy Amis. Yes. My address?" She gave her address as she started to cry. The woman listening to her paused until Joy composed herself enough to give her the address, her name again, and the name of her doctor. The woman seemed to take an inordinate amount of time to note down the information, methodically repeating Joy's name and the name of her street as though she had all day, and then she told Joy to lie down and stay comfortable until the ambulance came, but first to open the front door so the paramedics could get in.

The phone rang. "Honey, what's—?"

"I'm in labor, Rich."

"Now?"

Hearing the disbelief in his voice caused her to start to cry again. "My water just broke."

"Are you sure—" his voice still registered doubt.

"Of course, I'm sure!"

"Okay—I'm leaving right now, but it may take me an hour. Can you call the neighbor to stay with you until I get there?"

"I called 911. This can't be, Rich. It's not time."

"Honey, just lie down. Lift up your feet. Are you sure the ambulance is on its way?"

She nodded.

"Honey?"

"Yes," she said, "yes, it's coming. But they'll take me to the nearest hospital, not St. Agnes. I called Dr. Watson, but he's not there." She sucked in her breath. "I'm scared, Rich. It hurts. I know it's . . . I'm twenty-two weeks along today."

"Honey, you're going to be okay. I'm grabbing a cab now. Just stay on the line with me. Don't hang up. Can you get yourself a drink?"

"A drink?" she said, incredulous.

"Some water, honey. Maybe you're dehydrated."

Prologue

"My insides are being ripped out. I'm not thirsty!"

"I mean, maybe it'll—"

She barely heard him. "I know this isn't good. This is not good," she repeated slowly, as if explaining to the students in her class the meaning of going into labor in the sixth month. She could see their faces staring at her, some worried and others blank, trying to empathize with something so far removed from their daily concerns. She wondered whether the young man who periodically dozed through class would be jolted to attention by this news. They were supposed to have brought in their papers to read today—a critique of Nabokov's "The Visit to the Museum."

She could hear a siren. She got up off the chair and slowly walked to the window. A fire truck was coming down the road.

"They sent a fire truck," she muttered in wonder. She noticed a single branch of a blooming white cherry tree fluttering daintily in the breeze as the fire truck passed it. It was too early for the cherry trees to bloom.

"It's whatever is available," Richard said. "They'll have medics. I'm on my way. Just stay on the line with me, honey. I love you."

The pain had eased momentarily, and she pulled the cloth from between her legs. There was a pale, crimson stain on it. She planted her feet into the carpet, as though she could put a stop to the involuntary actions of her body just by willing it so. All that they had been planning for these past treasured months was slipping away. Her world was disintegrating, one cramp at a time.

The knocks on the door came just as the pain started up again.

Richard was beside her, wearing a blue mask and gown, bending to kiss her forehead. "My love," he was saying. "My beautiful Joy. It's going to be okay."

Again, she felt the shrieking pain in her belly. Another man was standing at the foot of the bed, holding up his hands, still dripping, as someone behind him tied his gown. Like Richard, the man was also wearing a blue cap. She barely recognized him without his thick, white hair.

"Dr. Watson?" she asked, trying to lift her head.

"Yes," Richard said, "he's here."

She heard the doctor talking with several people near him. She heard him say, "She's already dilated."

"No!" she snapped, looking up at Richard.

He rubbed her hand, glancing at the doctor and then at her, his eyes moist.

"No," she said again, angrily. "Leave my baby alone!"

The doctor came up to her and gently touched her forehead. "Mrs. Amis," he said steadily, father-like, "we're going to do everything we can. Take some deep breaths for me. That's right. Take another one." He looked at Richard. "It's fear," he said. Then he strode away, issuing orders.

She squeezed Richard's hand.

"Honey," he said, stroking her cheek with his other hand.

She started to cry, confused, but knowing that not even the doctor doing everything he could was going to work a miracle, now. She could feel her stomach tighten like a bullet, feel it again and again as she started to give in to the pain.

"Stephen, Stephen," she groaned, repeating the name that had become so dear to her.

Richard's face was next to hers, his eyes warm but his skin pale, trying to soothe her as he kissed her forehead again.

She shook her head. She didn't want to be touched. She screamed. That felt good. She screamed again, and that seemed to make everything stop, the stiffening of her stomach, the pain. She screamed until it all flowed into one long song, filling the roomful of strangers trying to take her baby away.

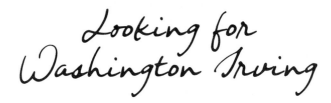

JOY

1

"I feel you're unhappy," Richard said, once they were in the room.

Joy unpacked her makeup case and headed for the bathroom to wash up after the afternoon drive to Granada. "Aren't you?"

"I thought it would be different, but it's not that bad."

She sighed. "I should have specified a room on an upper floor. It's the only way to get a view. Instead, I asked for a quiet room— and we get *this*. A view of the fire escape."

"It *is* quiet," Richard said, flopping down on the bed. "Don't worry about it, sweetheart."

This was just like Richard, always quick to settle, but it had never grated on her nerves so much as it had since the loss of the baby. She had a brief wave of extraordinary doubt that she and Richard were even meant to be together, but as always, she pushed it down.

They'd already had their first disappointment today. For

most of the drive from Seville, they'd enjoyed seeing the white towns of Andalusia across the countryside, cozily nestled at the foot of a hill and guarded by a towering Moorish fortress on the crest. Joy had feasted on what she had read about and imagined for so long—plains crisscrossed by glimmering olive trees, hilltop cathedrals, and ruined castles, fields of strawberries and buttery sunflowers. She'd devoured Washington Irving's travelogue, *Tales of the Alhambra*, when studying American romantic literature and had fantasized that a visit to Granada would be a life-changing experience. And, since arriving in Spain, she'd had a sense that something remarkable was about to unfold for Richard and her.

Irving's nearly two-hundred-year-old account of winding through hedges of aloes and fig trees to arrive at the gates of the fabled Spanish city amid a glorious sunset had, for years, intrigued Joy. She had expected Granada to similarly reveal itself to *her* from a distance, postcard-like, the lofty red walls and turrets of the Alhambra crowning the horizon.

Instead, on her approach to Granada itself, the bucolic landscape of olive groves and tidy farms had given way to a tangle of overpasses and confounding road signs that resembled the cluttered outskirts of Trenton more than the majestic town she'd envisioned. She was beginning to dread being confronted by a glut of Starbucks and Burger Kings as they had in Madrid.

After driving through several industrial-looking neighborhoods, they'd finally located the historic district of Albaicin, a far quainter part of town, and down an alleyway so narrow that cars were parked on sidewalks, they eventually came to the whitewashed, nineteenth-century former mansion where they had reserved a room.

At first glance, the hotel had looked as appealing as the brochure depicted—a vibrant Moorish lobby with tiled walls of blue and green, beveled glass windows, and an interior courtyard filled with orange trees and blooming jasmine. Their bedroom, however, was shockingly drab. A faded curtain covered the small window, and a frayed sofa looked as though a cat had recently gone at it with sharpened claws.

To Joy, hotels were like temples, refuges to house her spirit away from home, and she needed to feel comfortable with the room before she could enjoy the outside city she was visiting from the same prism of satisfaction. She'd ruthlessly researched hotels with local character for this trip and had expected at least some semblance of the historic city to be reflected inside this restored villa's bedroom. Instead, the rumpled gold bedspread and ochre-painted walls made her cringe.

She watched in dismay as Richard stretched out on the bed, obviously unfazed by the dreariness of the furnishings, when what she wanted was to march back down to the front desk to demand a better room. Although he was usually content with whatever accommodations they were given, his indifference this time seemed to indicate he was totally missing the point of this trip.

"Maybe they'll change our room if we pay them something," she suggested from the bathroom, unable to dismiss her own expectations, much as she wanted to for his sake. After all, he had lost a baby, too, and this was supposed to be *his* vacation as well as hers, a trip to help them heal.

She ran the water from the tap for a moment to let it warm, then rinsed her face and blotted it dry with tissues from the box on the sink, not wanting to soil the towels in case they changed rooms. She slipped off her blouse and bra and, wetting more tissues, rubbed them over her neck, chest, and arms rather than mess up the actual shower.

"Honey, the receptionist said all the others are taken," Richard called back.

She fanned herself dry with her hands and shook her head, loosening her blonde, shoulder-length hair from its ponytail. "They always say that unless we make a fuss," she said.

"There are only nine rooms, Joy. Anyway, this one's clean. It's not like we'll spend much time in here."

"But we should be able to enjoy it."

There was a pause. "It's fine, honey. Really. The bed's comfy."

She brushed her teeth. She knew she'd be better off adopting his attitude of making the best of the mediocre surroundings. He was usually less affected by the lack of the little touches that she seemed to need to complete her enjoyment of a vacation, but she was baffled by how easily he could settle for so much less than what they'd paid for, given the hotel rates. She'd been looking forward to being happy on this trip. Happy and relaxed. That was the whole reason for their coming, to shed some of that sense of loss, a loss far deeper than any she'd ever known. She already doubted it was going to happen in this room.

She wasn't sure why she was so irritated with Richard and suddenly so intolerant of their differing opinions on a subject they'd almost always differed on. She knew she was being petty on one level, but then again, she resented him being so lackadaisical about something he knew meant a lot to her.

She examined her breasts in the mirror. Their recent fullness due to her pregnancy was finally completely gone, although they still felt more tender than usual.

She stepped out of the bathroom. Richard was already undressed and tucked beneath the bedspread, watching television in a language he barely understood.

She sighed. "As long as there's a TV, Rich."

He flipped the dial of the television remote. "I've been driving all day, honey. I need to relax."

"I need to relax, too, but this room is . . ."

He turned to look at her, and seeing her nude from the waist up, he grinned. "Come on over here, sweetie. I'll help you relax." She ignored his invitation. With a TV and her half-naked, he'd be happy in a coffin.

"Come on," he prodded, his eyes twinkling.

Although she still found his gaze disarming after five years of marriage, she resisted his attempt to lure her to the bed, bothered that he wasn't taking her concern seriously. Instead, wrapping a towel around her chest, she crossed the room and opened her suitcase just enough to slide out the shirt and skirt she planned to wear to dinner, still unwilling to unpack in case they moved to another room.

Hearing him chuckle, she glanced up. He'd switched channels again, and an old episode of *Three's Company* was on, dubbed in Spanish and complete with laugh track.

"Honey, for God's sake," she said. "Let's go out and find the Alhambra."

Fixated on the screen, Richard seemed not to hear her.

She picked up her guidebook, her annoyance growing, and then went to the bed and lay down beside him, noisily flipping through the book to the pages describing the Alhambra—hoping to keep him from completely zoning out and to get him to refocus on her dissatisfaction with the room. She didn't want to start their stay in Granada on a sour note by continuing to harp on it, especially since he seemed perfectly fine with the accommodations, but she couldn't let go of her disenchantment.

It took a few seconds, but he turned to her and glanced at the page she was perusing, a view of a lavish palace chamber with an ornate stucco ceiling, bordered by a wall of blinding, gold-leafed, Arabic calligraphy.

"Wow," he said, looking at the photo.

Her anger started to melt away as he finally showed some interest in the Alhambra. She inched closer to him, so they could share the page. Then, just as quickly, he turned back to the television.

She put down the book and climbed on top of him, straddling his lap to obstruct his view. When he tilted his head to see past her, she gave him an impish smile and leaned over to block his view again.

"Honey," he protested.

She got off him and picked up the book, sighing.

"Okay, okay," he said, gently, turning to her. He rolled on top of her and pulled aside the towel to cup her breast. He started to kiss her neck, and she put down her book again and ran her hand over his hair, threading her fingers through the thick clump of it above his neck, trying to concentrate on its pleasing smoothness rather than on the ugly window curtain.

She felt somewhat foolish for making such a fuss about the room, especially since she was mostly to blame for it. When they were preparing for the trip, Richard had delegated hotel arrangements to her while he focused on ways to keep them safe, specifically to keep them from being targeted by thieves or gypsies. As she'd mapped out their route through southern Spain, marking the pretty towns and Moorish castles she wanted to visit, he was busy devising methods to camouflage money pouches and cameras.

"We just won't ride the subway, Rich," she'd said, resenting his priorities and the damper his overzealous attention to safety was putting on her enthusiasm for the trip. "Most thefts I've read about happen on the subway."

"They can sniff a tourist anywhere," he'd replied, experimenting with a contraption around his ankle: a bandana secured with Velcro.

To make things worse, there had been several incidents in Malaga perpetrated by Libyan immigrants two weeks before their scheduled departure. Although Spain had had no mass immigrations from other Middle Eastern countries, such as those that Northern Europe was currently experiencing, she'd sensed that the news report had made Richard even more wary of their upcoming tour. She suspected that, if it were up to him, he would have canceled the trip altogether.

Richard turned to glance back at the TV where perky Suzanne Somers was chattering in Castilian. Then he returned to Joy and planted little kisses on her breast, continuing upward to bury his face in her neck with more ticklish kisses.

She struggled to hold onto her determination to change the room, but she couldn't help dissolving in a fit of helpless giggles. "Stop!"

"*Mi amor,*" he said, breathing into her neck again.

She chuckled. "Are you romancing me in Spanish?"

"Just trying to impress you."

He ran his fingers in little circles around her navel, then bent down to kiss her stomach.

She tried to enjoy the feel of his hands and lips on her skin, but instead felt herself inadvertently shrinking away. "You know, Rich, I still feel him, feel his little thumps inside me."

He kissed her forehead tenderly.

"It's been months, but I can't shake it. Sometimes I wake up at night and can't catch my breath. It's scary."

He cuddled her closer and kissed her eyelids. "We'll make another one, sweetheart. Another Stephen."

"There'll never be another Stephen," she said.

He sighed. "No, there won't be another Stephen." He caressed her cheek. After some moments, his hand ventured out to touch her breast again.

"Honey, I'm tired," she mumbled, expecting him to catch her cue that she wasn't in the mood to make love.

Her pregnancy seemed like yesterday. Her water breaking unexpectedly, much too early, as she was vacuuming the living room, the labor pains in her back and abdomen ripping through her, Richard rushing home from Manhattan to get to the hospital, and later, the doctor's frantic rush to save the baby. Then the weeks that followed as the depression set in. Though the wound in her stomach had healed, her belly continued to cry out for its missing contents.

She knew, however, that her inattentiveness to his overtures was caused by more than just the familiar despair creeping into her. Over the past months, sex for her had mostly become a required chore, like grading papers or folding laundry—a mission solely aimed at conception. Whenever Richard reached for her, she responded as though summoned by the god of some fertility cult, her sights focused squarely on the end result. She suspected he sensed that her heart wasn't in it for the sake of pleasure, and that she wasn't entirely with him.

She'd gone back on birth control for a while after the stillbirth, although there was almost no need at that point since she was rarely in the mood for sex. She certainly hadn't wanted to get pregnant again and face a possible repetition of that terrible loss.

Not until some four months later, the pain of the loss numbed somewhat, had she begun to feel the stirrings of optimism and her drive to try again. At first her desire was like a faucet she could turn on at a whim. All it took was feeling Richard strong and reassuring beside her in bed to kindle her mood. He had been supportive and loving throughout the ordeal, and she wanted to give him a child as much as she wanted one for herself.

Even when it didn't happen immediately, she wasn't concerned, suspecting that her body was simply weaning itself of the vestiges of the previous pregnancy. She was thirty-five, and he was five years older, not spring chickens but surely still in their prime.

A few months later, however, she began to grow discouraged, wondering whether something inside her had changed as a result of the stillbirth. Although tests showed they were both healthy, that her tubes were in good shape and his sperm count sufficient to produce healthy children, she couldn't help obsessing about the "congenital weakness of the fetus," the medical reason given to them for the stillbirth. At times, she'd even begun to wonder whether she and Richard were somehow incompatible on a genetic level.

⚭

Richard had now moved slightly away from her and resumed watching TV.

"I'm sorry," Joy said, reaching out and stroking his hair again, wanting to shake off her ambivalence.

"It's okay," he replied absently, as though lost in his own thoughts.

She could feel herself pulling away even now, constructing walls between them. Perhaps it was due to her latent fears of a future loss, she rationalized, although part of her knew better. She was beginning to have the gnawing sense that Richard was not, after all, her true soul mate.

For some reason she couldn't understand, since the loss of the baby, she'd been retreating into her fantasy world more than usual. Especially when they made love. It was rarely Richard she was focused on in those intimate moments, but rather on some other acquaintance or colleague she found attractive or sensed was attracted to her. In the past, she would simply have accepted the regard of these men as a compliment, and she certainly had never responded to any innuendos sent her way. But recently, the images of these men bombarded her thoughts during sex, and it was getting harder to banish them. Although she obviously didn't blame Richard for her erotic daydreams of other men, she suspected they had something to do with his change during these past months.

The grief that had threatened to destroy her had also engulfed him, affecting him in ways she couldn't have foreseen. He'd obviously bottled up his feelings about Stephen; instead of crying and withdrawing as she had done, he seemed to conceal his sadness by creating ever steeper career goals and burying himself under overwhelming workloads. He would voluntarily take on difficult clients for his boss and consent to work-related travel more often than usual. At times he was distant, and at others he would lose his temper over trivial things. Some days he seemed to have morphed into a complete stranger.

Now, as they lay in bed miles from home, Joy reminded herself that both his behavior and hers were temporary, that a new baby would reestablish her feelings for him and for their marriage. It was, after all, the solid aim of family-building Richard had projected from the start that had attracted her—that and his robust awareness of what he wanted from life.

Back when they'd met, she'd been smitten by his innate pragmatic grasp of things. She'd been on the rebound from a previous relationship, yearning for some grounding, and he had been gallant, handsome, and sensible. He was a banker. Despite her years studying and working in Manhattan, she had never dated a banker and found his knowledge of the complex world of finance intriguing, the way he could summarize the current state of inflation or the reasons for fluctuating interest rates. He could analyze specific economic data or investments he'd just heard about as though he'd been studying them for years, and he had even mapped out a plan for his own financial security for the next decade. Drawing her away from her own, often exhausting, literary and philosophical excursions as a college English teacher, his solid attitudes were refreshing and sexy to her, all bravado and fortitude. It had certainly felt like great chemistry between them. Two years later, they had married.

Now as she watched him while still stroking his hair, she wondered whether opposites really do attract. Once again, she wanted to push aside the heartbreaking thought that perhaps the stillbirth had been some sort of sign—perhaps they weren't meant to be parents together, and this was nature's way of pointing it out.

Richard's lips against her ear now startled her. His warm feet affectionately rubbed her cool ones.

"Rich . . ." she started to object.

He nuzzled her face, his arms encircling her.

Touched by his efforts to be uplifting, she found herself returning to her previous hopes that a baby would change everything. She turned to him and lightly kissed his lips.

"Rich, do you think we'll be parents? Someday?"

"Honey, of course we'll be parents."

"I'm not so sure anymore."

"Don't keep thinking about it," he said softly. "Like the doctor said, it'll just happen. Like it did before."

"That's what I'm afraid of."

"Not that part. It'll be different next time."

His confidence was meant to bolster her, but she felt he was denying the legitimacy of her fears.

She turned slightly away from him. "I feel so alone."

He kissed her shoulder. "You're not alone. I'm here."

"It just feels so lonely, not carrying the baby, not having him growing inside me. My body seems useless now."

He shook his head. "It's normal, honey. You were pregnant and now you're not. But nothing else has changed."

She felt that was a callous thing to say. Of course, he couldn't understand what it meant to be pregnant and suddenly not to be, to feel your body couldn't fulfill its purpose, its promise. She used to try to tell him how wonderful it was to feel the baby's kicks, and he'd smile as she put his hand to her stomach to feel the butterfly-light thumps. But he wasn't as fixated on them as she. He was able to shift his attention to other things almost immediately.

"You weren't as connected as I was," she said.

"I wasn't carrying him," he said softly.

"I mean, you were more aloof. Like you couldn't get into the pregnancy."

"Honey, that's not true. I enjoyed every minute of it."

"I felt you weren't as interested—"

He interrupted. "Joy, don't do this. That's not true and not fair. I wanted that baby. But . . ." he stopped and took a breath, "we can't keep torturing ourselves like this. It didn't happen this time."

His face contorted slightly, and he ran his fingers through his hair. "There'll be a next time," he said, as though trying to convince himself.

She sighed. He was right. She shouldn't be tormenting them both like this. He felt as much anguish at their loss as she. He just handled it differently.

Maybe he was right about the baby too, that there would be a next time. She wanted to believe that. But even if she conceived and successfully carried a baby to term, what she really wondered was whether they could ever finally knit together their bond as lovers and partners and go back to how they'd been before.

Wasn't that the real reason she'd chosen to come here, chosen Granada, this jewel of Andalusia, to reignite love? She hugged him.

As if encouraged by her awakening energy, Richard lifted her hair and lightly bit her neck as he fumbled with the zipper of her jeans.

This time she yielded to his coaxing, snuggling closer to him, her fingers tracing the bulge of his arm muscles as he guided her hand gently to his waist, then downward, as if to verify his desire.

She pushed her hips into his, now eager to make love and to escape into her fantasies, guilty fantasies of other men, admittedly, but providing a pleasing buoyancy that fueled her. As if on cue, her dream of getting pregnant took hold, and she found herself embarking on her mission again, riding the narcotic, danger-ridden strains of a guitar coming from somewhere outside the window.

She stretched puma-like, fingers and toes reaching in opposite directions. Things really were different here. Even their love-making left her unexpectedly light and happy and more focused on Richard. She placed her palm on her stomach. Maybe this time some baby magic would work its spell.

Three's Company mercifully over, she got dressed, retrieved the guidebook from the floor, and lightly tossed it to Richard on the bed.

"Can you please get us to the Alhambra?" she asked.

Picking up her old copy of *Tales of the Alhambra*, she tried to make herself comfortable enough on the stiff sofa to settle into Washington Irving's world for a bit.

Since first reading of the "light, elegant, and voluptuous character" of the Moorish wonder that Irving had lived in for several months in 1829 and so eloquently described, the Alhambra had indelibly etched itself into her consciousness. When her doctor advised that she and Richard take a trip to get their minds off their devastating loss, she'd immediately thought of southern

Spain, of Granada. Despite the unsettling accounts of thefts and political unrest that Richard worried about, she'd doggedly pushed on with their itinerary, convinced that Granada would be the place that might cheer her up. Judging by the quality of their lovemaking just now, she'd been right.

Although she knew that her view of the place was overly influenced by Irving's romantic writings, for a long time now she had believed that such a place existed, and she trusted Irving not to mislead her.

"He started writing this while actually living here," she mused aloud. She looked up, but Richard was now tuned to a Spanish soap opera.

She groaned and dove back into Irving's reflections on the medieval Moorish era of Al-Andalus. The enterprising American writer and diplomat had been fascinated by the historical narrative of the Moorish empire and had documented the legions of myths of the Alhambra as well as added his own colorful anecdotes of his stay in the dilapidated Moorish palace.

When she looked up again, Richard was dozing.

"Great way to start off, Rich," she said, putting down her book. "Rich?" She went to the bed and, despite being miffed, crawled over to lie beside him.

She used to love to watch him doze when they were first married, the way he could catnap, his face placid as the Sphinx, his head sunk deep into the pillow so that it bunched up on either side to insulate him from noise. Gazing at his profile now, tracing the line of his straight nose and full lips, then moving down the long form of his body under the bedspread and back up to his smooth, brown hair, she tried to resurrect those past warm feelings instead of dwelling on her irritation at his not leaping up to sightsee or to help her change their room. She jiggled the bed a bit to coax him awake, but it was no use. He was beginning to snore.

"Damn it, Rich," she muttered.

She knew he would have preferred that their first trip to Europe together be to Italy, to Tuscany, but he'd wanted to indulge her Spanish fantasy. This would be *her* trip, he'd told her. The "new beginning" trip. The *new baby* trip. Although she appreciated that, this journey wasn't starting off right.

The doctor had encouraged them to take time off from their daily stresses. She was free between the spring and summer semesters of teaching English at Hunter College, and Richard had extra weeks of leave from the bank. Yet, despite all their preparations, Richard was showing a mystifying inability to open himself up to the adventure. His energy and inquisitiveness seemed to have mysteriously evaporated the minute they got to Spain, leaving him wary and stolid.

She found his reticence puzzling, especially since he and his younger brother had spent two years overseas when their father was a diplomat stationed in Athens. His parents were divorced by then, his mother having moved to California with her new husband, leaving the boys with their father. Richard and his brother had traveled around Europe during their school holidays, and Richard had talked fondly of the Scandinavian fjords, the Italian towns, and the Greek islands they'd visited.

What should have been a springboard to a love for international travel, however, seemed to have had the opposite effect on him, as if he'd never truly been to those foreign places. He now seemed willing to stray only so far off the beaten track, and halfheartedly at that, as if he were more comfortable in a limited world. It was becoming all too clear that any initiative to explore on this trip would be up to her.

She gazed at his face again, at his lips that, in their relaxed state, seemed perfectly drawn by an artist's pen. The first time they'd kissed, she'd been getting over those other lips that had never rushed but only slowly and sensuously teased. The insistence of Richard's kisses had at first felt too desperate, and she couldn't help but compare them to those that still haunted her. Yet his ardor had also left her no time to sink into old memories, and it hadn't taken long for him to spark her wounded flame, spurring her to fall in love again.

She jiggled the bed once more. Richard rolled onto his side, oblivious.

"So much for trying to impress me, *mi amor*," she whispered, thinking of those romantic words of Spanish he'd uttered earlier.

She got up from the bed, picked up Richard's camera, and quietly fled the room. Outside, she headed for the outdoor iron staircase where she'd earlier seen a sign pointing to a rooftop swimming pool.

On the rooftop deck, there was indeed a small pool sitting derelict and abandoned. The surface of the foggy water rippled lightly in the breeze, and the concrete around one edge was broken at a jagged angle.

She glanced about. There were still no signs of the Alhambra, even from this higher vantage. No ruddy towers or airy terraces, no white pavilions nestled in the groves and vineyards where the Moors were said to have enjoyed the sumptuous fruits of their gardens. Instead of the legendary slopes of lush prickly pear and wild olive that Irving had described, she saw only adjoining old roofs of dull-red tile or flat concrete. The sole signs of life were the rooftop clotheslines of men's drying white briefs and undershirts flapping to the rattle of air-conditioners.

Then, once her gaze settled, something else caught her eye.

From across several other flat roofs cluttered with household detritus peeked a pink-and-turquoise stucco mansion. A little farther off, an old building gleamed like a painted vase, its tawny walls ornamented with intricate Gothic stonework. A sliver of arabesque tile glinted from a half-open doorway below, revealing a colonnaded courtyard—undeniable evidence of the eight hundred years of Moorish presence.

She closed her eyes and listened. Even the breeze here above the cobbled streets seemed to carry a faint wail, an echo of the long-lost lamentations of the vanquished Moors.

Crossing from one corner of the roof to the other, she stepped around the decaying pool to snap shots of red tile and curling, wrought-iron balconies, swirling baroque plasterwork above doorways, and windows with looping trim like women's hair tresses. She shot the buildings from different angles, grabbing the late afternoon's waning light.

Renewed optimism flooded her. Her earlier impatience with Richard had been silly. The reality before her now had its own delicate charm. They *were* in the right place, lackluster room or not. Richard was right. They weren't going to spend much time inside. She'd ignore the mediocre furnishings and focus on this amazing city, on the architecture and restaurants and history.

Brimming with discovery, she hurried back down the steps, eager to express her gratitude to Richard for bringing her to this magnificent place. But she found him still asleep, sprawled in bed like an exhausted child, firmly clutching the television remote.

She glanced at her watch. It was too late to sightsee.

She slipped off her shoes and lay on the bed, thinking they could settle for a romantic dinner out. But her earlier enthusiasm on the roof started to dim as the familiar ache began to grow in her again, as on those nights when she awoke terrified from nightmares of being in labor.

2

The piercing aroma of fresh coffee tugged her from her dreams. She opened her eyes and eyed the saucers of cheese, ham, bread rolls, and maroon figs. Richard had ordered up breakfast as if he knew just the sort of meal Washington Irving wrote of starting his day with in Granada. Joy smiled, ravenous, her misgivings of yesterday all but evaporating in the pungent stream of coffee he was pouring into a porcelain cup.

They ate sitting in bed, Richard flipping the television channel from CNN to a local English channel that was predicting heavy traffic on the highways due to an international golf tournament in Seville.

"Good thing we drove in yesterday," he said.

"You bet," she said with a chuckle, thinking of his intolerance for traffic of any kind. Tournament-induced traffic would have done him in.

Feeling renewed after the meal, she showered and dressed. Then, packing cameras and guidebooks, they set off for the Alhambra.

Map in hand as usual, Richard led them up a narrow street where bars with lunching customers and shops selling all manner of colorful handicrafts, T-shirts, guitars, and ruffled flamenco dresses had obviously replaced a once-verdant hillside. Legend had it that King Ferdinand and his pregnant Isabella had camped in this valley below the Alhambra castle walls while their

Catholic army laid siege to the inhabitants of the last Moorish stronghold above.

Arriving at an ancient stone gateway with a large sign for the Alhambra above it, Joy and Richard proceeded up a wide, dirt road flanked on either side by babbling water channels reputed to be remnants of the ingenious Moorish irrigation and drainage system. The hill was somewhat steep, and she took his hand as they climbed. Farther up the hill, the renowned elm groves appeared, and finally, the towering red walls of the fortress itself.

The woman in the entrance booth, however, informed them that the next tour of the palace wasn't for another two hours. She told them to check out the gardens while they waited and turned to the next person in line.

More delays? Joy thought. But once in the manicured terraces and leafy promenades, she was glad for this interval. The bustle of the town below had abruptly given way to a lyrical quiet, and the clear air of the wooded hills was moist and cool. Water trickled through open earthen pipes from upper springs into lower gardens as fountains sprayed iridescent rainbows in a line down the center of a flowered courtyard. Scarlet and yellow rosebushes bloomed in spirals, while archways of red bougainvillea formed a stately, beckoning colonnade. In the distance above it all glistened the snow-capped cliffs of the Sierra Nevada.

"Amazing," Joy said, breathing in with deep satisfaction.

"Yeah," Richard said, removing the cap on his camera lens to take a picture.

Joy gazed around at the colorful splendor. This is what they'd come for, what the Moors had allegedly designed these gardens for—a total submersion in beauty so tranquil that a moment in a perfumed garden could last an eternity. Irving himself had declared in wonder, "Who can do justice to a moonlit night in such a climate and in such a place!"

She felt a swell of relief. How could she not believe that all their struggles as a couple who had lost a child, even before they were allowed to know him, would eventually yield fruitful results?

✤

They exited the gardens into a large, paved yard where others waiting to see the palace were gathered around a refreshment kiosk. Richard bought two bottles of chilled Alhambra Reserva, and they sat on the stone steps in the shade of the fortress, sipping the lager.

A few minutes later, Richard laid his head on her shoulder and yawned. "God, I'm tired."

"Rich, it's the Alhambra," she said, sensing his usual impatience with waiting for anything.

"Well, let's try to get in now."

He stood and stretched and started to wander toward the palace, beckoning for her to follow. The line to get in was long and the guards appeared to be checking passes.

"It's not time yet," she said. "They may stop us."

Even as she hurried to catch up, however, she sensed that Richard had grown uneasy. She guessed at the reason when she spotted the brightly dressed women weaving through the tourists and handing out sprigs of thyme and pink carnations in return for a tip. Gypsies.

Joy had long been fascinated by gypsies, by their ancient roots in India, and especially by those of Granada and their creation of flamenco. Richard, however, had warned her about their reputation as swindlers and asked that she not speak to any who might approach them.

A ruddy-faced young woman in a flowery dress now walked up to Joy and gamely pressed her arm, indicating that she wanted to read her palm. Joy shook her head, looking around for Richard.

But when she noticed the small head of black hair poking out of the bundle the young woman was cradling, she changed her mind. What could be the harm? She reached into her purse for some money to help the young mother. If nothing else, maybe the colorful soothsayer could predict a pregnancy in her future.

Before she could hand the young woman the change, however, a shrill curse pierced the air. Another woman in a red scarf was gesturing obscenely at Richard and yelling, "*Cabron!* (Bastard!)"

Richard returned to Joy, grabbed her elbow, and herded her toward the exit gate. "Let's get out of here."

"We'll lose our place," she said, the coins for the palm reader still in her hand.

"Those damned women stop at nothing!"

"Honey, just give them a dollar."

"You think they only want a dollar?" he snapped when they were out of earshot. "She was slipping her hand into my pocket for my wallet, practically squeezing my balls."

Joy didn't know whether to laugh or be shocked. They were halfway to the exit before she finally convinced him to turn around and get back in line. Although he was reluctant and on guard, he also seemed to understand that he had overreacted. This time she stuck close to him as they moved along with the throng toward the main palace. The gypsy women were nowhere in sight.

When they passed the guard, he barely glanced at their tickets.

"Nobody's paying attention," Richard said. "We could have gone in an hour ago."

"You're right," Joy said, suddenly too enthralled by what was before her to argue.

There was an audible collective gasp as they wandered along

with the others, everyone seeming to inhale in a single breath the vivid colors and artistry of each palace room, patio, dome, and fountain. They strolled through the banquet halls and court-yards, the walls intricately ornamented with Arabic calligraphy and flowers in filigree plasterwork painted yellow, cobalt, and sienna. At once opulent and serene, the façade of the chambers' beige stuccowork seemed to illuminate the lush, floral ceramics. Carving and color meshed perfectly, the flowers seamlessly lead-ing into the calligraphy as if beauty was intended to soothe rather than dazzle.

They climbed some stairs and found a plaque in one of the apartments that identified it as the governor's residence and the one Washington Irving had occupied during his visit.

"This must be where he wrote," she said, clutching Richard's arm.

There was Irving, notebook in hand, jotting down his impres-sions: the wooden eaves where the pigeons roosted, the patio where the elderly caretaker prepared Irving's meals, the garden where a pair of village lovers secretly met each night. Clearly, any-one who was lucky enough to stay here would never want to leave.

Descending a different staircase, they arrived at Patio de los Leones, where twelve white marble lions circled a fountain.

"Irving loved this fountain," Joy said. "They say the ghosts of the Moors visit this courtyard each night in search of their abandoned treasure."

Richard snapped a photo of her with the aloof, elegant lions and arcade in the background. She watched him intently focus his lens, zooming in for a good shot, and yet, other than his inter-est in photographing it, he seemed detached from all that was before them.

"Do you believe in ghosts?" she asked, almost to see whether he was listening.

He changed his angle and blew into his camera lens as if to clear it of dust, then exhaled in frustration and began to focus again. "I should have brought my other camera," he said.

All at once Joy felt that she was suffocating. She'd once thought that their love had been like this, as flowing and perfect as these circling lions he was photographing.

She turned to him, a lump forming in her upper abdomen, above her womb. She began to feel she was being smothered, not only here, but in her life altogether. "Honey," she said, panicking, "whatever happened to us?"

He lowered his camera. "What?"

"I—" She quickly caught herself. She stared at the lions, wild predators and dangerous despite their beauty. The longer she stared, the more she felt defeated, as if she could no longer trust in anything positive again. All that she'd once dreamed she'd have with Richard, someone to share her delight and passion with, was never going to be.

She held in her anxiety, not wanting to drag him into her turmoil and spoil the moment for both of them. What was she about to say, anyway? That she was having serious doubts about their marriage and had even been contemplating a trial separation?

The notion had occurred to her for the first time only a few days ago, and she'd dismissed it like so many other thoughts, but that notion had steadily built into a very real scenario as she felt his general aloofness in Madrid and Seville. Now she felt physically ill.

Still, she merely pointed to their surroundings. "This place was intended to represent paradise on earth. Look at all the carving and detail. Why did people stop creating beauty like this?"

He shrugged. "Too expensive."

She turned away from him. Somehow, she'd known he'd say this. She'd been thinking of the artistic spirit altogether, that people had lost the capacity to be creative with what little means they had as the descendants of the Moors had done, and his thoughts had gone straight to crunching the numbers, to the practical.

"Well, this was built by a bankrupt kingdom at the ebb of the Moorish empire," she said. "They used cheap materials like wood and plasterwork. None of it was meant to last, and they still came up with a masterpiece."

Seemingly amused by the extent of her awe, Richard smiled and snapped another picture.

She held back the tears welling in her eyes. If only we, you and I, she thought, could go back to that time of passion and grace, if we could go back to before all the unhappiness, to before Stephen. . . .

They moved on, Joy trying to convince herself that she was just suffering from delayed postpartum depression and that her volatile emotions were causing her to come to these bizarre conclusions. In spite of her visions of separation, deep down she knew she wasn't thinking right. Richard had planned this trip to Spain with her for her sake. And whether or not he showed it, he was probably enjoying himself in his own way. If she were a little more patient, she told herself, her distorted view of their relationship would pass, like so much ragweed pollen in the air.

They finally came to the Sala de los Abencerrajes. She'd been eager to see this room for its famed cupola, which was shaped like an eight-pointed star. The Moors were known to love mathematics, and this ceiling was said to have been inspired by Pythagoras's theorem.

She collapsed into one of several wooden chairs and dropped her head back to study the intricate cones of the ceiling. The fluffy, plaster ornamentation seemed to float down from the sky as if carved out of snowflakes. For an instant, she imagined scaling a silken web up into the delicate spirals, into a sort of heaven, a baby heaven, where her own little Stephen slept cradled in the spongy white.

Then, she was cuddling him in her arms again, looking down through her tears at his perfect infant's face. Wracked with agony at the news of his stillbirth, she'd waited in vain for his tiny lids to open in the delivery room, so she could stare into his eyes. She tried to picture him now, to trace again his doll's nose and mouth, sensing his little body hovering nearby. She was still unwilling to believe that his brief appearance in their lives had been for nothing. Stephen. My baby love.

Richard's voice broke into her vision. "Know how the room got its name?"

She lifted her head to stop him from continuing, but the blood rushed to her face. Dazed, she fought her way out of the blur before her eyes.

"'The Abencerrajes were a rival noble family of the caliph,'" Richard read from the book. "'The caliph invited the leaders of the Abencerrajes to a banquet, where he had them all—'"

"Richard! Not now!"

"It's true," he said, apparently unaware of her distress. "The whole clan was murdered right here. Heads piled up in the corner."

Upset that he could think of ruining the place with this grizzly detail, even if it were true, she sank into silence, jarred at being reminded of the terrible truth—creators of great art could also be brutal.

As she tried to reconnect to her earlier peaceful feelings, she spotted a young man across the room sitting on a chair like the one she was in. The man's eyes were closed, his spine perfectly erect, as if he were meditating. His black hair hung loosely to his shoulders, and a backpack was propped on his lap. He looked like a student from India, or a yogi, she thought, tuned in to somewhere deep within, absorbing the surroundings through his breaths.

Joy lowered her gaze and inhaled slowly, then exhaled. For a stark moment, she tried to copy him, to disappear into the very air of the room as this man seemed to be doing. She continued to breathe slowly: in and out, in and out. The room around her buzzed with tourists, but in her mind, she heard only an immense silence.

When she looked up, the man was still perched across from her, sitting straight and immobile as a sculpture, radiating otherworldly calm.

They left the Alhambra and strolled back down the road with the melodic water channels on either side. Immersed in the headiness of having finally witnessed the legendary castle, Joy thought of the composed young meditator who had seemed to be lost in the beauty of the room. She was grateful to have experienced those few moments of reverie as she'd tried to emulate him.

Inspired, she pointed to the map.

"Look, honey, Sacromonte isn't far. The entire neighborhood is built into the mountainside across from here. Let's see if we can catch a flamenco performance there tonight."

Richard looked skeptical. "Isn't that the gypsy quarter?"

"It's more touristy now. But it's famous for flamenco and the dancers are local gypsies."

"We saw lots of flamenco in Seville. We need to stick to safe streets here, Joy."

"But Sacromonte's the real thing." she said. "It's *authentic.*"

"It can't be that authentic if it's for tourists. And I don't want to fool with gypsies."

"Honey, everybody goes there to see the flamenco. Do this for me. I've been dying to see the gypsy dancers of Sacromonte. Washington Irving raved about them."

Richard raised his eyebrows as if trusting in Irving's "raving" about something was the height of insanity. "You're obsessed with that guy. Maybe you should have come here with Irving instead of me."

She chuckled. "Don't be silly."

"Gypsies are trouble," he said flatly.

"I know you'll love it," she said, already anticipating the evening of dangerous enchantment ahead.

3

"I can't get him out of my mind," Joy said, nibbling on a cumin-scented olive at an outdoor patio in the medieval Albaicin.

Since arriving in Spain, she'd fancied starting dinner like the Spaniards, trawling the bars for thimblefuls of sherry and tapas of olives, Manchego cheese, and Iberico ham until ten o'clock, when they'd choose a restaurant for their main meal. Inevitably, however, by eight their American stomachs were howling with hunger, and so each night they'd caved in and had their entrees early. Tonight, practically the only diners in the restaurant, they ordered paella for Joy and a fish baked in rock salt for Richard.

"Who can't you get out of your mind?" Richard said. "Someone I should worry about?"

She smiled, mischievous. "Washington Irving."

"Irving? Oh, yeah. That book."

"*Tales of the Alhambra.*"

Richard gazed into his wine glass. "I thought it was Hemingway you liked."

There were photographs on the walls of a bespectacled, paunchy Hemingway, cheering at a bullfight. He'd purportedly researched the topic for *Death in the Afternoon* in this very establishment, feasting on red wine and braised oxtail.

She shook her head. "Hemingway's obsessions were wars and

bullfighting. Irving loved Spain's beauty and romance, and he especially loved the Alhambra."

Richard swirled his goblet, inhaled, then took a sip of his Rioja Reserva, the red wine he'd chosen for them tonight. Despite eschewing wine recently in the event she got pregnant, Joy had indulged tonight, enjoying the full-bodied oakiness of it.

"Irving was an incredible adventurer," she went on. "He traveled through bandit-infested territory with only a friend and a single guard—unheard of in those days. *He's* my kind of hero."

Richard took another sip of his wine, again pausing to sniff and savor. "Hemingway too macho for you?"

"Too bloody. Real heroes are compassionate." Even as she said this, she was aware that her nuanced world was a little suspect to Richard.

"Well, we should have seen a bullfight in Seville, Joy, or at least in Ronda," he said, with an unmistakable hint of regret.

She made a face.

"I went to one with my father once," he went on, wistful. "Seville has the oldest bullring in Spain."

She took a gulp of her wine, wishing he hadn't brought this up, now. Although moved by his sentimental memory of an outing with his father, she couldn't stomach such cruelty.

"The poor bull never has a chance," she said.

"I shouldn't have let you talk me out of it."

She touched his hand. "We went to the Bandit Museum. That was fun."

He frowned into his wine glass.

How she had loved Ronda! They'd arrived at early sunset, the Puente Nuevo Bridge sprawling across the Tajo gorge below them like a spindly legged mosquito. The bridge highlighted Ronda's remoteness in past centuries, when the town had been better known for its ruthless highwaymen than for its pretty streets and spectacular views; and there had been the incredible Moorish Palacio Mondragon where Queen Isabella had delivered her daughter, one of the exquisite settings in which the willful medieval queen had managed to give birth. Why ruin the memory of the lovely locale with a gruesome bullfight? Any manner of death now made her think of Stephen and the stillbirth.

Several days before they left home, she'd felt an urge to go rummaging in the guest room drawer for the quilt she'd made for Stephen. She and Richard had picked out just the right turquoise-checked fabric together, as well as the thick padding and the embroidery stitch to use on her sewing machine. She'd worked on the quilt during her second trimester, finishing it just before going into premature labor at six months. As if she had known.

When it was all over, and they returned home from the burial, she'd slept with the quilt for several nights. Even though it had never touched the baby, it seemed to embody him. She'd brought it to her face and cried for a long time before putting it back into the drawer that day. As she remembered the blanket now, a somber sadness passed over her like a shadow, there and then gone, and she knew for a brief moment that she was mourning not only Stephen, but her marriage and life as it used to be, as well.

Richard was leaning forward. "Honey, forty percent of Spaniards don't think it's so terrible. They still swear by the memory of Manolete."

She tried to remember what they'd been talking about.

"Manolete," Richard repeated. "The matador who was gored to death in 1947."

She nodded, secretly harboring satisfaction that a bull had taken revenge on an all-powerful torero.

"That's something I'll never understand," she said. "How people so fun-loving and artistic can uphold such cruelty."

"Well, forty percent of the people polled admitted they

enjoyed bullfighting, and the rest lied when they said they didn't. Bullfighting is in their genes. The stands are full every time."

A svelte waiter in black leather pants brought out Richard's baked fish, presenting the snow-white hake peeping out amid the glittering salt crystals for their approval before taking it back to the kitchen to be filleted. A scent of lemon and fennel lingered in its wake, and Joy thought of Irving's accounts of delectable Spanish "repasts" in the cool shade of an olive grove: salted cod, roasted kid and partridge, figs, crusty bread, and a robust red wine.

"See how artistic that is?" she said, referring as much to her vision of Irving's picnics as to the aromatic fish they were just shown.

Richard smiled. "Well, these artists didn't think twice about gouging out eyes during the Inquisition or butchering each other in a civil war not too long ago. Lorca was dragged off and shot somewhere near here."

"That's still no reason for us to go to a bullfight," she said, giving him a light warning kick under the table to remind him not to dilute her joy at being in Granada.

She knew about the ghastly horrors of the civil war of the 1930s, a descent into barbarity that had wiped out hundreds of thousands of citizens. Granada's own Federico Garcia Lorca, arguably the greatest Spanish poet and dramatist of the twentieth century, was imprisoned and shot by the right-wing Nationalists in 1936 for his outspoken criticism of them. Not even his famous *Blood Wedding* had saved him. Yet, despite the unspeakable acts that had taken place on this beautiful spot, she couldn't let Richard's skepticism dispirit her.

"There's a bullfight tomorrow," he said cheerfully.

She overlooked the enthusiasm in his announcement, concentrating on the saffron-and-paprika-scented rice as perfect and round as pearls melting on her tongue between morsels of shrimp, squid, and *chorizo.*

"I'd like to go," he said.

"Well go, then," she said, savoring the smoky flavors.

She should have known this topic would come up the moment they walked into the restaurant. The walls leading to the patio were bursting with paintings of "illustrious bullfighters" and stuffed heads of "brave bulls."

"What about you?" he asked.

Ignoring his question, she held up a nugget of *chorizo* on her fork. "One reason pork is so prevalent in Spanish food is because it was proof that you weren't Muslim or Jewish. During the Inquisition, a kitchen without pork was practically a death sentence."

She popped the bite into her mouth, relishing the perfectly cured meat, puzzled that a thing so exquisite could be linked to such human oppression. Despite her infatuation with Iberian culture, it was beginning to seem that everything pleasurable in Spain had sprouted from some long-ago fountain of pain.

"You don't want to go?" Richard asked.

"You can't seriously expect me to see a bullfight?"

"*I'd* like to."

"Then, go," she said, shrugging, barely masking her disdain.

"But I thought we were heading for Cordoba tomorrow."

"We can take off later in the afternoon," he said, although she was not sure whether his look was one of disappointment or relief that she did not want to join him at the ring. "What'll you do while I'm gone?"

"I'll find plenty to keep me busy."

"Be careful, Joy. Don't take your credit cards."

"Rich, you're so darn worried all the time. I'll only be shopping, then sitting in a nice cafe while you're enjoying your bloodthirsty sport."

He smiled at her jab. "Well," he said, reaching over and caressing her cheek, "Carmen was killed *outside* the ring. And," he added with a seductive whisper, "the only blood sport I enjoy is with you."

She glanced at him cynically, sure that his sudden enthusiasm had more to do with his anticipation of the ring than with romance. She could barely stand to think that he could enjoy something so horrible. How could he be two people at once— kind and gentle and yet insensitive to such animal suffering?

The young waiter who came to pour them more wine enthusiastically answered Richard's questions on matador fighting styles. He obviously endorsed Richard's wanting to go to the ring, and in brotherly spirit, the two men chatted about bulls and Joselito, the current reigning matador.

The waiter beamed at them. "It is the real Spain. You will love it."

"I'll be going alone," Richard said.

The waiter looked surprised. "You should try it once," he said. "If you don't like it—finish," he added, with all the drama of plunging the final sword into the bull's spine. He smiled uneasily, as if he had little tolerance for the squeamishness of foreign women. "The bull likes to die that way. Bravely. He does not like to go to the butcher."

Joy smiled back. "I'll be shopping."

Richard shrugged as though equally baffled by his wife's lack of interest in the national pastime.

The waiter's eyebrows rose in abject disapproval. "What if there is a big war tomorrow? What if there is no tomorrow? Do you want to miss the corrida?"

Joy continued to smile.

After supper, she and Richard took on the lamplit streets.

Despite its substantial size and the crowds, Granada felt surprisingly intimate. Some roads were so narrow they could only be navigated on foot. Even the dogs on their leashes seemed purposely small so as to take up as little space as possible. Best of all, there was a palpable air of contentment, entire families out for a late evening stroll, teenagers whizzing by on motor scooters as if there were no school tomorrow.

She browsed through hanging shawls richly embroidered with bright flowers and birds, like the flamenco dancers wore. Like the gypsies. *Gypsies.* Her thoughts flew back to what she had read about the gypsies having moved into the caves of Sacromonte mountain after the Moors had abandoned them during the reconquest. Although Joy knew there was little chance of Richard going to the Sacromonte willingly, she simply had to find a way to take him.

"Does the lady care to ride?" Richard said suddenly, signaling to the driver of a flower-adorned horse carriage

Richard helped her into the colorful carriage. The white horse's mane was braided with blue and orange ribbons, and the husky driver proceeded to steer the horse down a quiet alley, away from traffic. Richard's spontaneous romantic gesture and the clip-clopping of the horse's hooves against the worn cobblestones delighted Joy, diffusing the cloud of his earlier talk of the darker side of Andalusia. When he took her hand, leaned over, and passionately kissed her as though to atone for his earlier bullfighting harangue, she relaxed into his arms, relieved by this lighthearted shift and impromptu make-out session in the back of the carriage. Maybe their vacation was finally about to start.

She couldn't help wondering now who the real Richard was: this gracious, attentive husband or the self-absorbed man he had been these past months.

Resolving to enjoy the moment instead of focusing on her earlier thoughts of leaving him, she settled affectionately against his chest, reaching up to stroke his cheek, her earlier foreboding beginning to dissipate as her heart unfolded to envelop him more fiercely than she had in a very long time.

4

a bullfight. Maybe a good idea. He'd get it out of his system, once and for all, so she needn't deal with it anymore. And, for a change, she'd have some unchaperoned time, time to leisurely explore the sun-drenched plazas and their aromas of toasted chestnuts, time to buy an ice cream or coffee. As she anticipated her afternoon alone, free from marital squabbling and gypsy fear, she began to feel the romantic pull of this place again. Maybe some dark-eyed Spaniard, totally at ease in this community, would invite her for a glass of Jerez and explain the city's sights to her.

Amazed by her flippant thoughts, she glanced around now as if to spot this dashing, fictional companion, but no one fitting this image was in sight. Only two elderly men, their hands clasped behind their backs in that melancholic way of old Spanish men here, were plodding up the street ahead.

Emboldened by her vision, she turned to Richard. "Let's walk over to Sacromonte since it's so close."

"Now? It's late."

"Honey, the evening's just starting here. If you don't like it, we'll turn back. I promise."

Richard scowled. "Do we have to do *everything* Irving did?"

She pretended not to hear him, moving onto the sidewalk to make way for a passing motor scooter.

"Joy," he said, as if explaining the obvious, "anybody who'd spend months sleeping in a deserted ruin had to have a screw loose."

She laughed out loud, feeling more reckless and hungry for adventure than she had in a long time. "Irving was perfectly sane. And look at all these people. *They* all go." She gestured encouragingly at the pedestrians—tourists and locals, grandparents to toddlers—climbing the narrow streets of the Albaicin as if they came here every night.

They arrived at a cobbled passageway with an old-fashioned street lamp and a sign that read "Sacromonte." An arrow pointed upward.

"Just a little farther, Rich," she urged, the second glass of Rioja she'd had at dinner propelling her onward into the jasmine-scented night.

He stopped. "These alleys are made for scooters. I don't want to walk back late at night."

She sighed. "There will be cabs, sweetheart."

Midway up the incline, she turned around to face him, panting with the exertion.

"Hey," she asked, "whatever happened to the risk-taker I married? There's a time to be prudent, Rich, and a time to just enjoy ourselves. We don't come here every day."

She waited as he bent to shake a pebble from his shoe. He was stalling.

She wanted to kick his butt right then, appalled by the change in him. Where was that gusto she'd been so smitten by when they first met? Up until recently, he'd seemed to have maintained at least some of that charismatic enthusiasm he'd displayed when he was wooing her. When had it all evaporated? Had he lost a piece of himself, too, with the loss of their baby?

"We're practically there," she urged. "Honey, stop being so frigging paranoid."

He stepped back into his shoe, ignoring her remark.

"It's like the waiter said," she continued, her voice with more edge than she'd intended. "We could all blow up tomorrow, Rich. You'll go to your bullfight, and I'll see Sacromonte."

She turned and resolutely started up the dimly lit street.

Years ago, she'd fancied herself someday linked to a thrill-seeking man who would share her wanderlust and with whom she would discover the world; a spirited, fearless man like Che Guevara, her hero in those idealistic college years,

For some months at NYU, she actually had her own Che, complete with flowing hair and motorcycle. His name was Francisco Esteban, a native of El Salvador, and he was attending the university on a scholarship.

She had gone back to school to do graduate work in English, and he was a teaching assistant, an avowed Marxist-Leninist earning his master's in public policy. By the end of the semester, they were in love, and he'd introduced her to the Socialist organizations on campus and made her aware of the folly of her lamentable "bourgeois" ways.

"*Rubia,*" he would affectionately chide, "Blondie, why spoil your beautiful face with makeup?"

Wearing makeup and feminine clothing was frowned upon by Francisco as a sly tool used by the bourgeoisie to make women feel powerless. He never tired of repeating this mantra, and oddly enough, once she'd given up lipstick and mascara, Joy actually had felt more liberated.

Material wealth was equally repugnant to him, so before long, she'd traded in her previous career goal of supporting herself as a teacher of English literature for a new agenda of educating the masses in whatever subject and wherever she was needed.

Despite his strident views, Francisco was exotic and intelligent. His comprehension of art, music, and a wide variety of Latin American literature, along with his tireless intellectual probing, opened her to the outside world in a way she'd never been before.

He read Borges and Neruda to her in Spanish, and although she didn't completely understand, she loved the lulling sounds flowing from his mouth. Under his tutelage she'd grown conscious of vast new horizons. Soon, Francisco replaced even Che as her hero; for Francisco seemed to embrace all of humanity in his urgent desire to better the planet.

She'd loved how he challenged her. Unlike her previous boyfriends, Francisco had big things in mind, and he made no secret that he wanted her to be a part of them. Together they were embarking on an exhilarating mission to rescue the world.

She'd certainly never doubted Francisco's love for her and had assumed his feelings for her were the equal of her adoration of *him* on those amorous afternoons in his rented loft listening to his sermons. Each time he took her in his arms, she wanted to be swallowed up by the universe he painted for her, to soar into oblivion through his lips, eyes, and dogma. He could coax the most abandoned love from her, rousing an uninhibited surrender that made her want to give herself to him again and again.

He didn't seem to care whether she was faithful to him. He told her she should be free and bold with her body, that she should *own* her sexuality. Although his saying this had been meant to empower her, she had no interest in being with any other men. She'd wanted to bear *his* children and share *his* life, dedicated to remaking society into a utopia devoid of poverty and misery. She pictured carrying out their life's work side by side and began to feel that her abilities were as infinite as she deemed his.

When he abruptly left for San Salvador one morning to visit

his ailing mother, she couldn't imagine not going with him. For a week, she had done everything possible to find a way to finish the semester early to follow him. She even considered dropping out of school altogether.

Then, on the day she purchased her airline ticket, she learned the truth from a mutual acquaintance. Francisco had *not* gone home to El Salvador to be with his mother, as he'd claimed, but to be with his wife when she gave birth to their second child!

In that sickening moment, Joy felt a tectonic shift beneath her. She cried herself to sleep for weeks, aching where her heart had been wrenched out, sure that she would never again find her footing. How could she possibly survive without him to tie her dreams to?

She couldn't bring herself to eat, remembering their shared dinners over wine and political discourse, meals that were preludes to love. She could barely concentrate on her studies. Her courses, exams, and career meant nothing now that her love, her entire future, was gone. There was nothing in her world to look forward to. A vast wasteland gaped before her with no recognizable landmark—only a vacuum devoid of reason or meaning.

How could he have been so duplicitous, and how could she not have sensed at least some sign of it?

For months, she'd plodded through her courses with indifference. She had no interest in dating, even casually. Something as simple as a Barry White song she'd listened to with Francisco would hurl her into a tailspin of such longing that she would almost collapse at the unbearable memory of his eyes, his lips. She put every ounce of energy she had left into graduating a semester early just to leave NYU and all the memories.

Then, on a blind date arranged by friends, she'd met Richard.

At first, she'd dismissed him as just another bourgeois predator on Wall Street, which was what Francisco would have considered him. Yet, once the memory of Francisco and his Marxist dreams began to fade, Richard's tangible life as a commercial banker started to make sense. Securing people's money and providing business loans and mortgages no longer seemed to Joy the menacing occupation Francisco had claimed it was. Furthermore, Richard was established in New York and wasn't going anywhere. It didn't take long before he became more than a healing solace to her. He was a safe landing pad after the disastrous turbulence she'd been through.

Although he didn't immediately ignite her passion with the same fury Francisco had, he was outgoing, charming, and witty; and there was a strong comfort in his steady presence.

Francisco had destroyed her ability to trust, so it took a while before she began to fully let her defenses down. Opening herself up to Richard's love was like opening a window onto a totally new landscape. It soon became clear to her that Richard was a solid, prospective mate, and that his was the kind of love she could depend on. His dogged pursuit of her both flattered her and made her feel secure again, his practical "bourgeois" outlook becoming the cure she needed to recover from the visionary Francisco.

The unexpected memory of Francisco tonight unnerved her. As she stood on this narrow path in Granada watching Richard mulishly lag behind, she wondered why she'd so readily traded in her dreams, traded in one extreme of a man for another. She'd settled, plain and simple. In her haste to get over the thrill-seeking Che, she had succumbed to the reliable Gerald Ford.

She watched him slip his foot back into his shoe and thought she heard him gasping, as if he were already out of breath.

"Rich," she called out, seething with desperation, "please hurry!"

⸙

Beyond the darkness appeared a brightly lit road with several tapas bars and seated diners at outdoor tables. With a crowd in sight, Richard looked reassured and no longer laboring.

She felt a sudden pinch in her bladder. "I need a bathroom. I'll slip into the restaurant."

Richard slid into a chair at one of the outdoor tables. "I'll be here."

The ladies' *servicio* was up some narrow stairs at the back of the bar. It was tight in the narrow room, and since two stalls were out of order and other women were in line to use the single toilet, it took time to get her turn. Then there was another line to wash her hands at the sink.

When she got back downstairs, the bar was lively, the usual discarded paper napkins and receipts beginning to coat the tapas bar's floors like snow. Outside, the table where she had left Richard was empty.

She looked around. "Rich?" she called, just loudly enough to be heard if he were nearby. Thinking he might have decided to have a drink while waiting, she went back into the bar, but he wasn't there. She peered inside the restaurant to the tables beyond the bar. The place was full, but she didn't see Richard. She glanced at the upstairs hallway. Maybe he'd gone to the men's room. She went outside and waited. Minutes passed. She took another look inside the restaurant, scanning the upstairs hallway and the bar again, then went back outside.

Screw it, Richard, she silently cursed, beginning to suspect he'd wandered off simply to avoid going to Sacromonte.

Richard had brought along the cell phone he used on his overseas business trips, but even if he were carrying it now, she hadn't memorized the number. Her own phone was only good for emails here, so she'd left it in the hotel. With no way to contact him, she would simply have to wait until he showed up.

❧

The few small stores near the restaurant were closing. Glancing anxiously up and down the narrow street and wondering how they could have missed each other, she spotted a sign for Sacromonte across the road. She stood totally still, torn by both the fear settling in her stomach at Richard's disappearance and by the urge to go forward to see where the sign would lead. Did she dare go alone, wander into the gypsy neighborhood at night?

She crossed to another alley where a few more stores were still open. There were strong vibrations coming from down the street, accompanied by whistling and muffled shouts of "Olé!" From the sharp tapping sounds, she knew there was a flamenco show taking place.

A fluorescent sign blazed above a door where a man was sitting outside, tuning a guitar. This was obviously quite near Sacromonte, or at least its fringes. She glanced back to where she had last seen Richard sitting at the outdoor table. Still no sign of him.

She turned and headed up the alley toward the sign.

"*Por favor?*" she asked the man in the doorway.

He put down his guitar. "*Buenas noches, Señora,*" he replied affably. "*Sí, sí,*" he said, when she asked if she might take a look inside to see where the music was coming from.

The whitewashed room was slightly stuffy from cigarette smoke, and a fluorescent light beamed from the ceiling. People were sitting on wooden chairs in a circle, and from where she stood, Joy got a clear view of the dancer, a woman in a bright-blue skirt with an orange shawl draped around her hips. The dancer's beguiling doll-like face belied her frown of concentration, her staccato foot-pounding at once in sync with the strums of the guitar and its counterpoint.

The audience included some Asians and a few Nordic-looking

blondes, so Joy assumed this was one of the "touristy" flamenco shows the guidebook warned against. Nonetheless, the music was catchy and the dancer fervent and agile. When the woman ended her dance and sat on a chair alongside the guitarist and singer, a young man with a shock of blue-black hair, wearing a dark suit, stood and took her place. Focusing his austere gaze on the floor, he began to follow the chanting of the singer with his own lightning-quick steps. His aquiline nose and dignified air reminded Joy of a Navajo, and she lingered a few minutes, gliding on the echo of his thudding heels. Like the woman before him, he exuded a visceral sensuality, bringing to life Joy's vision of the archetypal Spanish male. Spellbound by his powerful stomping and shimmering hair, she envisioned making love to him, melting into that potent energy.

"No?" said the man outside the door with the guitar as she left.

"No. *Gracias.*"

She crossed the street and returned to the restaurant where she'd last seen Richard, a quiver in her stomach and an edgy discomfort shimmering along her skin. She knew she shouldn't have left the restaurant without him.

5

" *I*s something wrong, *Señora?*"
She spun in the direction of the voice swimming to her through the darkness. A young man in a dark T-shirt and jeans, his black hair slicked back in a ponytail, was sitting at a table, holding a bottle of beer. He looked somewhat familiar, unless perhaps after a week here all Spanish men were beginning to fuse into one Andalusian face with dark eyes beneath sensuously knotted eyebrows. A backpack was propped on the table in front of him.

"Do you have trouble?" he asked in English as he stood with an air of concern.

Joy paused. The earnestness in his voice drew her toward him. He was tall, and she had to look up to meet his gaze. "I'm looking for my husband. He's wearing a blue shirt and has light-brown hair."

She realized that the wine at dinner had taken effect the minute she said this, divulging to a stranger the fact that she was alone.

"I saw him with you before, but not here," the young man said, taking a sip from his beer.

She wondered whether she'd heard him correctly. "You saw us before?"

"You were at the Alhambra today?" he said, placing the bottle on the table.

A Marriage in Four Seasons

The Alhambra? She wasn't sure what he meant, but then, slowly, she began to see the young man who had been sitting on a chair across from hers, deep in contemplation. She'd pegged him for a tourist from India. A yogi.

"In that room with the stucco, the room where the massacre took place?" she asked.

"Si," the man said. "La Sala de los Abencerrajes."

She felt her face brighten at the memory of watching him bask so serenely in the silence of that exquisite room and how thankful she'd been to find someone else as taken by it as she was. "I remember. You looked like you were meditating."

He smiled. "Too many people for meditating. That is my favorite room in the palace. I go there only to enjoy it."

She recalled how fascinated she'd been with the dainty airiness of the stucco ceiling, which had led to her poignant thoughts of Stephen, before Richard had ruined things by bringing up that horrible slaughter.

"Are you—from here?" she asked, noting that he seemed to speak with a different accent from the Spanish she'd been hearing.

He looked surprised. "Do I not look Spanish?"

"You do. Yes, you do," she said quickly. It was something she couldn't pinpoint, but she clearly sensed something different about him.

He chuckled, revealing as his lips parted, the glint of white, even teeth. "I'm from here, in a way, although officially . . ." He paused a moment. "From Morocco." He nodded upward to the illuminated Alhambra complex rising high from the adjoining hill. "I am descended from the Medinas. Some of my ancestors once lived there."

She glanced toward the fortress hill. "In the Alhambra?"

He nodded. "Many years ago. We still have the key to our house."

"A key?" she asked in disbelief. So that was it. He wasn't a local. She wondered whether he might be joking. She'd read that the last descendants of the Moors had mostly been evicted from Spain early in the seventeenth century. "*Moroscos?*" she asked. He nodded again. "*Si, Moroscos.*"

She stifled a gasp, hardly believing she was talking to someone whose roots went back to those fabled times. She hadn't imagined that any from that bloodline were still here.

She was both stunned and curious. "Does it bother you to go there? To the palace?"

He seemed to consider this, and then shook his head. "I come only to experience the beauty. It is beautiful, no?"

She inhaled. "Breathtaking."

He nodded, shutting his eyes as if peering back in time through some inner telescope. "I'm proud of those who built it," he said softly. Then he smiled. "My family believes the Muslims will get Granada back one day."

She looked at him, not sure how to respond, wondering if this was wishful thinking on his part or whether there were those who actually believed that Moroccan descendants of Moors would regain Granada from Spain.

After a pause, she said, "You speak such good English. And Spanish."

"I went to the *universidad* here. I'm an architect."

"You live here?"

He shook his head. "In Morocco."

"Where all this came from," she said, unable to hide her admiration.

He smiled. "There are beautiful buildings in Morocco, but no Alhambra."

She shrugged. "Not in New York, either."

"New York?" he said, glancing at her with obvious, unabashed approval. She noticed again how tall he was, although not as tall as Richard. His amber skin was what had given her the impression that he was Indian. She hadn't thought Moroccan.

He nodded toward a succession of cafes ahead. "Shall we look for your husband?"

She glanced around. Somewhere in the pit of her stomach, or perhaps in her head—she was no longer sure where the wine had settled—she knew she shouldn't stroll up the street at night with a stranger. Although the idea of continuing to search for Richard at night alone made her shudder, being escorted by a strange man was equally unnerving.

Then it occurred to her that she did need to prove to Richard that not everyone in Granada was out to take advantage of tourists, and this man seemed to want to be helpful. Besides, there were people everywhere. Hoping that she and Richard would get to Sacromonte that evening, she'd left her passport and credit cards in the hotel safe, and so she had little cash or anything of value on her that could be stolen.

She'd been yearning to discover Andalusia her own way. She had, after all, imagined meeting an amiable Spaniard tomorrow who would show her the sights while she waited for Richard to return from the bullfight. A Moor accompanying her was even better.

The young man told her he was Hussein from Rabat. She introduced herself and they started up the street.

From the adjoining hill, the Alhambra glared down, its ramparts lit like candles on a birthday cake. She imagined a pregnant Queen Isabella leading the campaign against Granada, round-bellied and exhausted, staring up at the starlit sky as she eagerly awaited news of the Spanish victory. She couldn't help but feel admiration for Isabella's determination, despite her aversion to the queen's merciless ambition. Not even pregnancy had impeded Isabella's resolve to conquer this coveted town.

"It must be hard to know that your ancestors once lived there," she said, hesitant to say Alhambra before a descendant of the people who had built and then been banished from this hauntingly beautiful place.

Hussein nodded, looking somewhat glum. "It is."

He slung his pack to his other shoulder, freeing his arm next to her. With his sleek, long hair and slender frame, he looked so young. This put her at ease, as if she were walking beside one of her own Hunter students.

They went to the bar next door. He waited outside while she stepped inside and scanned the bustling crowd.

"No?" he asked when she came out.

She shook her head, feeling silly and worried. How could she explain to this young man that she'd lost Richard in the short time it took her to go to the toilet?

They walked up more steps toward another restaurant.

"This is your first time in Andalusia?" he asked.

"My first time in Spain," she said, marveling at the fact that it had, in fact, taken her so long to come to this wondrous place. Again, she realized too late that she may have made herself vulnerable by admitting that her surroundings were all new to her.

Breathing deeply from the climb, she glanced at his face. She noted again the high bridge of his nose, the dark eyebrows that sloped toward his temple giving him a pensive air. Spaniard or Moor? Even the last, ill-fated Moorish king, Boabdil, bore the blood of both Spaniards and Moors. Boabdil. He had famously wept as he was forced to abandon his beloved Granada in defeat.

There was something about this man, an easy, unconscious virility that reminded her of Francisco. Maybe it was the wine or those nostalgic college memories a little while ago, or maybe simply the thrill of being in Granada and walking alongside this attractive stranger, that made her wish that, instead of the cotton shirt and skirt she was wearing, she had put on something more alluring, like the clingy dress still in her suitcase. Just a moment before, she'd felt he could have been one of her students. Now, her readily accepting his offer to accompany her seemed tinged with something else—attraction? She pushed the thought away.

There was no trace of Richard in the next bar, either.

Hussein was glancing around with an air of concern. "Maybe he went to watch flamenco," he suggested, tilting his head in the direction of the *tablao* she'd looked in earlier.

"I've checked that one," she said quickly, reminding herself that she'd lost her husband and needed to find him. Now. "I'd better go back to the first bar, but thanks for your help."

"There are others," Hussein said encouragingly, as if there were dozens of flamenco halls where Richard might be hanging out at that very instant.

"No. . . ." she began. Then she asked herself whether she actually needed to find Richard, just yet. Maybe he *had* wandered farther away than she'd thought. She began to feel as confused as Alice hunting for her white rabbit in a world where nothing made sense. Would Richard have actually gone to a gypsy show looking for her? Would he have assumed she'd gone off to watch flamenco by herself? His behavior had been so strange on this trip, she thought, that anything was possible.

Perhaps because she'd watched Hussein at the Alhambra and sensed they'd shared a kindred vision, she felt a certain trust in his earnest interest in helping her. "I guess we could look," she said, and followed him.

The man who had been tuning his guitar in the doorway earlier was still there, strumming softly under the fluorescent light. He nodded as they passed, obviously remembering her. His eyes lingered on Hussein a few minutes, his palm muting the strumming before resuming.

Joy wondered how this Spaniard from Granada felt toward descendants of Moors, people he would no doubt consider pretenders to the Alhambra, and how he would respond to the notion that his city would one day be taken back by Morocco, as Hussein had suggested.

Farther on, a brightly lit blue door opened out onto a wide, whitewashed terrace. She hadn't reached this far on her own before, but now Hussein boldly strode upward as if magnetically drawn to the loud thuds and clapping. She followed the guitar strums embracing her as she and Hussein approached, each strum tugging her toward the door.

On the moonlit terrace, she stopped again to catch her breath before the open door that, she now realized, was the entrance to an actual cave in the hillside. She looked back at the Alhambra on the adjacent hill to hold onto some shred of reality, and then she turned back to Hussein, who was waiting.

⚬

People inside were seated in a row of chairs against the whitewashed wall of a deep rectangular room. The rounded cave ceiling was decorated with shiny copper plates and cooking ladles that glowed a burnished orange and looked like they'd just been polished.

Although the audience here included tourists photographing the show, many in the crowd did look Spanish, all watching a slender, stern-looking woman, furiously stomping her heels.

The dancer was wearing a wide, ankle-length skirt, a part of which she had bunched in one hand above her knees to show off her stomping feet while her other hand was poised high behind her head, fingers curling gracefully to the rhythm belted out by the woman hand-clapper behind her. The dancer's face glistened with perspiration, and she seemed to be in a trance, her eyes half-closed, her jaw working with exertion. Joy could barely hold in her excitement at being in a true gypsy cave. She wouldn't have been surprised to learn that this dancer was actually the lady of the house, pausing in her cooking to dance for her guests.

Joy and Hussein stood near the doorway. He glanced down at her, and again she thought of Francisco and how they used to walk through Manhattan, dipping in and out of the Soho bars. They'd been gutsy and foolhardy in those days, and the inherent dangers of the city's streets late at night had yanked at the tight passion between them, leading them back to his apartment for fervent, sweaty sex.

She felt giddy at the memory as both she and Hussein continued to gaze at the dancer, the surrounding music sealing the two of them into a private cocoon.

"Flamenco is the dance of pain," Hussein whispered to her, nudging her to move in front of him so she could get a better view. "It comes from the Inquisition, the slaughtering of the Moors, the gypsies, and the Jews."

She nodded solemnly, although she hadn't thought of it in those terms. Flamenco always seemed to her a dance of the fiercely independent gypsy way of life, of rootless hardship, as well as being singularly Spanish, whatever that now was. She'd never connected it to the plight of the persecuted Moors and Jews, and yet now she saw that it must have been. The lamentation and wailing in the singer's voice was sparked by something far more wrenching than a precarious nomadic life. It was a primal cry of agony.

Joy heard herself echo those very wails—in yearning for her lost child and for the longed-for happiness with Richard that seemed more untenable than ever.

She grew conscious of the warm press of Hussein's chest against her back. She inched forward, away from him, a hot flush rising from her toes to her face. She dared not look back at him or acknowledge his, probably accidental, touch.

A moment later she pretended not to notice when his hand, perhaps unintentionally again, brushed against her arm and landed gently on her wrist.

She flinched, remembering how she'd enviously watched him that afternoon in the Alhambra as he surrendered himself to the brilliance of the Sala de los Abencerrajes. It now made perfect sense that, as an architect, he would let that marvel of design carry him on its magic as she had tried to do. As Richard could never seem to do, regardless of how magnificent he found the surroundings.

Hussein now appeared to be inviting her to embrace the dancer and hypnotic music his way, as if nothing else mattered but submitting to this marvelous spectacle before them.

She sank deeper into the fervor of the room and the beats of the dancer's pounding feet, felt each pulsing stomp reverberate through her own body. Closing her eyes, she let the room envelope her and coax her into its mystical landscape and throbbing pulse.

The image of Richard flashed through her mind. She brusquely turned around to face Hussein. "I must find my husband."

Hussein's eyes bore into her, his face going blank, but he obediently stepped back, making space for her to pass. They slipped behind the guitarist and hand-clapper and out the door of the cave into the crisp night air. The chill braced her, clearing her head.

The light from the street lamps illuminated the tops of the whitewashed alley walls below them, as though they'd been dusted with sugar. From here, the Alhambra across the valley and the lights of its gardens and summer pavilion sparkled. The air around her, as if filtered through some exquisite sieve, flowed into her lungs like pure oxygen.

Irving had described nostalgic nights in his dank palace chamber, listening to the gypsy singing from the Sacromonte caves. She felt him watching her now from his room in the Alhambra, sharing in and wholeheartedly approving of her enchantment. A ripple of pride rustled through her that she had actually dared to create her own exploration of Sacromonte.

Quietly, Hussein moved closer to her on the stoop above the steps. For an instant their faces almost touched.

He reached out and touched her hair, running his hand down to her shoulder. "Beautiful hair, beautiful blue eyes," she thought he said.

Joy steadied herself on the stoop. Hussein bent his head down to hers, his lips grazing her cheek as she instinctively turned her head away. Then, she found her way back to him, her mouth settling briefly against his, against his raw youth and her revived memories of Francisco.

Without a word, he gently pulled her toward him. She didn't resist when he lifted her slightly and pressed her against the wall, tentatively kissing her lips.

Her heart started to pound stronger, so fast and hard she thought she'd choke. She was certain he could sense the out-of-control drumming in her chest as her back rubbed against the wall in response to his pressure. Oh, God, she thought. This is how it was with Francisco, his lips . . .

Shaking off the vision, she placed her hands on Hussein's chest and pushed him away. What was wrong with her? What was she doing here with this man nearly half her age, a man she didn't even know?

Hussein straightened up, looking puzzled. He dropped his hands to his side.

She looked at him, embarrassed to have been so totally swept up in this ridiculous way, but before she could say anything, he pointed toward the dark ravine sloping down the mountainside.

"Look, *Señora*," he said. "That is where King Boabdil departed Granada, hidden from his people."

She looked to where his outstretched arm was pointing, her mouth smarting from the imprint of his. Had this really happened? Had she just cheated on Richard?

Hussein's voice, however, seemed tinged with a reverent sadness at this historic defeat of his people rather than regret for his actions just now. For him, perhaps, nothing untoward had passed between them. Or else the quick swing on his part was to spare them any awkwardness. Perhaps, to him, what just occurred had been simply a free moment of pleasure between two people that should remain private and thus without remark.

"And there," he added, pointing in another direction, "*La Cuesta de las Lagrimas*—the Hill of Tears."

The Hill of Tears, the alleged spot from which King Boabdil had taken his last look at Granada. The victorious Ferdinand and Isabella, in an act of surprising charity, were said to have granted the vanquished Moor permission to leave the Alhambra in secret to avoid having to pass before throngs of his conquered subjects.

"*El ultimo suspiro del Moro,*" he said.

She nodded, her pulse still racing. The last sigh of the Moor.

She turned to look at him again, but he was looking straight ahead, his face impassive. He was, she realized, unbearably good-looking. She was confused. Was it the thrill of kissing a stranger, of betraying her husband in this way, that had pushed her to go along with him? Was it that he had just showed her the other possibilities that existed for her? Other than Richard?

He offered his hand. She tried to ignore the warm feel of his palm against hers as she let him lead her down the rest of the dark steps. Although thankful for his discretion, she couldn't help wishing that he'd pushed on with his kisses and touches, brought her more deeply into his world, rather than allowed her to stop him.

She stepped quietly beside him, awkwardly keeping her hand in his, wanting to comfort him for the loss of his king and of Granada, wanting to comfort herself for the loss of her own innocence and to protect herself from the unnerving realization that she could so easily disengage from her life and move into the unknown.

6

She heard her name.

As she and Hussein emerged from the alley, Joy quickly tugged her hand free.

Richard was hurrying toward them in the dark. She instinctively turned to Hussein, still stinging from their one kiss and yet wanting to reclaim some of their brief, shared intimacy. He seemed about to say something, but stopped. It was too late, anyway.

She felt her shoulders droop. "It's my husband," she said.

Richard reached her out of breath. "Joy! Where the hell . . . ? I've been looking all over for you!"

She stumbled back from the sharp gale of his agitation.

"Christ, honey, I went into every bar. Where the heck did you wander off to?"

"I—I came out of the bathroom and you were gone," she said. "I waited around and checked back in the restaurant. Then I went looking for you."

"You were up there in the bathroom almost half an hour. I went up to look for you myself. I even asked the waiters, but nobody'd seen you."

"I'm sorry," she mumbled, "we must have crossed signals. I thought you might have gone looking for me in one of those other cafes."

Richard was now staring past her. Remembering Hussein, Joy

turned around. Hussein appeared even younger and more strik-ing than before.

"I'm sorry," she repeated, suddenly feeling weak but knowing she must introduce them to each other. "Rich, this is Hussein. He was in the Alhambra this afternoon at the same time we were. He was helping me look for you."

Richard continued to stare at Hussein, studying him closely. Hussein now appeared uncomfortable.

"This is my husband, Richard," she said to Hussein, almost ashamed to admit to her choice of a cranky spouse. Hussein stepped forward and offered his hand. Richard hesitated, and then perfunctorily shook it.

"Hussein is from Morocco, but his ancestors lived here, in the Alhambra," she said, a tremor of pride in her voice at having come upon an actual offspring of the Moors who built this place.

Hussein grinned. Richard was silent and looked unmoved.

From down the street came a spout of bright headlights and a choking rumble. A motorcycle was making its way toward them.

"Finally," Richard said. "I had the restaurant call the cops."

Embarrassed that Richard was making such a fuss in public, Joy broke into an uneasy laugh. "Honey, I'm sorry. I didn't mean to give you such a scare. I should have just stayed put."

A loud voice abruptly called from up the street.

She turned to see who it was. She could make out a man standing in the dark alley, a man with a guitar. She thought he must be the same one who'd been strumming earlier outside the flamenco *tablao*. She wondered if there was some commotion inside.

When she turned back around, Hussein was gone.

"Hussein?" She stared into the empty space behind her. The man up the street with the guitar went inside the *tablao*. From somewhere in the alley beyond, she heard light, rapid steps.

"Hussein?" She turned back to Richard. "Where'd he go?"

The helmeted policeman on the motorcycle reached them and slowed down, idling his sputtering motor.

"It's okay," Richard said to the policeman, putting his arm around Joy. "I've found her."

The policeman looked at her, then at Richard from under the visor of his helmet. "*Bueno?*"

Richard nodded. "Yes, thank you. Sorry to have bothered you."

"Be careful," the policeman said sternly. "Many thieves here."

Richard nodded in agreement. "Yes, sir. *Gracias.*"

The policeman appraised them a second more, then turned his bike around, revved up his engine, and headed back down the street.

Richard turned to her. "Who was that guy?"

"Who?"

"That guy with you."

"Hussein?"

"Joy, how could you just wander off with a perfect stranger? *Here* of all places?"

She shrugged. "I didn't know what else to do. I thought you'd gone to some other bar up the street. He saw me looking for you and offered to help. He's visiting, too, from Morocco."

Richard scoffed. "Morocco?" He shook his head. "I saw someone just like him hanging around with some other guys while I was waiting for you to come out of the bathroom. They were smoking joints and gabbing in Spanish."

"Hussein?"

"The guy with the backpack. The ponytail. I know the smell of dope."

"Oh, Rich, don't start now!" she snapped, resenting the accusation. She had just been in Hussein's arms and had certainly not smelled anything like dope.

"I'm not starting anything. I saw him smoking it."

"Hussein was sitting alone," she said adamantly. "I was looking for you and he said you might be in one of the other bars. We went to the Sacromonte to see if you—"

He stared at her in disbelief. "You *what?*"

"There was a show—" She started to explain, but the absurdity of what she'd done was already dawning on her.

"How could you have just gone off like that, and with someone you don't even know? You see the hustlers around here, honey. Didn't you hear the cop? The place is crawling with thieves! Men with nothing better to do than—you just let the wind blow you here and there—"

"Rich! I just wanted to see for myself . . . and Hussein is no thief. He was perfectly—" She caught herself before she could say *irresistible.* "He was helping me look for you. I was safer with him than I would have been on my own."

"Jesus Christ! That was crazy."

"I couldn't find you."

Looking flabbergasted, he shook his head. "I can't understand how I missed you." His voice faltered. The fear he must have felt was now apparent because he was trembling and seemed out of breath again, although he had been standing still for some time.

"I'm sorry," she said, suddenly softened by his concern. "Honey, I'm sorry you were so worried."

He shook his head again; then, he sighed and glanced at his watch. "Come on. It's nearly twelve, and we have to drive to Cordoba tomorrow afternoon. We need to find a cab from the main road."

⚭

She started to follow him, then stopped, not wanting to lose all that had happened this past hour, her reckless abandon, her resurrected feelings. Although she was already feeling guilty for some of her thoughts about Hussein and for having wished he'd continued with his kisses, a part of her still wanted to hang on to that moment.

"Wait," she said, tugging at Richard's shirt sleeve. "Just wait a minute, Rich. Look."

He stopped, then glanced up to where she was pointing.

"Look at how beautiful it is, Rich."

The ebony sky looked all the more inscrutable above the twinkling lights of the luminous palace across the valley. She'd read that those who'd once lived in the Alhambra had listened to the distant singing and clapping from the hill they were now standing on.

Washington Irving was known to have never married after the tragic death of his first love, a young woman who had died at the age of seventeen. But, had he ever tasted an Andalusian night through a woman's lips, she wondered, ever stood on the Sacromonte caressing a woman's body under a moon-drenched sky? Had he ever loved the Alhambra for something beyond its historical and architectural significance?

Still pointing, Joy noticed her wrist glowing in the faint light.

She twisted her arm a little, remembering the arching arms of the dancer in the cave. She stared at her wrist as if in a trance, remembering the dancer's elegant, curling fingers. Her own white skin looked oddly bare. Something was different about it. Something was missing. She kept staring at her wrist.

Her gold bracelet . . .

She tried to remember if she'd left it on the hotel's bathroom sink. She hardly ever took the bracelet off unless she was showering.

She turned to Richard, about to ask him whether he'd noticed her wearing it earlier. She stopped herself. The bracelet had been his gift on their first anniversary.

"What is it?" he asked.

Her heart skipped. She was positive she'd been wearing it, although she couldn't exactly recall seeing it on her wrist when they left the hotel. Then she remembered Hussein's brief touch as they stood in the tight space of the cave watching the flamenco dancer. She tried to envision the crowded cave and dancer once more, to feel Hussein's warmth behind her, his skin on her skin. He had touched her right wrist.

"Honey?" Richard asked again.

Maybe it was later, outside, when she had been so lost in her own sensory hunger, focused on his hands, his lips, on a moment that would never come again.

"Joy, are you okay?" Richard's voice sounded as unfamiliar as a stranger's.

She dropped her head and let out a deep breath. *Shit!* She was certain now that she'd been wearing it.

"Honey, what is it?" Richard reached out and stroked her cheek.

Shit! If Richard had just been more flexible, had just gone to Sacromonte with her from the start, none of this would have happened.

She turned away from him and tried to think. Her fingers started to tingle as she remembered the singeing heat of Hussein's palm. Had he taken it in that sweep of his hand she'd mistaken for a caress? Her pulse had been racing, her face flaming as she'd watched the dancer. He had probably picked up on her gullibility from the start, realized he had her in his clutches the moment he saw her fascination with his Moorish ancestry—or his claim to it—and had easily reeled her in.

Her heart began to pound again at her own stupidity. *Shit, shit, shit!* How could she have deluded herself, even for an instant, into feeling that she and that man had anything in common, that they'd shared anything other than a passing animal attraction?

She took a deep breath, trying to swallow her shame. She'd been lucky he hadn't forced her to do anything more. She wondered what might have happened if she had gone further than the kiss, if he would have stolen whatever he could find on her, including her wedding ring. She would never have let her guard down with a strange man in New York. No matter his age, looks, or story.

A thread of anger jerked at her again for having allowed Hussein to take advantage of her, and it included anger at him for having had the nerve to deceive her. She couldn't bring herself to say anything. She just stood in silence, next to Richard, trying to regain her composure.

Then the feel of Hussein's lips intruded again, bringing back Francisco's long-ago kisses. Her cheeks began to sting all over again.

An unbidden flush of pleasure started to rise in her, bathing her in silky warmth. She shut her eyes and savored it. Despite her disappointment, she'd just allowed herself an experience she couldn't have imagined in her day-to-day life back home.

She'd been given a gift tonight, a strange, special gift. Maybe from Washington Irving himself. She'd felt him with her tonight in some peculiar way, and he'd certainly believed in ghosts. He'd never doubted their nocturnal presence all around the Alhambra.

Her distress began to wane. Hussein had presented her with a part of Andalusia tonight, and as a result she had been awakened to a part of herself she had come to think was permanently gone. He had shown her how to give herself to those feelings of longing and passion, whether or not he knew it. Whether or not he even cared. Maybe he'd felt entitled to something in return. Her bracelet?

"Rich?" she said, anxiously turning to face him.

Richard looked at her. Something in her voice seemed to alarm him.

She forced herself to smile a little, wanting to allay his worry. She was beginning to feel lightheaded and dropped her head against his shoulder. *Lucky.* She'd been damned lucky tonight in being spared actual danger.

He hugged her close. "Honey, I was so worried. You just disappeared."

"Rich," she said again, wanting to apologize but not daring to tell him that he'd been right all along, that she should have listened to him and been more careful rather than put herself at risk.

"I love you," was all she said, the words tumbling out of her like a confession.

Caressing her hair, he said, "I love you, too, babe. I was shaken, that's all."

She exhaled, knowing she'd meant what she'd just said. She also knew that there were things in life that were impossible to explain, like how her love for her husband could have been so quickly supplanted by an impulsive attraction to a man she didn't even know, by a deep craving for something she had yet to identify.

She took his arm and together they walked in the direction of their hotel.

Belinda

RICHARD

⟨⟩

7

*H*e had spotted her outside the Kennedy terminal and had practically run up to her, inviting her to share his cab into Manhattan.

"I'm going to New Jersey," she said, a half smile on her lips.

"Well, how about a drink in the city? I have to take a train to Westchester from Grand Central."

He knew he was out on a limb, but he didn't care. Something deeply missing in his life was propelling him forward into uncharted territory, and he couldn't chance never seeing her again.

He'd met her the previous night at a London airport hotel. They'd been booked on the same flight from London to New York, which had been canceled. She was among the passengers being put up for the night at the airport Hilton. In line ahead of him to fill in the voucher at the reception desk for the complimentary room, she'd turned to face him.

"Would you have a pen on you?"

He'd retrieved it from his breast pocket, and as he handed

it to her, he was immediately seized by her bright smile and the yellow-green of her eyes raging against her olive skin. He had an odd, yet distinct sense that they'd met before, or perhaps she simply reminded him of someone he once knew, but the unmistakable connection unnerved him. She handed his pen back and introduced herself: Belinda Bericini.

"Richard Amis."

He was pleased to see her the next morning at the breakfast counter in the hotel lobby, and she'd smiled when he gave her a friendly nod. Later, on the courtesy bus back to the airport, she was sitting in the single seat behind the driver, head down as she busily checked her cell phone. He'd been booked in business class and had lost her in the throng of passengers on the plane. Until now.

In response to his invitation to buy her a drink, she tilted her head, but whether mentally checking transportation or other personal ties, he wasn't sure. Finally, she agreed, saying she could take a later bus to Paramus.

At a Midtown bar, he learned that she was single, taught preschool in Paramus, and was returning after a week at Oxford, where she'd attended a conference on early childhood education. She said she was passionate about teaching and couldn't wait to start applying what she'd just learned.

They somehow got to talking about traveling, and she mentioned her other journeys—to Yemen, Morocco, Uzbekistan, Albania, Burma, Thailand, Pakistan, Fiji. The list went on, none of them work-related. Whenever she had a break and saved enough money, she told him, she was off to someplace new. She'd traveled all of her adult life, even more than he had as the child of a diplomat. Certainly more than he and Joy had since their marriage. He was surprised to find that her talk was piquing his own interest to travel. Most of his "exotic" trips nowadays had to do with bank business, which he didn't relish.

Belinda

Belinda talked almost casually of sailing Omani dhows like Sinbad, swimming in the diamond-clear waters off Fiji, riding elephants through jungles in Thailand. This restive nomadic quality, together with her wiry black hair and green eyes, moved him to invite her to dinner; then he didn't want the night to end. Somehow it didn't surprise him when, with a somewhat puzzled grin, she agreed to spend more time with him.

He couldn't explain how his initial attraction to this woman had transformed into this dogged passion so quickly. She was certainly attractive, and probably younger than him by a decade, but it was something he'd felt in their conversations, something he'd been searching for before without even knowing it. She was fearless in an odd, haphazard way, exhibiting an infectious exuberance during their brief encounter in London and later over drinks in town.

As they spoke, he began to feel he'd always known her. They'd possibly even crossed paths on Manhattan streets any number of times. Although not one to give credence to fate, it seemed inevitable to him over drinks that he would take her into his life. Immediately.

There were countless ways to rationalize an affair, and many of them raced through his mind: the past few years of discontent with Joy after losing Stephen, the bitter arguments as he tried to help her through the depression after the loss, compounded by their work pressures and his travel. No matter how hard he had tried to reassure Joy that their future would surely include children, she couldn't get pregnant. It was as if her body were rejecting carrying his baby, sealing itself off from him. Although he'd tried to overlook her distance, he had come to feel dejected and, on some deeper level, no longer significant in her life. It was as though he had become only a means to an end, a sperm bank. He sometimes wondered whether it would even matter to her if he simply stopped showing up at home.

Still, it was with a sliver of hope that she would refuse that he asked Belinda if she'd ever been to the Dumas Hotel, a renovated art-deco building known for its charm. The bank kept several executive rooms for out-of-town guests or its own late-night work-aholics there. They'd only just met, after all, and he'd never been unfaithful to Joy. He'd never engaged much in casual sex even before he met Joy. But he'd been yearning to do this since London, and he knew this beguiling woman would become a part of his life.

8

$\mathcal{A}$lthough Joy usually waited for him to get home to have dinner, by her own admission she enjoyed rare evenings alone to grade papers or catch up with her reading without feeling she was neglecting him.

He called her from the men's room at the bar. "Hey, I'm back. You okay?"

"Hi, honey, I missed you. Good flight?"

He paused. "Pretty much. Anything new on your end?"

"I'm fine. Just working like a dog to turn in grades before next week."

He paused again. "Okay, then, I'll crash downtown. I've got early meetings tomorrow, and I'm bushed."

"Sure," she said. "I need to finish most of this tonight, anyway."

"I'll see you tomorrow, then." He hesitated, then added, "Love you."

He imagined her pleased by the news that he wouldn't be making it back for dinner, freeing her from preparing a meal for the two of them. Instead, she could stretch out on the sofa with a snack and a glass of wine and tend to her students' papers, the purring Ophelia on her lap.

The lobby was empty when he and Belinda arrived at the Dumas, but he still gave her the room number and rode up the elevator alone, asking her to follow separately. It seemed to take her forever to finally knock on the door. When he answered, almost surprised that she'd actually come, she gave him a quizzical smile, as if asking whether she should even be here; but he pulled her against him, holding her close for several moments, then lowered her onto the bed, cradling her head as if it were porcelain.

He caressed her neck, the thick coils of her hair. She reached up to unbutton his shirt as if she'd done this countless times before, her hand then continuing downward and unbuckling his belt. Before he knew it, they were naked, her body against his, warm and yielding.

As his other world faded, Richard was engulfed by an emotional calm he hadn't felt in a long while. Nothing else mattered but the soft hills of her breasts beneath him, her nipples the color of cocoa, her dark pubic triangle that beckoned. When he entered her, he was suddenly on another planet and in another lifetime. Still, he wasn't prepared for the ease with which he could deceive Joy or the sheer delight and tranquility he felt in this stranger's arms.

Afterwards, however, he was racked by violent, and embarrassing, hysterical sobs that seemed to come out of relief more than anything else. He cried and muttered incoherently, yet Belinda offered no sign at all of resentment that their stolen moment together had been hijacked by whatever was bothering him. Perhaps she understood that it was only with her, a stranger, that he could let it all out.

When she asked what was wrong, he told her all of it, how when Joy first became pregnant he'd never been able to feel enough of what she'd wanted him to, nor identify with that new part of him she was carrying inside of her. Even when they'd seen the head and tiny curled body on the sonogram, the technician eagerly pointing out a foot, toes, an elbow, he couldn't yet care for this fetus in the same way he did for Joy.

Belinda

He told Belinda of that moment in the delivery room, after the emergency rush to the hospital when Joy went into labor three months early and her moans had made him hate himself and even the unborn infant for putting her through that. He told her of his astonishment at what happened when the child burst into their lives.

It wasn't until he'd actually laid eyes on their son, he told her, that he'd felt his love for his wife transform, divide, and burrow one-half into the tiny body of the baby. He couldn't help retaining that image in the delivery room during the C-section when Stephen was wrested from Joy's belly by the doctor's bloody hands. It was only then that he felt the sweat that had accumulated above his sterile mask, nervous sweat that burned his eyes but that he hadn't noticed for the two hours of Joy's intense labor.

He told her how through the blurring sweat he saw, or thought he saw, something clearly move from Joy to the infant, some vague apparition. The sight of that shadow-like energy was inexplicably clear, as if his love for his wife had split in two, one half attaching itself to the little body in the doctor's hands. It was so astonishing that he had momentarily forgotten about Joy, despite her cries of despair at the shocking news of the stillbirth. He told Belinda that his own cries soon echoed Joy's.

Even when they'd both taken turns holding the small, perfectly formed corpse, he'd been stunned, marveling at this new love for the tiny, slippery being that was no longer. To this day, he said, he wasn't certain whether he had been hallucinating when he saw that shadow. He was also not sure he'd ever fully absorbed the magnitude of their loss in that awful moment. It had been nearly two years ago.

He told Belinda that for weeks and months afterward, he had spent each day waiting for its end, the minutes inching by at the office until he could leave. Once home, he would drop onto the sofa and mindlessly watch television to escape the reality he didn't want to face. He told her how he had tried to soothe Joy, to make their dinner, or to take her out. Sometimes she would join him on the sofa, silently curling up beside him as they watched other lives pass by on the screen. Nothing with children; only news, reality shows, or detective dramas. But, most of the time, she would remain at the dining room table with the enviable distraction of papers to grade. Finally, they'd get into bed where he would drift into a battered sleep, eased only by a double scotch.

It was as if their son had taken to his tiny grave all the strength Richard had left. On a good day, Richard said, his feelings were completely snuffed out, and he couldn't resurrect emotions much at all, even for Joy, who must have been even more devastated than he. On the occasions when he rallied and tried to comfort her, his attempts came out clumsy and deficient. It was as if they had both been run over by a truck and left to writhe in agony on opposite sides of the road, unable even to crawl to each other for help. His entire viewpoint seemed to shift from then on, he told Belinda. The world was a far more perilous and unpredictable place.

As the months passed, he told her, Joy seemed less and less interested in anything but her work at Hunter. Her students' needs and wellbeing became increasingly important to her, and Richard assumed that the pain of the loss of the baby was somewhat lessened by her tending to them. Similarly, her desire to have sex seemed to have totally vanished. His tender advances and hints were mostly met with stony indifference, as if it were as unthinkable as boarding a spaceship to Mars. She definitely avoided arousing him, even slipping into her closet to undress, insisting that it was warmer between the hanging clothes.

He knew he was as much to blame as Joy for the dribbling away of their sex life. Even when he did approach her, he did so tentatively because he felt he was supposed to, and not with the passion he'd previously felt. But at least he approached her, he said. At least he had tried. Something organic between the two of them just didn't jibe the way it used to, something he'd been unable to put his finger on, something she must have needed that he couldn't give her. That, he told Belinda, and the loss of their unborn child, struck and rattled like a loose rock in his own chest at unexpected moments.

He couldn't bear to admit to Belinda that he could not think of a time recently when he felt even a shred of Joy's ardor. On the rare occasion that she approached him, it seemed that all she relished lately in their sexual encounters were her quick, multiple orgasms, of which she seemed infinitely capable. An avid exerciser, Joy had a toned body that obeyed her every command. But mostly, he suspected that his very presence in the same bedroom had come to annoy her. He assumed this also had to do with her loss of the baby and figured it would pass at some point, although waiting for that moment had become damn near excruciating.

"You love her, don't you?" Belinda had finally asked.

He was silent, then nodded, unable to lie, but also aware that whatever he was creating with her would have to fit into the truth of his life as it was.

"That's good," was all she said, stroking his hair as if his answer, oddly enough, gave her peace. "Always remember that."

As she continued to caress him, there was no sign that she was disappointed or even discouraged by his outburst. She simply drifted off to sleep with her arm around him as if they'd been together for years.

A week after their first encounter, they met again outside his office on Park Avenue. Although on most Fridays he took the earlier five o'clock train home, he told Joy he'd be working late again. It was her book club evening, anyway, and she never got home before midnight from those meetings, eager to sleep off the dinner, wine, and female chatter.

Tonight, Belinda took him to an Italian restaurant, Giovanni. They went down two flights of stairs from the sidewalk and he had the feeling that only regulars would have known of its cavernous whereabouts. In his eagerness, he wolfed down the risotto and osso bucco he'd ordered—as good as any he'd had in Rome— and Belinda's choice of a lush Chianti slid down his throat like a balm. It seemed a positive omen.

She turned to him during dessert. "Where are we going with this, Richard?"

He swallowed more wine, savoring its hint of plum and cherry. "All the way," he said, as steadily as he could.

"Which is?"

"Wherever we want it to go."

She sipped her espresso.

"Where do *you* want it to go?" he said, hating the ambivalence in his tone.

"I asked you first. You're the one with the most to lose. I'm not married."

"Are you asking how I'm going to deal with my wife or with my feelings for you?"

"Both," she said.

"I'm totally wanting to get to know you better," he heard himself insist, staring at her face, afraid that if he took his eyes off her even for an instant she'd detect the faltering behind his gaze. "I've never wanted anything so much."

"And you're sure this won't cost you?"

"Cost me?"

"Your current life. Your wife. Your stable marriage."

"My marriage is on the rocks."

Her eyes seemed to penetrate him, although her expression hadn't changed. "Not entirely."

"This isn't going to cost me," he said.

As much as he meant what he said, and despite his suffocating, urgent hunger for Belinda, he knew he was lying. He also wanted Joy.

With the way his relationship with Joy had been lately, betrayal would certainly create an even bigger rift between them. He knew that he could still get out of "this" if he wanted to, could still get home to Joy and his life without giving up much. A few brief encounters could be forgotten. Yet, it seemed that he and Joy together had nothing at the moment besides a confused and lacking world. All they'd had previously was not just in jeopardy, but in doubt. And the lack he felt of love and desire and fulfillment—how much of that had he really had even before Stephen?

He was sinking into this guilty awareness of his unsolved issues, half praying for his good sense to snatch him back from the brink of temptation, when Belinda reached across the table and touched his lips with her slender, cool fingertips. He closed his eyes and realized, with a somewhat sinking heart, that he was hooked. In spite of his thought to the contrary just a moment before, he'd missed the moment when he could have escaped and spared himself, and Joy, of what surely must come next. Now that the moment had slipped by, it wouldn't come again. He'd crossed over into his new life, and like it or not, he'd have to deal with all the consequences.

He couldn't help asking himself, then, who Belinda really was and why she didn't seem to mind hanging around with someone not entirely available to her. She had asked him where this was going, after all, so she seemed to care about their relationship continuing, perhaps without caring that she could not have more than this: interludes. Perhaps she was some new breed of woman looking for a lover rather than a relationship. Maybe what she wanted was a sugar daddy, or maybe the conquest of a married man would boost her ego. But none of that seemed to fit what little he knew of her. She had asked where the relationship was going, and yet, hadn't seemed to need to know. She didn't seem to need anyone or anything, in fact. Like an amoeba, he thought, she seemed self-sufficient and content on her own.

He called Joy and told her he'd be spending the night in the office accommodations again, not unusual when he had a late working night; but instead of going to the Dumas Hotel, they took a cab to a West Side hotel Belinda suggested.

At first, he was too excited by the prospect of the night ahead to notice the shabbiness of the hotel, expecting to find it the same sort of surprise as the restaurant, unconventional but inviting. It wasn't. The room was depressingly Spartan, and it smelled of artificial spray and stale cigarettes. The loud window air-conditioner seemed to amplify the street noise.

Belinda, to his surprise, looked enchanted. "Not bad," she whispered, as she took in the unattractive room.

"Well. . . ." He started to say they could change rooms, but her happy smile made him forget his unease. "If you like it, it's fine."

She looked nostalgic. "It reminds me of a place I stayed at in Thailand, once. That was one of my best trips."

He shrugged. "I've seen worse in Kyrgyzstan." In fact, several months ago he had bitterly complained to the bank's overseas travel bureau that they do a better job of researching before booking their staff into dumps like that one in Kyrgyzstan. But tonight, he'd pretend they were in some mesmerizing stink-hole where this was the best to be had. He could see being in a hovel in Thailand, or even Kyrgyzstan, with this woman and not minding it one bit.

Belinda

He overlooked the natty bedspread, along with the thought that they might wake somebody in the next room through the cheap walls. All he wanted now was to be swallowed up inside her.

⁓

As he lay in bed after she fell asleep, he could still hear her deep, cadenced voice. There was a musky quality to it, as if her low notes carried a rich scent of amaretto. Maybe that quality came with her dark Italian hair and skin. Joy's voice was much higher and lighter by comparison, and she was fair-skinned and blonde. *Cerebral* was the word that came to mind to describe his wife. It seemed right, somehow, that Belinda was so different from Joy, that he was not tempted to compare them so much as to note their differences. In some ways, they were a species apart. Intellectual, artistic Joy; fiery, earthy Belinda.

He was aware, however, that Belinda had some of the traits he'd fallen for in Joy, mainly her love of exotic settings. Maybe he was doomed to desire this in a woman, to seek out the antithesis of himself, although by now he knew the pitfalls.

His differences with Joy strained their relationship more than he wanted to admit. He never felt adventurous or daring enough for her, especially in unfamiliar situations. Joy was always at ease confronting the unknown, whether it was walking into a room full of strangers or exploring a new environment. Whereas he'd always had an overactive instinct for self-preservation, Joy happily threw caution to the wind. Obviously, Belinda did the same.

Maybe his stubborn reserve was a response to his mother's restlessness, which had been on display until the day she finally packed up and left altogether. He'd never gotten over her need to pursue her own life beyond that of his father, his younger brother, and himself. Perhaps his choice of a steady career in business had been an attempt to salvage some shred of stability after the crushing upheaval of his mother walking out on them.

Both Belinda and Joy loved teaching, although on different ends of the spectrum: Belinda taught small children, and Joy taught college kids. Yet teaching was something he had little knack or patience for, even when it came to training his own assistants at the bank. By now, he'd surrendered to being the recalcitrant, adoring pupil at the back of the classroom, helplessly vulnerable to the will of the teacher, drawn to women who enjoyed leading the way.

9

"I couldn't wait," he said happily, quickly walking up to her.

"Darling!" she whispered, looking elated to see him.

The motel, the Adriatica, was on the outskirts of Astoria. He'd found this place in a travel magazine, suspecting Belinda would enjoy flowers on windowsills and the slightly shabby, old-world appeal of the quaint wrought-iron doorway and striped awnings.

She'd just given some teachers a workshop at an elementary school in a neighborhood in Queens. Before the violent Balkan events, he'd thought of it as a Yugoslav neighborhood. Now he assumed it was ethnically Croatian because of the multitude of Catholic churches. Even the motel seemed to have been air-lifted straight out of Zagreb and into this New York borough. The embroidered chairs at the reception desk reflected a bygone European elegance, and the place smelled like aromatic, aging wood. Belinda seemed captivated enough.

He'd been agonizing all day, imagining her scent, barely getting through a particularly stressful afternoon at work, and leaving an hour early to avoid traffic. Now here she was, wearing a pink dress, her hair in a ponytail, looking more like a schoolgirl than a teacher. He felt an inadvertent ripple of discomfort with her looking so prim and innocent when he'd had other ideas.

Once in the room, however, she undid her hair and came to him, laughing and fervent, once more the vixen. He started to undo the buttons of her dress, but overcome by desire, gave up and simply lifted her skirt. She seemed no less impatient, kicking off her panties and coaxing him into her.

She folded herself around him like a silken pretzel, wrapping her legs around his back, calves caressing his spine, her chest rising up to him. Although he was careful not to hurt her, she seemed to luxuriate in these convoluted postures, her eyes closing indolently with her moans.

"I feel I exist to excite you," she murmured, caressing the back of his head as if he were a prized lion, smoothing away the tension from his day, preparing him for love. She stroked his back, massaging his neck and shoulders as if he were an athlete whose muscles needed reconditioning.

It seemed important to her that he felt loved. She paid careful attention to the kinds of foods he liked when selecting a restaurant, to the mood he was in when recommending a wine. In truth, he never expected to be treated as this special by a woman. Conflicted though he was, he recognized that he was more than lucky. He was downright blessed.

Later, while Belinda lay in bed watching television, he went into the bathroom.

"Damn!" he called out.

"What?"

"A condom. Someone else's condom in the toilet."

She came into the bathroom, peeked from behind him, and started to giggle.

"Fuck," he muttered, flushing several times before the thing disappeared.

Back in bed, he glanced around the room at the threadbare carpet and the tear in the curtain. The European-inspired decor now had considerably less appeal. He thought of Joy's attention to hotel rooms whenever they traveled, how they almost always changed the room originally assigned them if Joy didn't like it. He'd become almost as critical of the accommodations he stayed in now, convinced that something better could be had with a little needling of the concierge; yet, while he and Joy shared this fondness for ambiance and comfort, it seemed to hold no attraction for Belinda. He was beginning to understand that she not only seemed bent on making do with an unsavory room—she liked it for that very reason.

Back in bed, he pulled hard on the starched white sheet to get it above his chest, smoothing it over the bedspread as far as he could to ensure that none of the outer spread touched them.

"How come it upset you so much to find that in the toilet?" Belinda asked with a grin, her black curls winding across his chest.

He looked down to the part in her hair revealing her ivory scalp. He kissed her there, wiping away the thoughts of Joy. "Because it's disgusting."

"Why?"

"It just is."

She laughed. "Does it bother you that others come here for the same reason we do?"

"Which is?"

"To satisfy their sinful urges," she said, a wicked look in her eye.

"No, it doesn't bother me that others come here to—share love."

"Then?"

"I feel the place hasn't been cleaned up well after its last tenants. That's all."

"Is it?"

"Sure." He thought a moment. "How else did you think I meant it?"

"Well, you might be feeling that this is a place where people come to fuck and that we're just like them. Does that bother you?"

He shook his head. "Of course not."

"Just the unsanitary aspect of it?"

"Yes."

"No guilt feelings or anything?"

"Guilty is the last thing I feel with you, baby," he said, but he knew that this was only partly true.

She shrugged. "Each of us comes into the other's life for a reason, Richard. The point is to make use of the experience, not try to figure out what the purpose of our having met is. Don't make it a bigger deal than it is."

He held her, saying nothing. Being with her *was* a big deal. At least to him.

"The Eastern belief is that nothing is permanent," she went on. "We, and everything else, are changing all the time. What we have together today we may not have tomorrow. What you have with your wife today may change tomorrow. Have you ever thought of that? That you'll leave me someday and have a satisfying marriage again with your wife? What if I were just meant to be a spark to reignite your marriage?"

"A spark?" He looked at her in disbelief. "My relationship with you is more than a spark. It won't just go away like that." He was annoyed that Belinda had virtually summoned Joy into this hotel room. "And I don't know what will happen with my wife in the future. Right now, we're going nowhere. But let's forget about that for now."

She sighed. "Some couples are meant to be together for the

long haul. Others not."

A few minutes later she started to gnaw at his stomach play-fully. "You're squeamish, know that? About germs, I mean."

"Because other people's germs disgust me?"

"Because you grew up in Manhattan, not in Ohio like me. Germs should be second nature to you."

He suddenly grew defensive. "People catch lethal viruses. A friend of mine nearly died from one."

She seemed to consider this, then lifted herself up. "So, we're not taking a shower later?"

"No."

She giggled, then seeing he was serious, she frowned. "Richard."

"That shower stall could be deadly."

Showering together was one of their favorite things, their way of saying goodbye: lathering each other, kissing under the flow-ing water, slippery, sudsy shower sex. Sometimes it led them right back into bed, making her late for her bus.

She moved to lie on the pillow rather than his chest. He pulled her back to him. "I want us to be smart, that's all."

"You just haven't been to some of the places I have," she said. "Try peeing in the bushes in Pakistan. Our bus stopped outside Karachi once to let us have a pit stop. Women went one way and men another. I was crouching in my baggy tunic, so I was covered enough, but I heard one of the other women scream, and the next thing I knew a snake as thick as my ankle was slithering through my own legs. I was too scared to move, but I remember it had a streak of green at the end of its tail, and I was sure it would rear its head and bite me."

He squirmed at the image of the snake's fangs in her flesh. "Was it poisonous?"

"Most snakes there are."

"Christ. What if it had bitten you?"

"It just slid on by. I guess it didn't like me."

He turned to find her eyes bursting with mischief. Sometimes, even when he knew she was teasing, she scared him. That other life she'd led had plunged her into experiences he couldn't even imagine and didn't really want to know about.

Several minutes later, he was back on top of her, going again where that fool snake had not.

Afterward, Belinda laid several of the motel's bath towels on the floor of the shower stall to completely cover the tile and any possible toxins.

"There." She nudged him under the water with her, bumping her soapy breasts against his chest, turning this way and that, all to show him what he would have missed had he not allowed himself the pleasure of a shower with her.

He chuckled in spite of himself. He would remember, next time, to put flip-flops in his briefcase.

10

"You hardly ever talk about love," he said to her one day. They were in bed in a hotel off Central Park, the Wainwright. His choice. Although not swanky, it was more refined than those she usually chose. It had Egyptian cotton robes and slippers in the bathrooms.

She cocked her head. "I guess I don't think about putting it into words."

"You hardly even say you love me."

She sat up and pulled back her dark hair as though to hear him better, a gesture he imagined her using to let her small pupils know she was paying full attention to them.

"You're right, I don't," she said. "Would it do any good?"

"What do you mean?"

"Would it make a difference if I kept saying I love you? To either of us?"

"I just like to hear you say it. Don't you want to say it?" He twisted the intricate silver ring on her middle finger, a piece of tribal jewelry she told him she'd bought in an Afghan bazaar. Its complex pattern seemed as convoluted as their discussion.

"You don't say it much, either, Richard."

"More than you do. Anyway, men don't verbalize love as much as women."

She burst out laughing.

"You know what I mean. Women are more emotional. I just find it interesting that you don't talk about love."

"Interesting or troubling?"

"Both." He turned and stared into her eyes. They appeared murky in the dim light, like lake water that has absorbed the rich minerals of the surrounding soil. He longed to dive in and hit bottom, to discover what was really there.

"What good would it do to say that we love each other all the time, Richard?"

He took a deep breath. "It would make us feel closer."

She rolled over on top of him, stretching out long and digging a space between his legs with her own. Resting her chin on his chest, she continued to stare at him. "But I do feel close to you. Why else would I be here?"

He smoothed stray curls from her face. "We have so little time together. It's all we can do to pop in and out of the sack. I'd just like to feel there's more to our relationship. Know what I mean?"

"No," she said, although he knew perfectly well that she had to know how much he missed her and that he was frustrated by these brief dates, which was how he'd come to see them.

She laid her cheek on his rib cage, the heat of her skin searing him. "I love you, Richard."

He hugged her tighter, quickly cheering up. "I love you, too."

She lifted her head and smiled. "So, what's next? Are we going to run off together?"

He stared at her.

"See?" she said, noting his surprise. "Why all the fuss? Why do you want me to profess undying love for you if you're not going to do anything about it?"

"I hadn't thought you wanted—"

"I don't," she said quickly. Then added almost to herself, "It's all meaningless."

He raised himself up. "Don't make it sound so hopeless. We can give this relationship meaning."

She shook her head. "It's not meant to have meaning. It's unnecessarily stressful to insist it does. Have no expectations or attachments, Richard. You'll be much happier."

He felt a swell of irritation. "Maybe that works for you, Belinda, but I can't help feeling attached to people I love. And I like having expectations in my life, something to work toward, something to motivate me."

She chuckled. "The only motivation you need is to enjoy yourself, to love what you're doing. Don't give abstract things unnecessary importance."

"That's not enough for me."

She shrugged. "Suit yourself, but life is unpredictable. It's unreliable and temporary. We're all much better off looking at things rationally."

He looked away from her, an exasperating gloom creeping into his bones. He felt abandoned, as if she had physically left the room.

"I feel so separated from you when you talk like that," he said.

She sighed, softly. "Separation is an illusion. Something we make up. We're never separate from each other."

"Well, I can't think of anything more absurd than to love someone and feel it's all meaningless."

"But that's what life is, Richard. Meaningless. There's nothing more than here and now, no other meaning," she said evenly. "We deceive ourselves into assigning things such significance. The only thing permanent in the universe is its transience. Life is revolving, coming and going all the time. That's the beauty of it. And we have to go with the flow. Just a constant moving along. Perfection. But it's best not to talk about it so much."

He did want to talk about it, though, or rather about them.

He wanted her to wonder if they'd ever have a future together, to worry about the precariousness of their situation, to tell him she'd be broken-hearted if they split up; but she only seemed concerned with the present and their brief times together. Most men would have been grateful for such an undemanding lover, but Belinda's detachment unsettled him. He was used to interdependence, like he had with Joy. He was becoming aware of his own rising neediness, and this made him uncomfortable.

One afternoon in Brooklyn—he couldn't even remember the name of the hotel—there was a sagging wooden curtain rod that made the entire room look lopsided, as if they were slowly sliding downhill. To right himself, he found he was tilting his head whenever he glanced at the window.

He would always remember this room because it was where she did this maneuver while crouching behind him on all fours. She told him afterwards that some village women in Burma had taught it to her. He asked her to do it again, marveling that an American woman tourist could wheedle such raunchy details out of secretive Asian women, and he couldn't see anybody, Burmese or otherwise, doing it any better than she.

He laughed after the first time, astonished and almost embarrassed that her tugging on him like this could be so pleasant. He couldn't begin to imagine Joy ever crouching that way or doing something so naughty. He told Belinda that, but to his surprise, instead of taking it as a compliment, she frowned and admonished him for being critical of Joy.

Later, as they were getting ready to leave, out of the blue she asked him whether he and Joy were planning another baby.

"No," he said, flatly.

"Why not?"

"We tried for nearly a year. It didn't happen. Now—I'm certainly not ready."

"What about her?"

"She doesn't seem to want to now."

"But you guys will in the future, won't you?"

He shrugged. "I don't know. We're just not thinking about it now."

"But she lost her baby. Can't you give her another?"

He looked at her, puzzled by her insistent tone. "I suppose I could, if it were safe and she wanted one—and if *I* wanted one. We tried once, and it didn't work. So, subject closed." He flashed back to those injections Joy had to give herself, the accompanying weight gain, the inevitable depression that seized both of them when each month turned up a negative pregnancy result.

"But don't *you* want one? Don't you want to be a father?" she persisted.

He sighed, impatient. "Not now. Can we talk about something else?"

"Sure." She fished around in her bag, pulled out a comb, fluffed up her bangs, then looked at him, a little sadly. "It's not fair for her not to have a baby if she wants one. Having a baby is an act of faith. A child creates hope for the future."

"I thought you didn't care about the future. I thought the present is all that matters."

"Living in the present doesn't mean denying the future. You just don't dwell in the future; but you consider it from here. Maybe Joy is the kind of woman who needs that positive pull. Having a child makes us go forward, no matter what. It opens us up to the universe in a way nothing else can."

"How would you know?"

"It's only logical. I don't have to have given birth to know that by having a child, we go with the flow of life rather than blocking it by closing ourselves off in fear."

He looked at her. Was he closing himself off in fear? He *had* gone with the flow of the universe, had put his trust in the future, but he'd been lashed by the cold-heartedness of that universe. That universe had imploded around him in that instant in the delivery room. His breath had been ripped out of him. He was still crushed by the weight of guilt at what he might have contributed, even organically, to the infant's death. A part of him and that universe he once belonged to had died and would never come back.

"Well, it's not up to us. We have to wait," he said, upset that they'd ended their intimate afternoon on this sad note regarding his home life.

"There are other ways—"

He interrupted her. "I know there are, but we're not interested."

"Don't you think you owe it to her—to both of you—to consider other options?"

"Options?"

"Artificial insemination? Or have you thought about adoption?"

"I told you, we're not interested."

"But have you looked into it? I have several friends who've had good luck with—"

"We're not adopting."

"Well, a surrogate, then. The baby would still be all yours. Lots of couples—"

"Belinda! Damn! You're pushing something you know nothing about, and you certainly do not know about *our* situation. I didn't come here to see a marriage therapist. You're ruining our time together."

Belinda

She started, as if awakened from a trance. He had never barked at her like that.

She now looked unhappy. "You have to be creative, sometimes. Don't limit yourself with old thinking. Create what's right for you." She picked up her things, glanced at herself in the mirror, and smiled. "You'd make an excellent father."

Before he could respond, she quickly gave his cheek a peck, as if to apologize, and led him out of the room.

11

"Why do we always go to hotels?" he complained one afternoon over drinks at a Soho bar. The bar was near the NYU campus and was so jammed with college kids that he felt out of place. Even Belinda, although dressed in jeans and a polo shirt, looked older than the rest, more like a grad student.

"I'd like to see your place for a change," he pushed, feeling rebellious. "Aren't you allowed to have guests?"

"As a matter of fact, I am, and you'd like my place." She'd already told him she rented the bottom floor of a house in Paramus not far from the preschool where she taught.

"Well, I'd like to see it. Let's meet there, next time."

"But I love hotels," she said.

"I just think your place would be more personal. We can cook dinner for a change."

She grimaced. "My cooking's not that great."

"I'll cook. I make a great *coq au vin*. It would be cozier, more real."

She sipped her beer. "Hotels aren't real?"

Despite his disappointment that the prospect of a shared domestic experience didn't seem to excite her, there was foam on her top lip that he wanted to lick.

"Hotels are temporary," he said. "I want to feel more permanence."

"Permanence?" She smiled. "Life isn't permanent, Richard. Life is a hotel. We're all just guests in this big hotel on our way to somewhere else."

"Don't go flaky on me."

"I'm just being realistic. Life is just one long space of waiting. Most of us are just waiting for our lives to start, waiting to be with the one we love, waiting for our children to be born and then to grow up. We're always just waiting. It's a human tendency, but we waste our lives that way. I find hotels comforting. By living in the present, we accept life's transience and live each moment fully. And we don't get attached to hotels. It would be different if we went to my place, or even to yours."

"We can't go to my place," he said.

"I know, but if we could, there would be evidence everywhere of your other life, pictures of your wife or the family dog."

"Joy has a cat."

"A cat?"

"Ophelia."

She smiled. "Shakespeare. But I couldn't make love to you with Ophelia looking on and surrounded by all those reminders of your other life. In unfamiliar rooms, we can be anywhere we imagine, create our own reality. And," she said, taking a breath, "hotel rooms remind me not to expect more than these moments with you. They remind me to stay in the now, Richard."

"Damn it, Belinda!" It frustrated him that she refused to think about them as an actual couple. "Our reality is whatever we make it. It's wherever we are. Reality isn't just my marriage or your work or the kids you teach. It's you and me, too, in the now and after."

She leaned back, raised her hands behind her head and rested her head in them as though it were suddenly too heavy to be unsupported.

His gaze traced the smooth crescent of her neck at the open collar. Then, to his annoyance, he noticed a young man at the bar staring at her, too.

"Do you have a headache?" he asked.

She opened her eyes. "No."

"You look tired."

She brought her hands down to her lap. "I'm fine."

"You know?" he said. "Sometimes I wonder what you see in me."

Her eyes widened. "Why do you say that?"

"You love the exotic, and I'm not that, at all. You're like a butterfly I'm constantly trying to net. Why don't you fly off in search of other butterflies? Wouldn't you be happier?"

"But I don't want a butterfly—"

"What *do* you want?" he cut in, hearing the interrogator's tone in his voice.

She shrugged. "You're stable. That's what I love about you. And you're always here."

"Here where?"

"Wherever I am, you're here for me. You're dependable and strong. I love that about you."

He sucked in his breath. He hoped this wasn't the entire story. He certainly didn't want to find that her attraction to him was simply because she saw him as "stable" or "dependable."

The young man at the bar was still appraising her. "Let's get out of here," Richard said abruptly, summoning the waitress for the check.

The waitress, a young girl with several pencils stuck in her twisted-up hair, looked at Belinda, then at him. He wondered if the waitress assumed he was a father coming to visit his jeans-clad daughter at college.

Belinda

The bed in the hotel creaked with each movement, and there was a ravine in the middle of the mattress that he kept sliding into.

"You know you're in the Village in a bed like this," Belinda said with a snicker.

"How do you find these places?" Richard asked, unable to hide his irritation.

"Yellow Pages."

"You're kidding."

"This one, I did. I don't know any place here, and I liked its name: the Concord. Sounds so posh, but I knew for ninety bucks there had to be a catch."

"The bed." He pounded a pillow between them in the middle to fill in the dent.

She folded her leg over the pillow and around him, curling next to him like a child. "You don't enjoy hotels, Richard? I thought you traveled a lot."

He thought about this for a moment. "As a matter of fact, I don't much like to travel."

She lifted her head with a start, staring at him as though to see whether or not he was joking.

"I don't," he admitted, almost disappointing himself by the truth. "When I was growing up, my dad landed in one embassy after another, and so my brother and I had to travel to visit him. Some of it was fun, I guess, but it was nonstop at times. And we had to fly to the West Coast to visit our mother several times a year." He'd already filled her in on his parents' divorce. "I actually feel best when I'm at home."

She inhaled. "Wow. I can't imagine life without travel. I once spent a week with a friend in Dubai. The Arab women there have their own wild parties at night, disco parties with dancing and painting their bodies with henna. They don't need the men, at all. They wear these long, gold-embroidered gowns—like sparkly fireflies. I never saw so many gorgeous women having so much fun in one place. In the West, we assume they're all downtrodden, miserable, and missing out on the freedoms the rest of us have. But I saw a bunch of joyful women having a blast."

Richard imagined the mad, estrogen-fueled scene. "I assume this was a moneyed bunch."

"It's not all about money. I also spent time with some village women in Africa. There was no water to bathe in for weeks. Amazing what you can adapt to. They were all so kind to me. They made me bathe first so I wouldn't run out of water. These experiences make me realize how fortunate I am here at home. And yet, I feel so alive seeing people cope with hardship."

"Well, I have no burning need to face the unknown so intimately," he said, butting in. "And I like clean places. Yes, clean. I admit it. Besides, I feel I've traveled to enough weird places vicariously through you."

She turned on her back as though to contemplate this, then climbed back onto him, straddling him and sitting upright.

He felt her heat radiating through his groin and cupped his palms over her breasts, reminded of the perfectly shaped Indian mounds in Arizona he'd explored as a kid.

"I can't imagine being confined to this sanitized country," she said, pursing her lips. "New York at least has personality. But God, Richard, the world out there is so different. The best night I ever spent was in the Himalayas under the stars. And the markets of Marrakesh, the food grilled in the streets of Delhi, the spices, the flowers blooming over broken walls, garbage rotting . . ." She crinkled her nose. "I even like the stink of urine in the streets."

She paused, and then her voice dropped. "Only once was I really afraid. In Yemen. I saw a woman being raped."

He thought he misheard her. "What?"

She nodded.

He removed his hands from her breasts and placed them on her knees.

"In Sana'a. Some mix-up in my visa landed me in a jail cell with a Bangladeshi housemaid who'd been arrested for stealing something. That night the jail guard came into our cell and climbed on top of her. Just like that. I called for help, but she shook her head for me not to. Thank God, it didn't take him long. When he left, the woman told me he did that every night, just came in and raped her, but it was better not to complain."

"Shit," Richard said, horrified.

"I was let out the next day and told the police what I saw."

"Did they do anything?"

"I never found out."

He stared at her. "*Shit*. What if he'd attacked you, too?"

She shook her head, her body seeming to recoil at the memory. "I guess he knew I would have reported him to the American embassy. We still have some clout there. Who could that woman appeal to? I just covered my head with my blanket like she did and waited for his grunts to stop. That's the only time I wanted to go right home."

He felt sick, then furious. He reached up and placed his hands on her shoulders, not sure how to hold her after this. "I'm amazed you ever let a man near you after that."

She shrugged. "I didn't have a boyfriend then, and so it didn't matter. I just handled it. Thinking how brave she was got me through it. She was like steel, you know? Just let him get on with it and leave. I couldn't have done that."

"Nobody should have to do that," he said, unable to hide his revulsion. "And you still travel to those places?"

She kissed him lightly on the lips. "If I didn't still travel,

Richard, I wouldn't have met you. Despite the danger of some places, I wouldn't give up traveling for anything."

He thought she would cry as she thought of that night that must surely have haunted her for years, but she was silent, withdrawing into herself. That silence scraped at his heart more ruthlessly than tears.

12

They were once again at the first hotel she'd taken him to on the West Side that had felt so sleazy at the time. That was six months ago. Now, remembering the crazy eagerness of the first night they'd spent there, he didn't find it as distasteful. It was early spring, and at six o'clock, it was no longer dark outside. It made the night, and his time with her, seem way too short.

Belinda was unusually restless. He could tell by the way she snapped the drapes shut, then immediately unzipped her dress, without bothering to face him. She had on lavender lace underwear, and he embraced her from behind, resting his chest on her back, kissing her neck, and undoing her bra. But he might as well have been hugging granite.

He sensed that she was upset with him. "Whatever I've done, I'm sorry," he whispered.

"You haven't done anything," she said, quietly.

He knew she was holding something in like a dam before water gushes through a crack. He pulled back, waiting for the deluge.

He glanced around the room. "Compared to some of the places we've been, this is the Waldorf."

"It's bland," she agreed, sounding unhappy.

"We can find someplace worse," he joked.

She was silent.

He continued to kiss her shoulder, sliding his lips down her arm. Her skin was soft and spongier than usual, as if she'd gained a bit of weight. He found that appealing. He was going to tell her so but wasn't sure whether her gaining weight might be upsetting to her, and so he said nothing.

"This place doesn't turn me on, either," he said finally. "Let's go."

"Cut it out, Richard. It's fine." The look in her eyes contradicted her tough words.

"What's wrong?" he asked.

She looked up at the ceiling, avoiding his eyes. Finally, she said, "An old friend called today. We traveled together a few years ago in Nepal. He's on his way to Africa. He wants to go out with me."

He winced. "And?"

"I told him I'd think about it."

He still had his shirt on but had slipped off his trousers and undershorts. Was she going to talk about her feelings for another man? He wanted to reach to the floor and at least pull on his underwear if this discussion was heading there.

He tried to sound unfazed. "No crime in meeting up with old friends. How long has it been since you saw this guy?"

"Rodney," she said. "Two years."

Two years. He should have been forgotten by now. "Well, is he, this Rodney, just a friend?"

"Yeah, he is."

"Meaning?"

She shrugged. "We had sex a few times, but I certainly wasn't in love with him."

His fingers went numb against her shoulders. "And?"

"He cared more for me than I did for him. He seems to want to restart something, though."

He dropped his hands to his sides. He spied his trousers at the foot of the bed and picked them up unceremoniously. "Should we talk?"

"I told him we could meet, but I made it clear that I was seeing somebody else."

His chest expanded. He almost smiled with relief. He put his arm around her shoulder and led her to the edge of the bed. The mattress tipped down at the foot end, so they had to scoot farther back toward the middle to be comfortable.

She drew her hair away from her face in that way that always turned him on. "Do you mind if I go out with him?"

He eyed her coolly. "Well, is it dinner or are you going to screw him?"

"It's just dinner, Richard."

"Then what's the big deal?" He closed his eyes a moment. "Why even ask me if that's all it is?"

"Because he's obviously expecting more. He just got back from Nepal. He's in the Peace Corps, now."

"On leave to look up old girlfriends?"

She smiled. "You sound childish when you're jealous."

"I'm not jealous," he said, not even convincing himself.

She cleared her throat. "He's looking for something, and he can be pretty insistent."

"Well, fuck. Are you going to be seduced?" He heard the hard edge in his voice. She obviously wanted to tell him something but was hedging. Maybe she was considering reviving something with this guy, but so far she seemed happy with *him*.

Or was she?

She was thirty. Was she thinking marriage, children,

permanence, after all? He remembered Joy's frantic obsession with pregnancy, like a missile seeking its target.

Maybe Belinda was looking at this Peace Corps hippie from her past in a new light. After all, the guy had just returned from Nepal, steeped in the transcendental sensuality of the East that so fascinated her, and he had probably mastered as many steamy sexual antics as she. Put the two of them together and who could predict the force of combustion?

Maybe his lack of escapades was beginning to make her rethink their relationship. Although she claimed to like it that he was stable, she thrived on risky new experiences, and if this guy wanted to sweep her off to Borneo or Kathmandu, not even the trashiest hotel in the Bronx could match that.

"Are you wanting something more, Belinda?"

"More?"

"Do you want to get married?" he asked, somewhat alarmed by his words.

She looked at him oddly. "Married?"

"Because if you are, we should talk about it. I can see marrying you."

"Richard!" she blurted out, aghast. "You're already married. I'm not thinking about that. Not at all!"

"Maybe I'm the one thinking it. Don't you want commitment? How's marriage for commitment?"

"You don't know what you're saying. Besides, I don't want to marry you."

It was his turn to be taken aback. He remembered Joy's tender caresses when he proposed, their kisses all the way home in the cab after dinner in the restaurant where he had presented her with an engagement ring.

"I don't believe you," he said.

She turned to him and gently took his face in her hands. "Richard, we have to stay as we are. This arrangement is why it works between us. We need to be free. We need to keep this whatever it's meant to be."

"Well, what is this meant to be, exactly? It sounds like you're not so convinced of our relationship all of a sudden."

"That's not what I'm saying. We have a great relationship. But you're married to the person you should be married to." She shrugged. "I'm not the marrying type."

"But it's not working out with me and her. It hasn't for a long time. You know that."

"Everything has worked out perfectly for you. Your wife is perfect for you. You just don't realize it, now."

"Why are you so sure of that? You don't know anything about Joy. And what the hell am I doing here with you if things are so *great* with her?"

She looked at him calmly. "I'm perfect for you in other ways. We always end up with who we're meant to be with at any given time. Someday you'll understand."

"Bull!" He'd had enough of her mumbo-jumbo concepts. "You don't want *me* anymore. Is that it?"

"Richard," she said in a tone and with a glance that made him feel like one of her preschoolers who'd just spilled juice. "I'm not a lifetime partner for you. Not for you or anybody else. I want my freedom too much."

"And I'm supposed to live with one kind of woman and screw another? Because you don't want to stick with me? Because it inhibits your so-called *freedom?*"

"I'm only going to dinner with the man," she said firmly, ignoring his outburst.

"Bullshit!"

Belinda, the exasperated teacher of unruly boys, looked at him a long moment. He half expected her to raise two fingers for a time-out.

"So, why the hell do you hang around with me when my love scares you so much?" he demanded. "When you could have such an exciting, *free* life with somebody else?"

"Because, Richard," she said, without hesitation, "as I've told you before, you're the most dependable man I've ever known."

There it was again. *Dependable.* "That's it?" he asked, deflated.

"That's enough. What more do I need?" She smiled, then after a pause added, "And you're a great lover." She stuck out her tongue. "Besides, you're funny."

He was a little surprised. Funny? Maybe she found his cynicism funny. It only seemed to get on Joy's nerves.

He realized that the only way he could win this confrontation was to appear to be above her going out with this guy from her past. "Then go," he said. "Go to dinner with the guy and see what happens. You'll know what to do."

She smiled wearily, obviously relieved that he'd given up.

All at once he wanted out of there, out of that miserable room, out of the hotel. *Fuck hotels!*

He wanted to breathe the fresh night air instead of the lingering staleness that seemed to cling to him now. More than anything, he wanted to be away from her, from the dangerous hold the smooth olive skin of her shoulders had on him. He was unnerved by these new stirrings of jealousy and angry that she'd evoked feelings he hadn't experienced in years. He needed to catch his train and head back to his marriage, back to reality, but before he could pull on the trousers that lay limply across his lap, she drew him to her.

This time when they made love, the sweat streamed down his back and between their bodies. He closed his eyes, not wanting to look at her, only to feel their mingled wetness, imagining that he was a river swallowing her up. The Ganges, the Amazon, the Nile. He wanted to be those rivers, to drown her so that she'd always, and only, live inside of him.

He furiously pounded away, burying his face in her moist neck.

13

"We'd planned on tomorrow night, Richard," Belinda said over the phone, sounding upset. "You know I need to see you. It's important."

"Belinda, I'm sorry. This thing . . . I can't get out of it."

"You could have said you're busy."

"If I could have made an excuse, I would have. These are old friends, just in town briefly. Joy made plans with them. I'm sorry. I'll make it up to you Sunday night."

"I'm busy Sunday."

"Doing what?"

"I have a commitment."

Knowing she was just being difficult, he was silent. He couldn't help smiling through his annoyance. He loved her even when she was being unreasonable, which was rare.

"I'm not the one doing the double-timing," she said. "We had plans to see each other, and you broke them. I've made other arrangements for Sunday."

"With him? Mr. Peace Corps?"

There was a pause. "It's none of your business." The coolness in her voice was unmistakable. He could picture the look in her eyes, that steely resolve to be uncooperative.

"It is my business," he said gently.

"Your business is to keep your appointments."

Belinda

"Baby, why can't you just tell me now over the phone? I'm all ears. You know I'm dying to see you, but I just can't see you tomorrow."

"Well, I'm not available Sunday."

"You're lying."

There was a stillness.

"You know you're being stubborn," he went on. "It's not as if I'm intentionally—"

There was a click on the other end.

"Hello?" He waited, but there was only an eerie silence.

He glared at his phone. "Damn!"

He'd learned to handle the arguments with Joy with a certain humor, a quiet aplomb. Even when she won them, he could walk away feeling somewhat vindicated at having put up a logical defense. However, he hadn't yet learned how to ease out of a quarrel with Belinda, and this failure left him peeved and uneasy. *Damn!*

The argument was silly. Belinda had made dinner plans with him, and he'd inadvertently agreed to an engagement with Joy the same night, with old friends they rarely saw, Joy's college roommate and her husband. They hadn't seen them since Joy lost the baby, and Joy had been looking forward to the dinner. He was also hoping that seeing her friend would help Joy finally get some relief from her unending grief. Maybe she'd be heartened by the fact that the couple, who had been unable themselves to have children, seemed perfectly happy.

He didn't know why Belinda was refusing to meet him on Sunday.

He had stayed home this morning, Friday, to finish working on his taxes. Now he was suddenly exhausted. That five-minute tiff over the telephone had seemed to last forever, and he was left staring at the receiver, baffled. Should he call back and apologize?

Should he try to get out of his dinner with Joy and their friends? Call Belinda back and insist she reschedule dinner with him?

When he called her number, however, it went to her voice-mail. He waited a few minutes and redialed her, but he got her recording again. She was obviously not going to answer his calls now. *Damn!* It had never crossed his mind when he first embarked on this rousing new venture that he'd need nerves of platinum.

Mr. Peace Corps. The prick!

Richard had no idea why Belinda didn't call the man her ex-lover, since that's obviously what he was. But she hadn't said anything more about him that night, and he hadn't asked.

Now, this morning, a fight. He didn't count any of their other haggling as real fights, but this certainly felt like one, and Joy was indirectly the cause of it. In a way, it was perhaps time that he and Belinda had a real fight. It seemed unnatural that in their time together, they'd never had much to argue about. Perhaps this fight was proof that they were, in fact, a couple, arguing over the inane things longtime couples find to argue about.

He rifled through the stack of papers on his desk, glancing at the phone, his fingers itching to dial her number, but he'd wait. He'd let her cool down a bit.

He felt a rubbing against his leg. The cat wanted to jump into his lap. He reached down and nudged her away. Joy insisted that he imagined his allergies to cats, but his sneezing increased whenever any cat came near. He stood, ran his fingers through his hair, and stalked out of the study.

In the kitchen, he flipped open a can of beer and rolled some turkey into a tortilla, biting into it between impatient gulps of the beer. Damn phone. He couldn't get that click of her hanging up out of his mind. Such a little thing, but his stomach twitched.

Back in his study, he continued preparing his taxes so his accountant, Ed, could file them next week. Ed had already filed for an extension, but it was the beginning of March, and Richard had never filed this late. He was always, as Joy claimed, annoyingly punctual, not only with paying bills, but with appointments and even casual meetings. Obviously, keeping a mistress and marriage afloat had caused him to slip.

He leafed through the documents, occasionally glancing at his phone as if he could will the thing to ring. Belinda hardly called him anyway, and so there was no reason to think she would now, except that he'd told her that Joy was out. It was usually he who called her, and since she always carried her cell phone, even in class, there had never been a need for her to call when he was home. Now, he wished she would ignore their past agreement about not contacting him when he was home and phone him. Even if she were still angry, he wanted to hear her voice, hear the breathless catch it had when she said his name, as if it were somehow unlikely that it was him on the other end.

He tried calling her again, but she still didn't answer.

He tried to push her out of his mind, but she crept back in. Not only the sweet feel of her, but the things they did together that he hadn't done with anybody else, and certainly not in that unbridled way.

Chocolate. It was the image he most often had whenever he kissed her. He imagined losing himself in her arms as if in one big pool of chocolate.

Once, when he'd described these feelings to her, she smiled. "Chocolate?"

Although the chocolate association amused her, she couldn't seem to appreciate its potent reverberations in him. She didn't seem to value her own loveliness enough or give much weight to his obsession with it. Perhaps she was used to men hungering after her and took his admiration for granted.

He glanced at the yellow pad on the desk under his hand.

He'd been jotting down words without thinking: *chocolate, desire, potent.*

He ripped the page off and shredded it. Once again, he started to jot down the itemized list of deductions on a separate piece of paper and tried to make sense of the forms in front of him.

Damn fight!

✴

The front door opened.

"Rich?"

"I'm in the study," he called.

Joy's footsteps tapped around the kitchen. Soon, she came into the study and draped her arm around his shoulder, kissing the top of his head. "Tax time? Ouch."

"Yeah," he said, reaching back to catch the strands of blonde hair falling across his eyes. Her hair smelled faintly of her fruity shampoo, and she was wearing the Chanel perfume he bought her for her birthday. It so disarmed him that he almost wanted to set her down on his lap and confess all to her.

He sometimes wondered whether she noticed the change in his behavior, his nights of working late, his friendly distance from her; but if she did, she showed nothing. He wondered whether she would be secretly thankful to learn that he now had somebody else catering to his innermost needs.

"Have a good day?" he said.

"Just a little shopping. Feel like going to a movie?"

"What movie?" he asked, suddenly eager to get away both from the numbers in front of him and the intrusive thoughts of Belinda.

"The new sci-fi in which everyone turns green and annihilates everybody else."

He looked up in surprise. "Let's go!"

She chuckled. "No, silly. Actually, there's an Italian film at the Avalon. *Sweet Dreams*."

He should have known, he thought. He pictured himself sitting through one of Joy's obscure art movies. "I just started on this, Joy."

"Well, why not take a break? C'mon, honey. It's my last week of vacation before school. Let's do something fun."

He sighed. "Let me finish a little more here. I'll try and hurry. I can't promise, though."

She started to leave, then paused. "Honey?"

"Yeah?" The tone of her voice put him on guard.

"I've been thinking of that trip we talked about a while ago. I'm ready for a change. Maybe Italy? I can plan some time off next semester. How about you? It's been two years since we went to Spain."

He pursed his lips. They'd talked about making another trip to Europe. Something to get them out of their rut, but that was months ago. That was *before*. He couldn't leave now, not with Belinda in his life. Besides, after hearing about Belinda's travels, he couldn't imagine traveling anywhere that would begin to compare with her adventures. Although he had no desire to explore in the vagabond way she did, travel had now become so synonymous with her that it was impossible to imagine going anywhere without her. He wanted to travel, but with Belinda.

"Sure, but let's talk about it later, Joy. I'm too focused on this right now to think about anything else. But let's keep it in mind."

"Okay. Just thought I'd mention it." She added, "Did you find the surprise I put in the fridge for you?"

"Surprise?"

"I left you a note. I defrosted the chili I made last week. I knew you'd be getting hungry with all that paperwork."

"God, I'm sorry, honey. I didn't see it."

He loved her chili. He'd been too distracted with Belinda all morning to think of a proper lunch. Joy had obviously thought of him this morning before heading downtown while he slept in. "I didn't even think to look. I just snacked."

"No problem. We can have it later," she said, shutting the door gently behind her.

He started filling in some figures. Travel now? No way, he thought, but going to a movie was a good idea. Her idea of a good movie was not exactly what he considered quality time with Joy, but they could bond over popcorn and cheese-smothered nachos. An Italian film, slightly quirky and with minimal plot, the kind she found inspiring and sometimes persuaded him to go to with her just to get him to see something besides his usual gritty thrillers—the kind Belinda might enjoy.

It occurred to him that it would be ideal if Belinda and Joy went together. Belinda had a playful streak that would challenge Joy's intellect, and they would both be in tune with the film's Continental flavor. In fact, deep inside he wanted them to meet. He wanted to believe that each would like and admire the other, that he somehow had brought together two compatible souls. He wanted them to understand his need for each of them. Mostly he wanted them both to forgive him. Although he'd managed to bury his guilt these past six months, occasionally when he felt weak, especially when Joy was thoughtful, like just then with the chili, his situation ate at him.

He pushed aside the tax papers and decided to take Joy up on the movie. Artsy-fartsy flick, so be it. He needed to get out of the house and out of his damn head.

"Joy?" he called, grabbing his jacket from the hall closet. "Hey, honey, let's catch that movie!"

Belinda

After they returned home, it took him until past midnight to finish compiling the tax data for Ed. When he headed upstairs, he was too tired even to drink his customary scotch. He was surprised to find Joy still awake and watching television in bed.

Usually, he was the one stretched out on the bedroom sofa watching a late-night game or the news, and she who turned in early. He'd gotten used to having the last hour or so before sleep to himself, when he could slump, dazed, in front of the television screen and fantasize about Belinda.

"All done?" Joy asked, as if she were intentionally waiting for him.

"Still up?" He pulled off his shirt.

"It's the least I could do with you slaving away downstairs."

Again, he smelled the Chanel, freshly applied. She was wearing a pink silk nightgown he hadn't seen in some time. It gave him a twinge. Was this for him? Christ! He had no stomach for intimacy now. Not with Joy.

Since Belinda, he hadn't made love to Joy more than a few times. Much to Joy's relief, he liked to assume, but he felt the signs tonight: waiting up for him, watching television, which was normally his domain, and the special nightgown and perfume. He wondered whether it was the movie, an admittedly pleasant concoction that had left them both mellow, or maybe she did feel, absurdly, that she had to repay him for working so late on the taxes. He was so completely saturated with Belinda tonight, though, that he doubted he could muster the ability to make even mediocre love to Joy.

He thought back to the start of his affair, to how smugly he was able to rebound between adultery and matrimony, to sail steadily back and forth over the calm waters of his two women; but he was too deeply moored to Belinda now, anchored in the swells of that nomadic soul of hers. He could almost see her face, a mild smirk on her lips, chiding him for his cowardice in the face of Joy's expectations.

He took longer than usual in the bathroom, showering and brushing his teeth, even clipping his nails, all in the hopes of finding Joy asleep when he emerged. But she was still wide awake, reading. Even the cat was perched at the foot of the bed, also waiting, it seemed.

It didn't take them long—it never did. In this way they were still, luckily, compatible. As he shifted away from Joy and drifted in and out of sleep, he was surprised at the distinct feeling of contentment that cradled him, despite the initial stab of remorse for having betrayed Belinda.

There was a calmness about Joy, a seemingly angelic serenity, her cheek flattened against her palm, mouth slightly open and trusting. He felt at ease knowing he'd done the right thing, and they had been better together tonight than they'd been in a long time, she attaining her bountiful orgasms while he sank into a welcome moment of forgetting all but the comfort of being with her in their own domain.

He was aware now of her hand reaching out to him, her fingers softly sliding over his thigh. Maybe something *was* changing for them, bringing them closer. His slight wonder at her touch gave way to gratitude. He was glad to be in his own bed, in his own bedroom, beautifully decorated by his wife. This was the way he'd always wanted it, the way it was meant to be. He and Joy, side by side. He *did* love her. This security lulled him into his dream world.

The next morning, Joy's face was still peaceful. She was beginning to stir, her eyes moving beneath rosy closed lids as if in desperate search of something, but her breaths were still even. Something in his throat caught. He held back the urge to touch her cheek.

Belinda

The cat scampered and skidded ahead of him as he headed downstairs to the kitchen to make coffee. He ground the coffee beans—something he enjoyed doing each morning, savoring the rich scent of the Arabica—then filled the coffee maker with water and turned it on. He placed two mugs on a tray and filled the antique sugar bowl and cream pitcher for Joy, marveling at how little it had taken to bind him to his marriage again.

He began to wonder what the hell had gotten into him these past months. How could he have ever thought he could lead a different life than this one that he and Joy had built these past years? What Belinda had said was true on some level. Joy was a perfect wife for him. She knew when to push him to be more open and when to let him revert to his innate reserve; and outgoing and cheerful, she was the force behind their social life, making new friends and introducing them to him.

He felt ashamed of the way he'd responded to her suggestion that they take a new trip together. They'd enjoyed the earlier trips they'd made to Mexico and Quebec and the trip to Spain. What made him think they wouldn't enjoy going to Italy? He'd always enjoyed how she picked out their lodgings and the places they should visit, prodded him to be pluckier, and discovered new places off the beaten track. It was one of the things he'd admired about her from the start, her inquisitiveness. How could he have so flippantly and selfishly dismissed her desire to explore Italy?

His cell phone abruptly rang from its charger on the counter. He reached to answer it before it woke Joy.

"Richard?"

He paused, hearing that little question in her breath that almost sounded like a hiccup. There was complete silence for a moment, a vacuum of confusion as he held his breath.

"Richard?" she repeated softly.

He cleared his throat, but before he could whisper Belinda's name, warn her that Joy would be getting up any minute, she suggested they meet on Wednesday for dinner, after her parent-teacher conferences were done. She would call to let him know what restaurant.

All at once he was enveloped in the sweet scent of coconut oil from the hair of Sri Lankan brides, the crashing African waters of Victoria Falls. He felt himself surging upward, lifted beyond the silent kitchen in his house.

He smiled and hopped onto that roller coaster again. He'd just been handed a box of luscious chocolates. Rich Godiva.

14

$\mathcal{B}$elinda didn't call on Wednesday, and when he tried to call her in the afternoon, he was surprised by the recorded message that said her line had been disconnected.

He tried her number several more times, wondering whether her phone was out of order or whether, for some reason, she'd changed her number and hadn't yet told him. Maybe she had finally listened to him and traded in her antiquated phone for a new one. He doubted she would have changed her number, though. He considered the possibility that she had simply lost the phone and had thus canceled her line for safety purposes, but she would have let him know, he told himself. He kept trying her number, the only one he had for her, but there was always the same message: "This number is not in service."

By Thursday afternoon he started to worry. He'd forgotten where she lived. He only drove her home once, and that was late at night and not long after they had started seeing each other. They'd always met in the city. He tried looking her up in the directory, but she was unlisted. Besides, there would be no listing if she had only a cell phone, like a lot of folks did these days. Shit! He couldn't believe his stupidity. She lived with a family in Paramus, but she'd never given him a name or address. Not that he'd ever needed it. She'd always been accessible by phone. For all he knew, he now realized, she could be living with another man.

All he did know for sure, and he now wondered if he could even be certain about this, was that she worked at a preschool in Paramus; but he'd never seen it, didn't know the name, and didn't have the address.

He started by looking up the names of all the preschools in the area and making calls to them. By the sixth one, he got lucky. Yes, he was told, Belinda Bericini had taught there for a number of years, but she'd quit two weeks ago. She had taken a six-month sabbatical. No, it wouldn't be possible for the school to give out her home address.

Six months! He could feel his face dissolve at the news. Six months!

Perhaps she was going to tell him about the sabbatical when they next met. Perhaps that was the reason she'd been so annoyed when he'd canceled with her, and maybe her phone being disconnected had something to do with that. None of this made sense, though.

On Friday morning, he began to imagine that something terrible had happened to her. He decided to report her missing to the Paramus police precinct, but he changed his mind. He didn't want to be on record just yet. Besides, since she had informed her employer of her leaving, the police wouldn't consider her absence of immediate concern. Furthermore, the police might even start to wonder whether she might be purposely keeping her whereabouts from him.

Finally, on a Google search on Saturday morning, he came across a short article on preschools in Paramus, and there was a listing for the preschool teachers at her school. There was an address for her! Marigold Street. Several other streets nearby had names of flowers, as if they were all part of a subdivision. He immediately got into his car and drove there.

He vaguely recognized the house, a split-level about forty

years old. He rang the bell several times, but there was no answer. He walked around to the back and found windows into what appeared to be a basement apartment with a separate door. He assumed this was where she lived. He knocked loudly on the door, but nobody answered.

He drove around a few more streets and returned to the house in an hour. This time a middle-aged woman with short brown hair opened the front door.

She looked surprised when he asked about Belinda. She seemed hesitant to divulge any information to him at first, but obviously sensing his anxiety, she relented.

"She left night before last," she said.

"Left? Where to?"

"Africa."

Like a madman, he drove away. Deep down he'd known all along that she had gone to someplace far away. And not alone! He was all but certain of it.

He felt the jealous rage take hold and rise inside him, ripping the breath out of him. She ran off with that bastard! Off to some cholera-infested, third world place with no toilets. It was just what turned her on, sinking into the underbelly of humanity to live life to its fullest, as she'd put it so many times. Those were times he should have taken her at her word and realized how crazy and unpredictable she was. Belinda Bericini, who didn't give a fuck about safety, good health, or civilization.

Finally, nearing White Plains, he found a quiet street near his neighborhood and pulled over to the curb. He cut the engine and leaned against the steering wheel, taking deep breaths. A deep sadness enveloped him. He closed his eyes and wiped his tears, his shoulders going limp as he sank into his new reality.

A Marriage in Four Seasons

At last, in mid-April, six weeks after she disappeared, he received a message from Belinda, a postcard inside an envelope addressed to him at his office. It showed the scene of a marketplace in Dakar, Senegal. On it she'd written simply: "I'm in Dakar for a while doing research and may end up staying even longer. Please find new happiness in your life without me, Richard. Remember, separation is an illusion. I'm with you in every moment and wish you love and peace. Be happy. Belinda."

His head started to throb. He held on to the card, turning it over several times, smelling it, absurdly expecting to inhale the exotic scents of the pictured market. He didn't know what had possessed her to write to him, and he resented the intrusion of this note. He had finally settled down a little, his initial pain blunted by longer days at the office and stiff drinks before bed, but it all flared up now as he read her overly slanted script and saw her face take on that pixie look it did whenever she tried to hide her emotions.

He sniffed the card again, shutting his eyes to the burning anger for that Peace Corps charlatan who was undoubtedly with her now, screwing her brains out. He knew with the utmost certainty that he'd kill the guy if he ever saw him.

Yet each time he breathed in the card, the smells of spice and sand that were clearly of his own imagining calmed him.

He knew he had to let her go, let a part of his heart be broken and buried as it had been with Stephen. In her world, nothing was permanent, as she kept asserting. Nothing. Not your child, not your wife, lover, parent, job, *nothing*. The only lasting thing in life was its very transience.

Separation is an illusion. She'd said it several times. Fuck! He should have taken it as a warning.

15

*T*wo months later, it seemed like forever since he'd read that postcard, smelled it, cried over it, tried to tear it to pieces; but unable to bring himself to destroy the card, he had stashed it in his desk drawer behind some files.

On a warm, summer night, he and Joy went out to a movie. They went to the mall theater in White Plains, so they could park indoors. She suggested they see *Turning Corners*, the Canadian film on failing minority schools in Quebec, but it was sold out. They looked for another film, but none of them appealed to her, and she refused to consider anything with even a whiff of violence. The discussion spiraled downward until, after several minutes of disagreeing over films, they decided to go home.

In the car, he was frustrated. "Sometimes you're so close-minded, Joy. There were plenty of other films we could've seen."

"Well, I just can't watch all that blood and gore you're strangely drawn to."

"It's not all blood and gore," he said. "There was a mystery that looked good. Sometimes I just need to take my mind off things."

"What is it with you these days, Rich? It's easier for you to zone out on any inane, violent movie than to sit and have a meaningful conversation. You're so in your own world all the time. And you're always in a bad mood."

"Me?"

"Yes."

"Look who's talking," he said.

"I wanted to have a pleasant evening, not be battered by vulgar, gratuitous bloodletting on the screen," she said. "Why can't you understand that? All you care about is what you want. You've become someone I barely recognize."

He was surprised by her anger. "You haven't exactly been upbeat yourself, Joy. You're pretty miserable most of the time."

"You'd be miserable, too, if you were me," she snapped. "And if I'm so miserable, why don't you do something to help?"

"Come on. I haven't tried to help you? I've tried to cheer you up, but I've come to the end of my rope, Joy. You won't let anyone help you. You're living alone inside your own head. You just want to be unhappy forever. Well, I can't go on like this."

They continued to snipe at each other, falling almost unconsciously into one of the random arguments they'd been plunging into lately, barely remembering what it had been about in the morning, only that they were both still pissed off.

She looked at him. "Then don't. Go find someone else to make you happy!"

He was silent.

"Just go find someone else and leave me alone."

"I will," he said flatly.

"I mean it."

"Okay." After a pause he added, "Maybe I have."

At first, she didn't appear to realize what he had said, but then she turned to him. "What?"

He stayed quiet.

"What did you say?" she asked again.

"Nothing."

"You did say something."

"I said maybe I will find somebody else."

"You said it funny. You said maybe you had. Isn't that what you said?"

His throat grew tight.

"Do you have someone else?"

He stared ahead.

She paused, then said, "Wow, Rich. Is that what this is all about, this change in you?"

He remained silent and focused on the road.

"What's going on?" Her voice came out cold but calm. "*Do you have someone else?*"

Finally, he sighed. "I don't have anyone else, Joy."

"You just said you did."

He knew he couldn't take back what he'd uttered a moment ago. He was acutely aware of the possible outcome that his next words would bring, and so he had to navigate as best he could. On the one hand, as had been the case so many times before, he felt a sudden desire to come clean once and for all, but he also knew the costs of doing that.

"I'm saying," he said, his voice low, "that I did have someone else. A while ago. Not now."

She continued to stare at him, looking confused.

"It's over," he said quietly.

She seemed to have slumped in her seat, as though she was about to plummet to the floor.

He turned into their neighborhood, his heart beating fast. "I'm sorry, Joy. It's the last thing I thought would ever happen, but it did."

A deafening silence crashed around them. "When?" she asked, her voice thin as a needle.

"A while ago."

"*When* a while ago?"

He sighed. "Last year. It lasted a few months; then she left."

"She left? What does that mean?"

"She left. Left me. Left the country."

She stared at the road in front of them.

A light fog was touching the ground like wafts of cotton candy that parted for his headlights.

Her voice drifted out into the dense white outside the window. "Who is she?"

"You don't know her," he said gently.

"Someone from your office?"

"No."

"Who, then?"

"Just someone I met. It was crazy, Joy, but it's over."

She gave a little gasp as if struggling to breathe. They were already parked in front of their house. He reached over and carefully put his hand on hers. She jerked her hand away and hit his arm, hard.

He flinched. "Joy, I'm sorry."

"You're sorry?"

"Joy—"

"Just shut up. I don't want to hear any more."

He was silent.

"Bastard!" she shouted.

He stared ahead at the garage door, which he hadn't yet bothered to open.

She stared up at the roof of the car. "I can't believe this. All the healing we'd worked on after Stephen's death, all the slow, painful reclaiming of my life."

"I'm—"

"This can't be true!" She started to cry, covering her mouth with her hands.

He stared at her, helpless. A hollow fear ground into his stomach, bringing a sour taste to his mouth.

"On vacation in Spain, you were so distant, so—so indifferent. I couldn't understand why you weren't enjoying anything."

"It was after Spain."

"You wanted to be anywhere else but with me."

"Joy—"

"Please, just shut up!" she screamed through her tears.

Somehow, they got into the house, both shell-shocked by the exchange. She didn't speak another word to him, just grabbed her work papers and headed off to the study. He lay on the living room couch with the newspaper. Neither went near their bedroom.

The next morning, having barely slept, Richard heard Joy leave the house early, drive out of the garage in the dark. He watched the sunrise from the living room couch where he'd slept, then headed off to the White Plains station to catch his train.

She didn't come home for dinner and got in after ten. Again, she slept in the recliner in the study, and the next morning they barely passed each other. She didn't respond to his attempts at communication.

They stayed like this a few more days, Richard trying to give Joy her space, but he knew that at this point she didn't care about his thoughtfulness or his own remorse or pain. He could have dropped dead in front of her and she would have calmly kicked his corpse as she stepped over him.

Finally, they did give each other basic information, a few words here and there about their respective daily schedules, neither broaching the topic of Richard's confession. Fortunately, he had a business trip to Chicago scheduled the following week and would be gone a few days.

He tried to call her a few times from Chicago, but she didn't answer. For the week after his return home, she seemed cordially indifferent to him.

⚘

A few weeks later, she suggested they go out for dinner.

"You bet," he said, overcome by a surging relief that she was finally taking a stab at normalcy. They went to their favorite Mexican restaurant and ordered margaritas.

She barely touched her tacos.

"Is something wrong with your food?" he asked.

She glanced up, her eyes looking ahead, past his face. "I've applied for a position in a private girls' school in Virginia. Assistant principal."

"What?" he said.

"They'll let me know by the end of the month if I get it."

"Joy," he said, dropping his fork. "No. Come on, sweetheart. Please don't do this."

She went on quickly. "If they do offer it to me, I'll take a leave of absence from Hunter."

He placed both of his hands on the table. He vigorously shook his head. "No. How can you just leave? And to teach at a high school? You've been teaching at the college level for years. And Virginia? The South? No way, Joy. We can work this out. I know we can."

She obviously sensed his confusion and hurt, and for a moment she looked as if she might even take back her words, but she went on. "Look. I need to get away for a bit. I need the change."

He blinked a few times. "I can't believe you're saying this.

Belinda

What about me? What about *us?* Our life here? I don't want you to leave."

She sat back in her chair and calmly picked up her drink. He realized that she'd made up her mind.

"It's only a short distance away, and it's only for a while," she said as though to reassure him.

"No, it's not. You're leaving me."

She exhaled. "Rich, don't make this more difficult than it is. I need to be away to get back on my feet. You won't begrudge me that, will you?"

He stared at her. "How can I—Joy, please just reconsider. I'll give you all the space you need here. Just please don't go. Let's work it out together. We'll do therapy—anything. You haven't thought this through."

She stared at the white froth in her drink, took a sip, picked up her fork, and ate a few more bites of her tacos.

"Joy?"

"Yes, I have," she said quietly. "I have thought it through."

A sad, resigned smile hovered on her lips.

Roxelana

JOY

⎰ ⚭ ⎱

16

She'd always imagined Turkey as if she were experiencing it through shimmering silk. Even as Istanbul's airport terminal greeted her with rank cigarette smoke and the disarray of flight information in Turkish, English, French, and German announced over the sputtering loudspeaker, it all seemed to filter through a diaphanous veil, an endless brocade of civilization. Despite the stench of disinfectant lacing the air, the squeals of children, the bark of baggage handlers, there was a timeless feel to the afternoon. She could have landed in the same spot a century ago and found the same bushy-mustached men alongside women in fluid robes. Even the reek of diesel fumes from the tarmac and passengers chatting on state-of-the art cell phones couldn't mute the resonance of Turkey's illustrious past.

Since her divorce three years ago, Joy considered herself "back" whenever she traveled, returning to her real home whenever she touched down on foreign soil. She came alive, got a stronger foothold on life. Maybe experiencing life in two different areas throttled her mind into high alert and out of the self-pity she sank into more often than she liked to admit. Travel jarred her out of her rut, but it was also simply the fact that everywhere else seemed infinitely more real than her current life in suburban Virginia.

She scanned the crowd in the "Arrivals" area as though someone were waiting for her, then walked on alone as she always did in new places.

She had specifically asked Richard to meet her in Istanbul rather than fly over together so that she could spend this bit of cherished transition time in private. Despite their divorce, they were spending the next two weeks in Istanbul together, although Richard's plane was not due to arrive for another two hours. He had telephoned yesterday from New York and told her not to wait at the airport for him, and so now, with her passport stamped and suitcase retrieved, she changed five hundred dollars into Turkish liras and headed for the exit.

She'd dreamed of living like this her entire life—between different cultures, time zones, and realities, never bound to any particular spot. She'd loved this sensation of floating free, especially since her first trip to Spain. Even later, the troubles that had shredded her and Richard's married life seemed to momentarily dissipate each time they were lifted out of familiar surroundings, the alien environment sharpening and stimulating her perceptions.

She exhaled, shoving the memories of previous vacations with Richard into the hollow of her past, and walked out of the airport into the Istanbul sun.

After they finalized their divorce, she and Richard had spent six months totally apart, not even a phone call between them. Her idea. She couldn't stay in touch and disconnect at the same time, and she wanted to make a clean break. No reminders. No lingering fights. When they'd met in the attorney's office to sign the papers, however, it was obvious from the look in his eyes that Richard was not past the pain of separation, perhaps hoping that she'd change her mind and call off the whole thing. Only after those initial six months did she feel sufficiently detached herself to finally call him late one night, and even then only after several glasses of wine. She'd been disappointed to find him out at that hour, but she left a message on his answering machine.

He called her back the next day and told her he'd been at a ballgame with a friend, a male friend, and although she didn't ask, he volunteered that he had no significant relationships. She didn't either, although she didn't divulge that. After that first phone call, he was the one to call her several more times. Once he even broached the subject of their reconciling.

She knew he was lonely. He'd never cultivated strong male friendships, relying mostly on her for their social life, but she told him she was happy. They could still see each other, but as friends.

Although he agreed, she sensed that keeping their relationship to mere friendship would be hard for him, sensed that to him the marriage wasn't over. In a way she was relieved because part of her was still attached to him, but she was also sad that he seemed unable to move on. Since then they'd resumed friendly, albeit infrequent, contact. On a few occasions she'd met him in New York for the day, even visited his small East Side apartment. Twice he'd driven to Virginia to see her and sightsee in Washington. Platonic visits, all. Separation was a process, she was finding out, and the road to complete uncoupling would not be as automatic as she'd hoped. Their years of companionship seemed to cling to her like weights she wasn't able, or perhaps didn't want to let go of.

With a stack of mid-term papers to grade, she'd turned over

the task of hotel bookings in Turkey to Richard. His choice of the Pensione in Istanbul, described as a row of renovated seventeenth-century attached houses converted into a "boutique hotel," located around the corner from the major sights, sounded perfect. He'd remembered her preference for hotels with local ambiance. Next week they would head for the ruins of Ephesus and the seaside resort of Antalya where the sprawling Marriott and its beautiful beach awaited them. Until then, she was looking forward to a simpler, more authentic experience of Constantinople.

The taxi driver veered off the main street and drew up to a row of quaint, blue-painted houses. PENSIONE was painted in yellow on a plaque next to the glass front doors.

The driver pointed out the window and declared with a flourish, "*Aya Sofia.*"

Joy looked to where he was gesturing and caught her breath. Through a line of gracefully pruned trees stood the unmistakable reddish colossus of domes and minarets, the Byzantine Hagia Sofia, once the largest Christian basilica in the world.

In the hotel's lobby, she was offered a glass of hot tea and some pistachio sweets while the reception clerk did her paperwork. Paintings of medieval Istanbul hung on the walls, images of languid women in silken gowns lounging under fruit trees; men in intricate robes carrying curved swords and strolling through gardens; a portly, turbaned sultan offering a doe-eyed maiden a rose.

A young porter picked up her suitcase, escorted her to the elevator, and up to a third-floor, Victorian-looking room. He threw open the maroon curtains.

"*Aya Sofia,*" he announced, echoing the taxi driver earlier, as he pointed out the window to the imposing sliver of red wall and minarets visible through the trees.

She smiled and tipped him. His pride in the historic building—the one-time church that the Ottomans had converted to a mosque in the fifteenth century and that had become a museum with secularization in the 1930s—was as evident as the driver's had been. Perhaps they assumed a Westerner would be most interested in a once-Christian landmark.

The porter left, and Joy stared a moment longer at the domes and minarets before kicking off her shoes and dropping onto the wide bed, where afternoon sunlight splattered the velvet coverlet. The mahogany dresser and satin-upholstered chairs ironically conjured up a cozy English cottage, although she was in a Turkish hotel, smack dab in the midst of some of the greatest Byzantine and Islamic monuments ever built.

Waiting for Richard. What on earth had she been thinking?

She'd been surprised when he'd called, out of the blue, to tell her that he'd learned from a mutual friend that she was planning this trip.

"Want company?" he had asked.

"Company?" She'd assumed he was joking.

"I thought we could travel together, like we used to."

She paused, wondering what had brought this on. "I'm going with a group. It's a cultural tour. I'll have plenty of company."

"A group?" He'd sounded skeptical, and she pictured his eyes twinkling in that way they did whenever he was amused. "Why not ditch the group and go with me?"

She had laughed.

He persisted. "It'll be fun to discover it ourselves, and we can see the things we feel like."

She'd prepared herself to travel alone, but the enthusiasm in his voice was infectious, and he knew how she hated group tours. Although the sadness of their lost marriage had remained submerged in her belly, she'd never seriously contemplated going back to him; but since he seemed to finally want to be friends, there was no reason not to try for that.

"I'll get back to you," she had said, imagining herself exploring the ancient alleys of Istanbul under his watchful gaze, and then pictured being cooped up with a bus full of strangers for ten days. Could being with Richard be worse than that? Despite being well aware of their past conflicting travel interests, she'd also enjoyed their camaraderie and shared curiosity in new foods and historic details of the places they'd visited. She considered his proposal for a few days, then called him back and invited him to join her.

Now it seemed like the wackiest idea she'd ever agreed to. In place of the usual euphoria of freedom that travel brought her, there seemed to be this void sucking her into the bed, as if she could curl up and disappear into the mattress and never have to get up.

Although part of her wished she hadn't let him talk her into his joining her, another part needed to come to terms with their divorce, to prove to herself that their now-separate lives needn't mean a total end to their past, parts of which were good. She assumed he still wasn't dating anybody, since nothing was impeding his coming with her. When he asked whether to book two separate rooms at the hotels, she'd been shocked at his suggestion that they might share one. She calmly declined and left it at that, although she couldn't help wondering what exactly each of them was expecting from this reunion.

At the last minute, she had packed the half-full container of anxiety pills she hadn't needed in a year. Just in case.

She lifted her duffel bag onto the bed and took out two books, a friend's dog-eared guidebook and *Roxelana*, a biography of the beautiful Russian slave girl who had become the consort of the renowned sixteenth-century Turkish sultan, Suleyman the Magnificent.

She read a few pages of the biography, to the part where the scheming Roxelana conspired to kill her husband's beloved grand vizier; then, losing track of the same paragraph for the third time, she rested the book on her chest, closed her eyes, and surrendered to the pull of the soft pillow. She had hardly slept on the nine-hour flight over, and the last thing she wanted was to start off the trip jet-lagged and irritable.

17

"*M*adam!" A man's voice pierced her dream.

Startled awake, she leaped off the bed and opened the door. It was the hotel porter. Behind him stood a tall figure.

"Hey," Richard said, grinning above the porter's head.

"Hey," she answered, still half asleep.

"Can we come in?" Richard asked, as if this were the most natural thing in the world.

She moved aside, and Richard stepped around the porter and into her room. Despite having just awakened from a troubling dream—of Richard, no less—she was almost glad to see him and gave him an affectionate hug.

"You're looking good," he said jovially once the porter had left.

She smoothed her hair. "I fell asleep. What time is it?"

"Almost six. We got in early."

"Good flight?"

"I slept," he said. Then he added, "They gave me a room on the floor below, but they're fixing the shower, so they wanted me to wait downstairs. I told them I could come up and see you, but they insisted on sending someone along to make sure you knew me. I thought you might have told them that—you know, you know me." Despite his smile, she sensed his disappointment that she hadn't informed the concierge of their relationship beforehand.

Richard looked surprisingly youthful and invigorated, his hair neatly trimmed and the lines around his eyes crinkling with enthusiasm. He'd also obviously lost weight since she'd last seen him, his face and chest leaner. Although he'd always claimed not to relish traveling, whenever he'd gone on overseas business trips, he returned looking energized. She used to joke that only he and James Bond could get off a ten-hour flight looking so unruffled.

He walked over to the window where the Hagia Sofia gleamed sienna in the late afternoon light. He gave a slight whistle. "What's that?"

She smiled. "The Hagia Sofia." It was now her turn to say this.

He stared at it, nodding, then turned to her. "So," he said, "how does it feel to finally be here?"

"It feels great," she lied. Although she had perked up from her earlier low mood, grains of unease still churned in her stomach.

"This city's huge," Richard said.

"And this location is good. You chose well, Rich."

"I hope so," he said, looking up at the ceiling fan. "They don't have air-conditioning."

She glanced at the fan. She hadn't noticed the lack of air conditioning. "It's May. It shouldn't get too hot."

Richard slid off his jacket. "I should have asked. We can change hotels if it gets too bad."

She chuckled. "Let's not start that."

He looked skeptical as he unbuttoned the top of his shirt. "The things you take for granted."

"Here," she said, twisting the antique iron handle on the window and pushing open the glass panes. It was warmer than she'd expected in spring, but there was a breeze. "The night will be cooler, and these are big windows," she said cheerfully, although she was already disheartened by his misgivings. In the past, accommodations hadn't bothered him as much as they did her. She used to be the finicky one.

"It'll be okay," he said, glancing back out the window and then returning his gaze to her. "It's great to see you, Joy."

"Same here," she said, trying to convince herself that, indeed, she was still happy to see him. "You must be tired. Do you need to rest?"

"Hell, no," he said. "I've been sitting all day. Let's go out and investigate."

Surprised by this atypical show of sightseeing bravado, she smiled, pulling her sneakers out of the suitcase.

He stood and waited while she put them on, seeming at a loss as to whether to sit on the chair or the bed or to be more deferential and stand. He hadn't yet remarked about the lack of a television in the room.

He picked up the book she was reading. She expected him to ask why she still carted books across the ocean in her suitcase when it was just as easy to look things up on her phone or iPad. Ever the pragmatist, always moving on to the newest gadget to simplify his life, he never understood her tactile and visual preference for old-fashioned paper.

"*Roxelana?*" he asked.

She tied her laces. "Suleyman the Magnificent's wife."

"Sounds familiar," he said.

"She was a Russian slave girl who married the sultan."

"It's a porno movie," he said, as though he hadn't heard her.

"What?"

"I pass the billboard on my way to work: *Roxelana XXX.*"

She raised her eyebrows. "Well, she was pretty enterprising. Ottoman sultans never had just one wife before Suleyman."

"Oh?"

"They just took harem girls who bore them sons. But Roxelana wasn't satisfied with being a mere concubine and insisted on becoming the official wife and mother of the heir."

Richard leafed through the book.

"She was ruthless," she went on. "Anyone who opposed her was eliminated. Even her own son, the one who should have inherited the throne, was removed. She had her favorite alcoholic son, 'Selim the Sot,' succeed his father instead."

"All that in here?" he said, looking impressed as he closed the slim volume.

She nodded and stood. "Let's go."

"Let's check on my room first," he said.

They walked down one flight to his room. The door had been left ajar, his suitcase placed on the bench at the foot of the bed. His room was decorated differently from hers. In one corner stood a chair and a lamp with yellow crystal beads dangling from the shade. There was only a single bed, however. A bachelor pad.

"It'll do," Richard said, looking less than content as he glanced up at the ceiling fan. "No TV?" he added.

"No TV," she repeated, overcoming an urge to smile. And no remote, she thought.

Walking beside Richard down the tree-lined street beyond the hotel felt natural. She hated to admit that she was comfortable in his presence, able to talk and joke as if they'd just picked up where they left off three years ago. Minus the misery of those final few months.

Although the years apart had been peaceful for her—no pent-up fuming—she had often missed the familiarity of being married, the Sunday omelets, his making her coffee in the mornings, his reading up on politics and then recounting it back to her like a bedtime story. She missed the feeling that there was someone there for her no matter what. But then the reality of his affair would come crashing around her and flood out all the positive memories.

"Oh, gosh, look!" she said suddenly, interrupting her own thoughts.

The Hagia Sofia was looming above them, immense lead-colored domes and red walls surrounded by four needle-like minarets poking at the evening sky. Despite its Christian origins, the minarets had converted the mammoth structure into a thoroughly Islamic sanctuary.

"The world's largest church for a thousand years. It was turned into a mosque in the fifteenth century," she said.

Richard stared up, looking impressed. "Are we on the European side or the Asian side?" he asked, scrutinizing his map.

"European."

He looked surprised. "The most famous Islamic landmarks are in Europe?"

"Ottoman rule extended to both continents. It's the Sultanahmet District, but it's Europe." She pointed toward the six minarets of another large mosque farther away and highlighted against the rosy sky. "That must be the Blue Mosque."

"You've really studied up on this," he said.

"I've been planning this trip for a while."

Before he could say anything, a delectable whiff of smoke permeated the air.

Richard inhaled, an eager grin spreading across his face. "Shish kebab?"

She breathed it in, too, amazed by how quickly history and sublime architecture had been eclipsed by the intoxicating lure of food assailing them from an outdoor restaurant.

"Two doner kebabs and two Turkish beers," Richard told the waiter once they'd been seated in the restaurant's garden and had perused the menu. They had a view of the Hagia Sofia on one side, the reddish walls now deepening to russet in the sunset. Strings of white lights, like a regiment of fireflies, meandered through the branches of the small trees neatly planted around them.

"Nice flowers," Richard said of the white roses placed on their table. His recent interest in gardening had been apparent from the blooming pots on his Manhattan balcony during her last visit to his New York apartment.

She sniffed the fragrant blooms. "Turks love flowers. They call roses the 'sweat of the Prophet.' Even tulips were developed here."

"Not in Holland?"

"They were introduced to Holland years later. They were brought here first as wildflowers from Central Asia by the Ottomans. They're painted on all the tiles."

Richard listened intently, still looking relaxed despite the long trip. Bachelorhood seemed to agree with him, and, although he'd never mentioned it, she couldn't help wondering again whether he was dating anyone regularly. She'd be surprised if he didn't occasionally go out with women.

Forcing herself back to the present, she said, "There was a Sultan Ahmet who loved flowers so much that his reign was known as the 'tulip era.'"

He smiled. "Yeah?" Then, he cleared his throat. "As a matter of fact," he said, his tone shifting, "I'm grateful you agreed to my coming with you, Joy."

She shrugged. "We once talked about coming here."

"But you had your mind set on coming alone."

"I'll be going other places alone."

He nodded, looking as though this realization saddened him.

The tables around them were filling with customers and their children. Although the sun had already set, people seemed to be ordering tea and ice cream rather than dinner.

Her stomach rumbled. "I didn't eat much on the plane, so I could enjoy my first Turkish meal here. Remember my attempts at rolled grape leaves?"

"They were good."

She made a face. "They were horrid. You just forgot."

"I didn't forget. You're a wonderful cook."

"You didn't used to think so."

He raised his eyebrows. "Yes, I did."

She chuckled at what had once been vexing spats. "I used to get so angry whenever you'd say, 'That isn't the way my mother did it.'"

"Well, that was back in the beginning," he said. "One of our first fights."

"We had so many first fights—and seconds and thirds."

"We don't fight now," he said, looking hopeful.

She couldn't help laughing. "There are two hundred miles between us."

Before he could answer, their waiter appeared with the smoking skewers of lamb on frothy white rice.

She inhaled, then picked up her fork and sampled the meat. A delectable jumble of garlic and allspice melded in her mouth.

After a few bites she said, "I dreamt about you this afternoon."

Richard looked up from his food. "Something sexy?"

She glanced at him, impatient. "Not every dream involves sex. You were pushing me down a bumpy road in a wheelbarrow. Puerto Vallarta, I think."

"A wheelbarrow?" He glanced upward as if trying to recall. "Didn't we rent a moped there?"

"It was scary. I felt like we were out of control, going to be lost."

He stopped eating. "But I wasn't lost, honey. I didn't want us to separate. I wanted us to stay together. Your dream proves that."

She stared at him. He didn't seem to get it, to comprehend the kind of pain he'd inflicted on her.

"I know," he mumbled sheepishly. "I screwed up."

There was an awkward silence, and she felt her neck grow hot. They resumed eating.

"God, this is delicious, isn't it?" he blurted out, as if desperately looking for common ground.

Yes, it was she who had pushed for the divorce. He had screwed up. Big time.

Those years hadn't been easy. Her heart caught: Stephen. A dream come true, then obliterated. She still felt that gut-numbing blow whenever she thought of losing the baby. Nothing seemed to make sense in those moments. How could a rational person ever accept the ruthless taking of such a joyously anticipated child? There had been no way to reasonably explain any of it.

They'd tried for another baby, their anticipations dashed monthly and turned to disappointments until she was finally convinced it was useless.

"Good, huh?" Richard said now, seeming to sense her sinking mood, his face pleading with her to get back on track.

"Yes," she agreed, somewhat soothed by the soft texture of the lamb and its delicate, unusual spicing. "Really good."

She couldn't help drifting back to that rocky year, her uterus still swollen and both of them mourning their lost child.

Then she'd learned of Richard's infidelity. Infidelity. The word rolled in her mouth like a marble she wanted to spit out.

How obscene to describe plain old cheating in such elegant terms.

She pushed around the rice on her plate as she pushed around the shards of anger in her mind. She saw Richard take a bite, but he was staring into his plate as he chewed, perhaps as lost in the past as she was.

Even before Richard's cheating, however, she'd found it difficult to reorient her relationship to him once the prospect of motherhood was gone. She'd hoped, naively, that a child would fix things for them. A family had been such a cornerstone of her initial attraction to Richard that facing life without a child to bind them to each other had changed the premise of their marriage. It had seemed almost crucial that they reinvent their relationship to move into this new, childless blueprint, and they might have eventually succeeded had it not been for . . .

Bastard! How could he have—and after the death of the baby?

She tried to keep her mind on the fluffiness of the rice and the rich seasoning of the lamb, then on the melting pinks and purples of the sunset behind the Hagia Sofia, but the hostility kept creeping in.

Without that other woman, there might have been something of their life together to salvage. She had defined the end.

Once they were divorced, Joy could hardly believe it. She and Richard—their marriage—over. She had swung between outrage and grief, one moment feeling she'd been flung into a scorching flame and the next like she was clawing herself out of some frozen underground cave.

She lied to friends, telling them the separation was amicable. Those who stayed in touch after she moved away were solicitous and caring, the same friends who rallied to support her in the wake of the lost baby and—those few who knew of it—of

Richard's straying. Joy was clearly the wronged one, in their view, and they were quick to stand by her while duly expressing hopes for a reconciliation. She was touched by their loyalty but couldn't console herself with it. There wasn't an easy verdict in her and Richard's case. Both had come up short. Padlocked into her sorrow after the baby, she'd pushed him away, left no room for him, and he had retaliated with frustration and, finally . . . Bastard!

She had been distant, yes, but they had each catapulted the other over the brink.

The stars were now filling the cobalt sky, and the rest of the restaurant's outdoor tables were taken. A young man at the table next to theirs was bouncing a toddler on his knee, popping bits of spongy Turkish bread into the child's mouth. Across from the man, his young wife nursed an infant beneath a large floral head scarf. The couple took turns cooing to the giggling toddler.

"Been going out any?" Richard asked. "Dating?"

"Some," she replied, trying to sound offhand. She had suspected this would eventually come up, but she was surprised that it had so soon. They'd never openly asked each other about other relationships.

"Anyone in particular?" He looked down at his food as though to dodge her response.

She paused. "Last summer I spent time in California with a guy I met rock climbing."

He looked up. "Rock climbing?"

"Yep." She wasn't sure whether he was more surprised by the news of her rock climbing or by the mention of a man in her life.

He looked intrigued. "I didn't know you were into that."

She wondered if he even heard the part about her companion. "I was working on my vertigo. It killed my arms and legs the first few times, but I got the hang of it. It's never too late to start over." She hoped he would get her drift. It was never too late to start over with another man.

"Sounds challenging."

"It was."

"Did it work? For the vertigo?"

"It helped. And the guy," she added, "helped even more."

He went back to his food, again avoiding her eyes.

She was surprised, herself, by the vindictiveness of her response.

"I joined a gym and do some horseback riding," she continued. "I have my work and new friends."

He didn't look up. "What about the rock climber?"

She smiled, sure that he'd return to this sooner or later. She was tempted to hurl something at him about the guy being a fabulous lover. Or maybe she'd tell him she'd had several lovers, give him a taste of his own medicine; but to her surprise, she wasn't inspired to concoct any lies, juicy or otherwise.

"He was handsome," she said, still wanting him to suffer a little, but then she started to chuckle at the sad truth of it all, the part that still disappointed her. "And boring."

Richard looked up, relief coating his brow.

"You?" she asked. "Anybody—"

"Nah," he said, shaking his head, "not since us."

She said nothing but was amazed by the weight in her own chest lifting at his response.

"But something was wrong," she said, folding her napkin, unable to stop herself. "For us."

He cleared his throat. "I was gone too much."

"You were too rigid."

He looked surprised. "I tried to be accommodating."

"Not with me. Maybe you were with that—with whoever she was."

He looked away. "That was a passing thing."

"Passing thing? Is that how you still see it, Rich?" She ironed the crease of the folded napkin with her palm to control herself. She didn't want to rehash any of this, but why not let him know how much he'd hurt her, hurt them both, by his twisted, narcissistic behavior?

"Maybe you'd like to reimburse me for my year-plus of therapy," she said under her breath.

His brow furrowed. "I didn't mean it that way."

"How did you mean it? Did you think things could ever be the same between us?" Before he could answer, she put up her hands to stop him. She didn't want his answer. At that point, anything could have ignited the tinderbox of their lives. They both knew his cheating was only the final blow.

"Look, I made a mistake," Richard said, lowering his voice. "I feel terrible about it. You know that."

"I don't know it."

"Joy—"

"You know how many times I tried to convince myself that you were just a nice guy who strayed? I know you were affected by Stephen's death and how I shut you out, I admit that, but you were a snake, Richard. You just went your own way. I didn't even know my own husband. How stupid could I have been?"

"Joy—"

She pushed her plate away and forced herself to smile. "Anyway, it's done. We're on vacation in Turkey, here to have fun."

"Yes," he said. "So, let's drop it and try to enjoy this."

She thought of how Roxelana would have handled a rival for her husband's affection. The sultana would have had the woman summarily strangled by one of the palace's notorious deaf-mute assassins. The corpse would have been flung into the river and nothing more would have been said about it.

"Indeed," Joy said, relishing the vision of her rival having a silk cord snapped round her neck, her imagined gasps as she sucked on the last ounce of precious air, her skin turning ashen. For, oddly enough, she had remembered the woman after Richard confessed to the affair: striking black curls and eyebrows, pert nose and chin. They'd been at some function in the city, and the woman had come up to them—could Richard have invited her?—smiling and pretty, and quite young. Joy had soon forgotten about her and their friendly exchange that evening until after Richard brought her up again months later in that miserable confession. It had to have been her. Joy had sensed something about the woman at the time, maybe in her over-eager friendliness, but she couldn't pinpoint what had bothered her and certainly hadn't suspected she had any link to Richard. Sipping her beer, Joy forced the pleasurable image of the assassin's cord around the woman's throat to recede.

Apparently, he'd lost touch with her when she left the country with another man. Richard had insisted that the fling was over and that it would never happen again.

But if he'd forgotten the woman, it was only the beginning of the obsession for Joy. For months she'd fixated on her—or rather, on the woman and Richard together. She could barely look at Richard without the searing image of him making love to someone else blazing before her, someone else's naked body in his arms.

As painful as it was, she couldn't help replaying the imagined, lurid scenes in her head, simultaneously hooked and sickened, unable to turn them off and yet hating every second of the reel playing before her eyes. She didn't want to know, and yet she tortured herself with questions. Why had he sought an affair to begin with? Was the woman, other than the fact that she was younger, that much prettier, smarter, better at sex? Had she been the one to tempt him or vice-versa? Once she even dared ask Richard what it felt like to make love to her, but he'd refused to talk about it.

"Did you ever consider leaving me for her, Rich?" she asked.

He sighed as though he'd been preparing himself for this. "No, I didn't." His shifting eyes told her he was either lying or else trying to spare her feelings. She wondered, a little meanly, whether he was contemplating heading for the airport.

"You could have started something new. Maybe she was more fertile—"

"No," he said flatly.

"I found a postcard from her before our divorce. I was sure you'd follow her."

The postcard had been stashed in his desk. There had been no return address, and it had said that she was staying in Africa. The card had rattled Joy, thinking of the woman marooned far away and daring to contact Richard so openly. She wondered at the time whether Richard would mention the card, but he never had and neither had she.

"No, I wouldn't have left, Joy. And I didn't."

"Why not?"

He sighed again. "I didn't want to leave you, honey. I loved you."

Honey? Did he intentionally say it, or was it out of some old habit? She was not sure how she felt about being referred to as "honey."

"Well, you were obviously ready to risk losing me when you got into it."

"I never imagined losing you. I wasn't going to go that far."

"How thoughtful," she almost sneered.

His face looked drained. He reached out and gently placed

his hand on hers. "It was a mistake, Joy. I can't change what I did, much as I'd like to. Can we try to put this behind us? At least for now? Please?"

She took a deep breath. "You're right," she said, sliding her hand out from under his.

With the time that had passed and the fact that she'd agreed to travel with him, she knew she shouldn't be kicking his butt so hard. She'd promised herself that she wouldn't bring up the past, but she obviously hadn't been thinking realistically. Although at this point she had no idea how to channel her feelings into a more constructive conversation, she reminded herself again that it hadn't only been the other woman. It was also her and Richard's inability to match up their ragged edges and sew up the rent in their life together.

They finished their meal talking about where they'd go the following day, whether to start out with the Hagia Sofia and the mosques or explore the bazaar. She couldn't wait to shop in the exotic, renowned market, but they decided on the sanctuaries for their first day.

As they walked the few blocks back to their hotel, the street humming with bustling shoppers and people strolling, she began to feel more upbeat. When he walked her to her room, she touched his arm. "Sorry about dinner, Rich. Old wounds. Jetlag. But I'm glad you're here."

She waited for him to suggest that he come inside for a few minutes or that she go down to his room, maybe order drinks in the hotel's bar downstairs—some sign that he wanted to be with her for a while longer. She needed some sort of reassurance that they could make it through the next two weeks without driving each other insane by unwittingly drawing each other back to the past, but he only said, "Meet you at nine for breakfast?"

Mustering a smile, she watched him walk away down the hall.

A Marriage in Four Seasons

❧

She sat on the crisp bed sheet that had been turned down by housekeeping, the two pillows fluffed invitingly, a small chocolate placed on each; but she suddenly felt less like sleeping than like having a glass of wine. Only there was no mini-bar in the room and no room service. A big disadvantage, she had to admit, of boutique hotels that didn't cater to travelers who expected amenities.

She opened the window and peeked down into the alley. Except for the noise from a few stray cats, it was quiet, and it was still warm out. She wondered whether Richard had gone to sleep or whether he was fretting about the lack of air conditioning and TV. Since it wasn't yet ten o'clock, she considered going down to his room to see if he felt like a nightcap. He didn't used to have qualms about getting dressed and fetching snacks from the hotel bar if there wasn't one in the room, one of the perks of traveling with him.

She decided against it. It was safer to end the night on the neutral tone they'd just parted on than to risk reopening their history. She would have ventured to the hotel bar herself, as she often did when traveling alone, but in glancing through the hotel directory she saw there was no bar, and the restaurant served only breakfast. So much for a nightcap.

She turned on the ceiling fan and closed the window to shut out the sounds of the cats, which started to remind her of her own Ophelia, now dead. She'd lasted ten months after the divorce. Joy had grieved her death as if she'd lost another child, those old memories rising again like demons. She'd wondered whether the cat had really died of grief, never having adjusted to the move to Virginia, or maybe from missing Richard, although he'd never interacted with her much.

Changing her mind, Joy reopened the window. She needed to stay connected to the tangible activity outside to avoid being pulled into some miserable dream like the one this afternoon, being wheeled around by Richard and feeling out of control.

When she first moved to Virginia, she'd found the colonial brick homes and open spaces of her new countryside surroundings endearing. There was a freshness to the rolling terrain that was vastly different from the older, lived-in look of the New York boroughs and suburbs. Although she missed New York, she'd found enough to do in the Washington area to distract her from both Manhattan and Richard.

Her first Virginia winter was so mild that she barely wore her coat, and that in itself seemed to signal a new beginning. She was renting a small townhouse not far from the school where she taught and didn't even have to shovel the short driveway the one time it snowed. The snow seemed to melt within hours in Virginia, not pile up into the glacial, soiled peaks it did in New York where it stayed until March. The southern warmth brought an early spring, with dogwood and cherry blossoms busting out of pale-green branches like pink-and-white popcorn. The long freezing winters of New York were almost a forgotten part of someone else's life.

She had a short drive to work rather than a train commute each morning, and even when she drove into Washington, she hugged her purse less and walked less quickly than she ever had in Manhattan. The absence of frantic, rushing crowds eased her nerves and enabled her to pause and enjoy the open skyline of the city with its sparkly turquoise skies.

The second year was different, however. Virginians seemed ruder, the winter colder. She began to feel nostalgic for the crisp Park Avenue buildings, the Madison Avenue galleries, and the eateries on every corner, especially her favorite deli on 47th

Street. The Washington streets were as devoid of food as if there were a famine. This third year, oddly enough, she'd even begun to miss her marriage.

She felt adrift, not uncomfortable alone, but not entirely at home with only her work. She enjoyed her freedom and yet longed to feel settled. She seemed to be at a crossroads. Perhaps this was what had drawn her to Turkey, this historic intersection crisscrossed through millennia by Greeks, Byzantines, Central Asians; this place that awkwardly bridged both Europe and Asia and wanted to be both. A place conflicted, like her.

Staring out at the glittering lights of Hagia Sofia, she finally drifted off.

18

*J*oy leaned against the outer stone wall of the Topkapi Palace gardens overlooking the Bosphorus Strait. The aqua water lapped thirstily against the marble, exhaling its heady sea scent. It was their second full day in Istanbul, and everything absorbed the azure of the sky: the stone ramparts along the river, the shimmering water. She imagined those hapless harem women of the past who, if suspected of deceiving the sultan, were said to have been sewn into sacks and hurled into this same beautiful waterway in the middle of the night.

They'd just finished the first half of their palace tour, viewing the emerald and ruby-encrusted scabbards of the sultans' swords and the royal jewels that dazzled like lasers. Joy was equally impressed by the massive cauldrons of the kitchens, huge tubs that could have cooked a dozen sheep at once, along with the blue-and-white Ming china collection that shone as if it had just been washed and tucked back into the cabinets. Five hundred years ago, these kitchens had purportedly fed ten thousand people at the festival of the circumcision of Suleyman the Magnificent's two sons, the banquet menu apparently so tantalizing that the exact recipes used were still preserved in the museum.

After lunch they were due to view the harem, those legendary living quarters of the sultans, their families, and legions of female slaves.

She and Richard crossed the courtyard to the palace riverside cafe, where they ordered the signature Imam Bayildi, eggplant simmered in tomatoes and onions, and two glasses of icy raki, the Turkish anisette liqueur.

"It was Roxelana who convinced Suleyman to move the harem from the separate women's building into this Topkapi complex," Joy said. "Before her, all women and children lived apart from the sultan in the Old Palace. When Roxelana had Suleyman change this tradition, his subjects accused her of bewitching him."

"Sounds like she did," Richard said, pouring the customary vial of water into their glasses of raki to make the liquor cloudy and milder than if simply sipped over ice.

Although Roxelana had been an extraordinarily strong-willed temptress, Joy couldn't help feeling pity for her, along with the other beautiful women chosen from across the empire as gifts for the sultan, for having to waste their lives in this "gilded cage," as it was known, with no other ambition than to gain and retain their master's affection. The faded beauty of the Topkapi gardens further amplified the sense of the stifled lives led here by the pampered, conniving slave women and their royal children. Would Roxelana, she wondered, have attained such prominence had she, like Joy, been unable to bear children?

"You had to be a slave woman's son to become sultan," she said. "Ironically, most of the slaves were Christians from Eastern Europe and Russia, which seems to have made the royal family mostly non-Turkish after a few generations."

"It makes sense," Richard said. "Slaves were cut off from their origins. Without competing local noble families, the Ottomans totally centralized their power."

She stared at the river. Richard had always understood the rules of power. It reminded her of how he often had to have the last word in an argument, as if to maintain his position in their relationship.

"Concubines fought to propel their own sons, at the expense of all their half-brothers, to accede their father's throne," she said.

He nodded. "It brought the dynasty down in the end. Isolation in the harem eventually drove all the offspring nuts. Down the line, the poor bastards got weaker and less exposed to the outside realities and more vulnerable to being controlled by savvier political forces."

Joy imagined a mob of crazy little princes stampeding down the elegant corridors.

"Whenever the palace women used to come out to the gardens, any man found on the premises was instantly killed by the royal gardeners," she said.

Richard whistled. "Did they use hoes or scimitars?"

She rolled her eyes, a smile escaping. "Silk cords around the neck." Although in the past she would have found his glibness annoying, now it somewhat lightened the horror of this detail.

Lunch arrived, and the sweetness of the eggplant drizzled with olive oil, raisins, and pine nuts perked up her taste buds. Imam Bayildi. "The cleric swooned." She closed her eyes, empathizing with that long-ago cleric said to have fainted over this dish, giving it the well-deserved name.

The sun in the breezy cafe felt good. Yesterday had been overcast and drizzly, and they'd escaped the moody skies by touring Istanbul's three main mosques: the Hagia Sofia, the Sultanahmet, and the Suleymaniya.

The Suleymaniya, considered Istanbul's greatest mosque, had been designed for Suleyman by the famed architect, Sinan. With its gray marble and granite colonnades, it was the most forbidding of the three from the outside, but Joy had found a tender poignancy to the placement of the domed mausoleums of Suleyman and Roxelana side by side in the garden, Suleyman's larger one and Roxelana's smaller one. Even in death, the lovers seemed to be straining toward each other.

"You weren't exactly bowled over by the Hagia Sofia," Richard said now.

"It's a little schizophrenic," she said, not adding that this aspect of the sanctuary reminded her of their current relationship.

Though clearly a masterpiece, the Hagia Sofia seemed to her to have lost its essence in its transformation from cathedral to mosque, as though trying too hard to announce its conversion. Although the name of Allah was prominently displayed in all corners in large gold letters, the naves and Byzantine mosaics were stark reminders of the building's Christian past.

By contrast, the Sultanahmet, the Blue Mosque, had a deeply Eastern feel to it, the ethereal stained-glass windows organically blending into the tranquil blue mosaics of the walls. Even its chandeliers, suspended like strands of pearls above the kneeling worshipers, seemed to effortlessly lift the murmured prayers into the sky.

"Kemal Ataturk had the right idea by westernizing this place," Richard said. "It would have taken centuries to push Turkey forward if he hadn't dragged it out of the Middle Ages after the First World War."

Joy glanced at some women at a nearby table who were modestly dressed in Islamic scarves and long coats. "I'm not sure he was so successful in his westernizing," she quipped.

"Well, the rest of the Middle East still hasn't recovered from the Crusades. By allying himself with Europe after World War I, Turkey benefited."

She tilted her head. It still amazed her that Richard reached these verdicts so easily. Life for him seemed to always be black or white, neatly boxed and labeled for expediency rather than bubbling with the myriad possibilities that constantly swam before her.

"You sound smug when you say these things, Rich. Aren't we all basically the same, just looking for some peace and joy in our lives? Why keep judging others by our own arbitrary standards?"

He shrugged. "I'm just saying it was time for Turkey to leave the old empire behind, and Ataturk was the man to do that. It was time to move on to something that worked, and the West was leading the way."

He rose abruptly as if to avoid a clash with her unspoken thoughts. "Come on. They're calling us for the tour."

She swallowed the last of her raki and followed him, grateful, herself, to be sidetracked.

Their guide stood before a set of tall iron doors.

"Welcome to the forbidden harem." He produced a chunky ring of keys. The group included two German couples and a Japanese woman and her daughter.

"We men today are lucky," the guide said, unlocking the doors and bolting them shut behind them like a jailer. "Once, any man who entered here other than the sultan or eunuchs was killed." As he said this, he made a swift gesture toward his pelvic region as if to indicate the emasculation of the eunuchs.

Joy drew back at the image of chopping off testicles.

"This was the dormitory of the special African eunuchs," the guide said, leading them down a hallway. "They slept in shifts so that the sultan's women were guarded at all times. There were often more than four hundred women living together in Topkapi."

Joy glanced at the ominous palace walls. A massive women's prison! She couldn't help thinking this, despite the fact that she'd just criticized Richard for being judgmental of this culture's past. There was a pulsing quality about the rooms, as if the occupants had left the stone floors and faded walls only hours ago rather than over a hundred years earlier. A dizzy feeling of despair locked into her, brought on by these silent pathways and corridors.

"The luckiest ladies were led down this hall at night to Sultan's bedchamber," the guide added with a knowing smile.

Luckiest ladies? She could think of better words to describe those women: wretched, even terrified. To all but a few, their master was mostly a stranger, after all.

The guide drew their attention to the next two rooms, which had been occupied, he said, by the first and second of the sultan's favorite concubines who had borne him sons.

"These favored *kadins* were especially fortunate," the guide asserted. "One of their sons might be the future sultan."

Again, Joy marveled at the arrangement that those "fortunate" women were made to live under. Rival concubines in adjoining bedrooms, sharing the only man they were allowed to love, if they did love him, their lives constantly at risk from jealous competitors. They must have developed cores of steel, she thought.

One of the German women asked what Joy had been wondering: "What happened to the women who didn't bear the sultan children?"

The guide shrugged. "They were not important."

Joy flinched. Women existed to produce heirs. Boys. Women who lost their babies or who couldn't conceive were expendable.

They exited through the gate to the outermost palace courtyard, where a fresh breeze welcomed them.

"Is it possible to find something so awful and yet be absolutely fascinated by it?" she said.

Richard shrugged. "These women seemed to live pretty darn well."

"They weren't here by choice. And those poor eunuchs."

He shrugged. "They were slaves. Finding favor with the sultan was their best assurance for staying alive."

"But they also had feelings. Humans haven't changed that much over the years. Those women were sex slaves."

He raised his eyebrows in mock horror. "Now who's being smug?"

"Okay. But that's what they were." She gestured at their surroundings. "At the same time, look at all that was created, all the art, the gorgeous buildings . . . people without feelings and sensitivity couldn't have done this."

"They had feelings, but their values were different from ours."

He drew her attention to a man carrying a small boy dressed in a blue satin cape and a pointed hat trimmed with white fuzz who looked like a first-grader at a Halloween party. In the cape and hat, the boy resembled a miniature prince, contentedly sucking on an oversized lollypop.

"That kid has just been circumcised."

She stared at the child. "How do you know?"

"I read about it. Those are special outfits. Parents bring them to the Topkapi afterwards as a reward. They purposely put it off until the kid's older, so he can remember the experience and celebrate it. It's not likely to get them into the European Union."

She glanced at him. "Come on. Circumcision is holding Turkey back from joining the EU?"

"You know what I mean."

"I don't think that has to do with the politics of joining the EU."

"They want to be European, but they're Asian to the core, celebrating manhood like that. They could do it at birth."

Although Joy didn't like the idea of performing this procedure on an older child, she found it equally absurd to attribute the European Union's not accepting Turkey into the fold because of the timing of boys' circumcisions.

"Maybe European prejudice is keeping them out," she suggested.

"Their old ideas are keeping them out."

She glanced at Richard's profile as they crossed the gardens and headed toward the gate and the city outside. His proclamations were starting to get to her again. Although he did have a point about Turks clinging to archaic traditions, that was *all* he seemed to see.

"Some traditions serve a purpose, Rich, at least in this society. I'd rather concentrate on the amazing things here instead of seeing these people as less than we are."

"I don't see them as less than we are. I see them as refusing to evolve."

They walked on in silence. Although a part of her regretted picking on him like this, and he did have some valid points, she could feel herself starting to withdraw from his overly pragmatic views.

∽

After dinner, they took a cab to the Ciragan Palace Hotel to have coffee on its famed waterfront terrace.

The marble floor of this former Ottoman palace shimmered like a lake, and there was a respectful hush as if the grounds were still occupied by the royal family rather than elite paying guests.

"A cut above the folks staying at our place," Richard joked.

"I'm glad we're not staying here," she said, appraising the smartly dressed clientele.

"Too rich for your blood?"

"Too many unhappy ghosts." She gazed around at the opulent terrace. One deposed sultan was said to have been jailed here by his brother for twenty-eight years. Every single exquisite palace in Istanbul seemed to have doubled as a prison.

They ordered coffee and a slice of Turkish almond cake. She stared at the lights of the Uskudar district across the river, wondering how it must have felt for a royal prisoner to watch the bustling activity of ordinary free citizens just a short distance away. She'd felt imprisoned in her marriage once. She knew the feeling of wanting desperately to be free.

Richard turned and gazed at her. "Has it really been three years?"

She realized he was referring to their divorce.

"Sometimes I think it's the craziest thing we ever did," he continued. "Why *did* we do it?"

"Get married or get divorced?"

"Divorced. I know why we got married," he said, roguishly raising his eyebrow.

She ignored his attempt at flirtation.

"We couldn't get along," she said simply.

"That's not true."

The waiter brought their coffee and cake.

"Well, I remember it differently," she said, refraining from mentioning the small matter of his affair. She took a bite of the syrupy, grainy cake. "How do you like it?"

"I know we disagreed on some things," he went on.

"It's got nice texture. And the almonds make it moist."

"We should have been more patient," he said.

Now she looked straight at him. "What's wrong with you, Rich? We had problems and your solution was to screw around!"

He looked as if he had just been punched. She'd been trying to keep things nice, but she couldn't let this one go. He started to say something, but she shook her head.

"Like you said, we're done with it." She took a sip of coffee. "The coffee's delicious."

Richard slurped it the way he slurped anything hot. "They don't roast the beans enough."

She sighed. "Right there is how we're different, Rich. You see the negative first. We just don't seem to be seeing or tasting the same things. We're on different wavelengths."

"Because I like my beans *dark?*"

"Because you always grumble."

"Come on, honey, not always," he said with a half chuckle. "And I don't see us being so different as you say. Never did. That's why I wanted to come on this trip with you, Joy. To show you how much alike we are in our interests and to find out whether we can, you know, make a go of things again. Move on. Change things."

She almost dropped her cup, spilling coffee onto her skirt, which she dabbed at irately with her napkin. She had no idea what would prompt him to say this.

"Well, that definitely isn't part of the plan, Rich. This is supposed to be a friendly trip together to end our past on a good note. There was never any intention of getting back together. Not for me."

He stared at her.

"At any rate," she went on, "coming on this trip is showing us quite the opposite of what you claim. We're really very different."

He leaned back in his chair, his expression softening. "Everybody's different in some ways, Joy. It's called complementing each other."

There it was, that warm glint in his gaze that she had always found so compelling. It was one of the things that had attracted her to him when they first met, how transparent his eyes were and how his feelings were laid bare in them; and their playful, seductive twinkle.

"Besides," he added, "I like the way you're different from me. I still don't understand why it upsets you."

She didn't answer. He was clearly in denial.

"Speak to me, Joy."

She sighed again, wondering when they had stopped really talking to each other, stopped listening. "You exhausted me, Rich."

"But why couldn't we have talked about it *then*, for Christ's sake?"

"We always disagreed. Have you forgotten? It was such an effort just to find common ground. I couldn't handle the arguments. And you changed so much."

She took a breath, feeling the old anxiety creeping into her veins. Small fishing boats bobbed on the other shore of the river below streetlamps, safe from the tempest of her anger. She tried to push her emotions aside, told herself to just pull back and tolerate their differences for the moment, to just take it easy and spend a pleasant, or at least productive, evening talking things out like two adults, the way Richard seemed to want to do.

"It's true, I have changed," he pushed on. "You have, too. We all change. If things don't change, they die."

Now it was she who couldn't help chuckling. "Since when did you become so Zen?" She sighed. "Okay. We're not married anymore, so let's try to get along. We have two more weeks. So far, we seem to be doing okay."

He stared at her, obviously as aware as she that they were not "doing okay." Yet he might have had a point about wanting to "change" things, as he had put it. She, too, wanted to leave behind their previous pain and move on as friends, but he still annoyed the heck out of her with his insularity. If she was going to change, he had to change, as well.

"Rich," she said, suddenly serious, "what you're suggesting about getting back together is absurd."

To her surprise, he smiled good-naturedly. "Not at all. All I want is a chance, Joy."

She looked away.

A Marriage in Four Seasons

❧

This time when he escorted her to her room, the hotel hallway was dark. As she reached inside her purse for her room key, he gently slid her purse strap down her arm and bent to kiss her neck.

Astonished, she pulled away. "Come on, Rich! We agreed. We're *friends*."

"Let's go inside," he whispered.

She was embarrassed by his sudden affectionate urging, and yet she also felt a rush of excitement. She drifted a moment, allowed his hands to gently sweep her hair off her neck. He used to do that a lot, mostly before they made love. He'd lift her hair, and then cover her neck with tiny kisses. It used to turn her on.

Her purse slipped to the floor.

"Remember that time on the sailing trip in Mexico?" he whispered. "Making love on that beach?"

She inhaled that memory, a stirring in her groin: the warm afternoon on the near-deserted island off Puerto Vallarta, the high dunes they hid behind for that delirious, instinctive moment when they'd strayed from their sailing companions to a remote part of the beach, yanked off their swimsuits and made quick tequila-fueled love. She smiled, remembering how the intoxicating excitement of doing something so risky, given the surroundings and company, had made it all the more thrilling.

"I remember," she said, lightly pressing her lips to his ear. He gently pulled her to him.

She reached down to search in her purse for her key. Once in her room, she'd let whatever was going to happen, happen.

But an abrupt, cracking sound came from down the hall. Her gaze darted through the dark, but nobody was there.

"Let's go inside," Richard urged.

She glanced at him, her breath trapped in her throat.

"Come on, honey," he coaxed.

There was a wilting inside her. "I'm—I'm not ready, Rich."

"Joy, just for a minute," he pleaded.

She pulled back slightly. "Let's slow down. Let's just have fun now, like we planned."

"Honey, we can have fun any way we want," he whispered, lightly stroking her cheek. "Let's go inside."

Something in her had cooled. "Rich, I don't want to. Not now. Please."

He stared at her, but whether with disappointment or love, she didn't know.

"Don't be upset," she said, feeling compassion for his fumbling tenderness.

"Okay," he said, pulling back.

"Are you angry?"

He shrugged. "Does it matter?"

"I'm just not ready."

He sighed. "Fine."

The boyish irritation in his voice made her smile. "Rich," she said, somewhat lost.

He was already walking away.

"Rich," she whispered, "sleep well."

19

*T*here was a loud crash above her.

"Rich?" She sprang upright in bed.

She heard the sound again. It wasn't a crash, but a sharp rap at her door. She remembered that Richard wasn't there. She was alone in a hotel room in Istanbul.

"Coming!" She grabbed her robe in case it was the house-keeper, who might barge in if she thought the room was vacant.

She opened the door to find Richard.

"It's nine-thirty, kid," he declared. "You don't want to miss this."

He went over to the window and slid open the drapes. Sun-light and pungent aftershave ripped into the room's somber shadows.

Still groggy, she squinted at the burst of blue sky above the Hagia Sofia.

"I didn't sleep well last night," she protested, miffed by his boisterous sashaying into her last moments of peaceful dozing.

"No?" Richard was studying her as if it had been years rather than mere hours since he last saw her. She couldn't tell whether or not he was pleased by what he saw, and she was self-conscious because she had not yet washed her face or brushed her teeth.

"I slept like a baby," he said cheerfully. "It's the Dolmabahce today, remember?"

She'd forgotten their plans to see the palace. What she was remembering right now was her father coming in to wake her in the mornings before school, smelling deliciously of aftershave as Richard did now. She savored this warm correlation with her dad, this sweet, dormant memory revived.

Despite hungering for another hour of sleep, she headed for the bathroom. "You go on to breakfast. I'll get ready."

Richard intercepted her, playfully reaching for her arm. "I miss waking up next to you."

She halfheartedly tried to evade his touch, but he managed to slip his arm around her waist and draw her close. He softly kissed the top of her head, and they stood a minute, hesitant as teenagers.

"Let's finish what we started last night," he whispered.

"Rich," she said, nudging him away.

"Joy, I'm trying to seduce you, for Christ's sake."

"Come on, Richard."

He grinned. "Can I at least watch you get dressed?"

"No!" she said, turning toward the bathroom. "Go on. I'll catch up with you downstairs."

She could sense, even if she didn't see, his disappointment. For a second, she almost turned back to him. What harm could a kiss do?

He'd already backed off, however, obviously heeding her wishes. She heard the door open and close behind him, heard his light steps clipping down the hall.

She continued to the bathroom, still smelling his tangy cologne on her skin. She briefly wondered what would have happened had she played along with him just then. She felt her stomach tingle. Would she have been aroused, as she'd clearly been last night? What had last night been about, anyway? Why hadn't she held on to that moment longer?

"Shit!" she muttered, no longer in the mood for sightseeing. Maybe they should have just hopped into bed and found out what this was all about, followed that spark to see where it led.

She slipped off her nightgown and gazed at herself in the full-length bathroom mirror. The overhead light sliced sharply into her right thigh and shoulder, changing her into a distorted Picasso nude. She stared at her breasts, still nicely rounded; and turning, she took in her buttocks and small waist. She'd gained a few pounds, but she didn't mind. She turned back full circle and glanced at the small, still-visible C-section scar above her pubic hairline. She'd always treasured it. It was all she had left of Stephan and her one pregnancy. She stepped into the tub and under the hot shower to wash away the sudden onset of trenchant sadness.

One of the last residences of the Ottoman sultans, the nineteenth-century Dolmabahce glittered along the Bosphorus like an immense alabaster wedding cake. It was all that the Topkapi was not, lavishly maintained with expansive, vibrant carpets and furniture. It looked every inch like a baroque French palace.

"Those must be the largest stalactites ever commissioned," Richard said, pointing to the Baccarat chandeliers stretching across the ceiling of the vast throne room. "The crystal factories of Europe must have all but gone to war over the opportunity to illuminate this place."

"Pretty amazing," she agreed, although she found herself floating back to his arms cuddling her in the room earlier. Richard seemed absorbed by the brilliant crystal before them now, rather than the nearly romantic moment they'd had.

When she did turn her attention to the setting, she couldn't help feeling somewhat dismayed by all the fine Italian and

Russian paintings and Rococo furniture before them. Despite the palace's gorgeously preserved opulence, or perhaps because of it, she found it blatantly devoid of the magic of the desolate, haunting, older palace.

"It doesn't seem very Turkish," she said as they descended the outside steps facing the river. "I prefer the Topkapi."

"That's because you like old things," he said with a smile. "This was only built in the 1800s."

Clearly, Richard related better to this newer, more European-style palace, elaborately restored to its former glory, than he had to the starker, more Eastern Topkapi. He was fascinated by this carefully furnished harem, the eight-foot long bed of the towering Sultan Abdul-Aziz, the special room for the sultanas in labor, the separate one for them to give birth, and a particularly well-appointed bedroom with a silken blue bedspread and canopy, where each newly circumcised prince slept. Yet, to her, these rooms were not half as evocative as the empty and eloquent chambers of the Topkapi.

Richard's mind always shot for the practical, she reminded herself. It was what he'd been trained to do and why he was successful in the world of finance. To Joy, the older palace's unfurnished rooms were far more evocative, freeing her mind to fill in the phantom spaces.

Emptied, the chambers had easily conjured up the secluded women and their eunuch guardians, the "cage" where the sultan's young brothers were sequestered away from the rest of the palace lest they try to overthrow their older brother, the grounds where the Christian slave boys trained to become future Janissary cavalrymen. Even the bejeweled Roxelana had seemed to glide alongside them down the Topkapi's corridors, resplendent in her power despite her former slave status.

It had been precisely the absence of concrete evidence in the

Topkapi that Joy had found so inspiring, like a blank page on which to write history, or even the future. Her own future.

As they watched the river slosh against the Dolmabahce's garden walls, enjoying the sunshine and fresh breeze, she said, "This entire empire was ruled by slaves. Palace women and Janissaries."

"Our own government's ruled by slaves posing as bureaucrats. Only they aren't strangled when they make mistakes, like the Turks were. We taxpayers are."

She shook her head, smiling. "Nothing's ever the same once you've regurgitated it, Rich."

He looked pleased to have amused her. "It's simple. This was a court run on rigid codes. When the codes were discarded by so-called reformers, the entire structure collapsed."

"You've read up a lot on Ottoman history," she said.

"I've always liked military history. The Ottomans were military geniuses."

Joy realized that there was still much about Richard she didn't know. For an instant, this thought reminded her of his betrayal and how he had so thoroughly hidden his affair from her. But it also reminded her of good things. Richard's knowledge of the tangible world had always fascinated her. It had made her feel safe at the beginning of their relationship when much of life was still in flux for her. She was surprised to feel a giddy wave of desire surge through her again, as she had earlier in the hotel room.

"Rich?" She was about to suggest they go find a quiet place to just sit and talk and get to know each other all over again.

"Yes?"

She was suddenly self-conscious. He had suggested being a couple again and she had rejected it, and he had suggested sex and she had rejected that. She couldn't help worrying where this was going, where she was being swept, who might get hurt and how much. Yet it had been a long time since she'd felt this overwhelmingly drawn to Richard, and she wanted to find out how he really felt about her, why he kept hinting that he was still in love with her, and whether he truly believed they could start over.

"Are you tired?" she asked, surprised that all these thoughts came out as this clumsy question.

He looked at her. "Are you?"

"I think I'd like to go back . . ." she started, then stopped. "This morning, in my bedroom, I felt you wanted to say something, like you had something specific on your mind."

He seemed about to say something when a bellowing horn blasted. They turned toward the sound. A fearsome-looking contingent of soldiers dressed in ceremonial medieval Ottoman uniforms with glinting sabers, pantaloons, and tasseled helmets was marching down the walkway toward them. Their menacing stance, framed by the effeminate Beaux Arts pink gates of the palace, was almost comical. She moved back toward the gardens for a better view, hoisting her camera to take pictures of the flamboyant headdresses and swords as other onlookers gathered to watch the spectacle. The performance lasted a good five minutes.

When it was over, she looked around for Richard and found him off to the side, talking with two men dressed in jeans and black T-shirts. One of them, his head somewhat too big for his neck and shoulders, was handing Richard a card.

"Very beautiful, and an excellent price," she overheard the large-headed man say as she came up to them. The other man, bald and older, was nodding.

Richard looked intrigued. "We hadn't planned—"

"Best prices in Istanbul," the large-headed man was saying. "Shipped straight to America."

Richard turned to her. "Want to look at carpets?"

"Now?"

"He says they have a warehouse."

"Straight from factory," the older bald man said, glancing at Joy, his eyes lingering on her hair. His gaze seemed overly penetrating, almost insolent.

Richard turned back to them. "Better prices than in the bazaar?"

"Bazaar?" The younger, large-headed man's face contorted at the idea of buying a rug in the famed market. He dragged his finger across his throat and the older man smiled ruefully. "Bazaar," the younger man repeated and redrew his finger against his throat with emphasis.

"That bad?" Richard said, looking amused.

"They cheat you in bazaar," the younger man said solemnly. "Not good quality also."

Richard led Joy a few steps away from them. "Do you want to go to their warehouse?"

"But we were going shopping in the bazaar together," she reminded him.

"It might be good to check out their prices first. Then we can go to the bazaar and compare."

She stared at him. "I don't want to spend my afternoon with strangers," she whispered, "or be pressured to buy anything."

He glanced at the men, then back at her. "These guys sell wholesale. Here's their card."

She reluctantly looked at the business card encrusted with gold letters, trying not to show her disappointment at Richard's willingness to forego exploring the exotic bazaar with her in favor of a trip to a warehouse in the company of some hard-selling carpet dealers. The card didn't prove they were reputable vendors. Her thoughts flew back to Spain, to Richard's nervousness whenever he spotted a gypsy, his suspicion that there was a con artist on every corner. She remembered the mysterious young man in Granada and her missing bracelet.

"I'm not going anywhere with them," she said. "We'd planned to shop alone."

He hesitated a moment, then said, "Okay. I'll see you back at the hotel."

She looked at him. "I didn't mean *you* should go with them. We have no idea who these men are."

He smiled. "Relax, Joy. This isn't New York. They're only businessmen."

"Or crooks," she whispered. "You can't go. It's the stupidest thing I ever heard."

Richard looked puzzled. "What are you afraid of, Joy? You used to like adventures, remember? Just wait for me at the hotel. I'll take a quick look and then we can go to the bazaar."

She stared at him, genuinely nervous. He hadn't always been so trusting. "What if something happens to you?"

"Nothing's going to happen, Joy. Take a taxi back to the hotel and I'll see you later."

"Rich," she said, her voice catching, "what on earth are you trying to prove?"

He gazed at her a moment. "Maybe that I can enjoy life?"

He turned away before she could answer. They weren't married now, so apparently her objections were no longer relevant.

He flagged her a taxi. As he shut the door after her, she detected a spark of exhilaration in his eyes, as if he were embarking on some male-only expedition that women couldn't fathom. It was so utterly foolhardy she could hardly believe it.

He patted her hand, cheerfully. "I won't be long. I'll call you."

20

She returned to the hotel, barely able to contain her irritation. She almost wanted to high-tail it to the bazaar by
herself, shop at her leisure, and get whatever she liked; but
the idea of being inside an enclosed market in the midday
heat after having just been in the cool riverside gardens of the
Dolmabahce palace wasn't appealing. A swim in the hotel's
picturesque swimming pool was what she felt like. She hunted
through her suitcase for her swimsuit. She'd swim and read in
the charming garden.

She had a better idea. A *hammam!* Why not treat herself to
one of those invigorating Turkish steam baths? She'd wanted to
try one since they got here, but due to Richard's lack of interest
in exploring public baths, she'd put it aside. Now would be the
perfect time to go.

Ingres's famous paintings of Turkish bathing women flashed
before her, the pink flesh and hedonistic glances of the reclining
nude odalisques of the imagined women's bath that had for centuries fired up the imaginations of Western painters. Lady Mary
Wortley Montagu, wife of the eighteenth-century British ambas-
sador to the sultan's court, wrote of her own visits to a hammam
in Istanbul, vividly describing the Turkish women lounging
naked in the steam as they experienced the ultimate in pamper-
ing and relaxation. There was one around the corner from the

hotel. An exotic, indulgent Turkish hammam. Now, they'd see who was being adventurous.

The young blonde woman at reception assured her that the nearby hammam was indeed a clean and modern public bath, and said that, today, the hours women could go were, conveniently, in the afternoon. Ignoring the receptionist's hints that she'd be better off going to a hotel spa, she set out, the euphoria of adventure trampling any tentativeness. She walked to the corner, turned, and came to the elegant doorway she'd noted this morning on their way to the Dolmabahce.

Inside the ornate, green-tiled hammam entrance, however, she was surprised to find only an unimpressive little vestibule with a few wooden stools. There was a crude sign with a female silhouette. She followed the direction of the arrow.

A woman splashing water on the floor of a hallway came over and raised two fingers to indicate the two-lira fee. Joy handed her the money, and the woman gave her several green-and-white striped towels and pointed her down the hall.

There were small cubicles along the hallway. Joy went into one and wondered what hammam etiquette was. Did one bathe naked or wear some sort of underwear? She changed into her two-piece black swimsuit for now and placed her folded clothes on a shelf. Wrapped in a towel, she slipped her feet into one of several pairs of wooden clogs in the cubicle, picked up her purse, and clip-clopped down the hallway.

The vast bathing chamber of gleaming, white marble walls and columns was misty with steam. Deep cracks in the marble columns and floor made it look as if it had been in use for centuries, but it was clean and smelled of herbs and soap.

Beams of afternoon sunlight filtered down through perforations in the high-domed ceiling, illuminating the women already sitting or lying on a raised platform in the center of the room.

Most of the women seemed to be wearing some form of undergarment as they were being scrubbed by female attendants wrapped from the waist down in green and white towels like the ones Joy had on.

A robust bath attendant with heavy, bare breasts took her handbag, then grunted and gestured for her to lie down on a mat spread on the marble central platform. Joy quickly complied, removing her towel and stretching out on her belly. Warm water immediately spilled over her head, shoulders, and back, drenching her. She drew back in surprise, but the attendant murmured encouraging coos in Turkish and doused her again.

The attendant rubbed a loosely woven coarse loofah with a thick, square bar of soap and began to scrub Joy's back in strong circular sweeps as if her skin were a hardy wooden washboard. At first, Joy recoiled from the harsh pressure, but after urging her muscles to relax, she started to get used to the relentless, steady strokes. The attendant re-lathered the loofah and commenced again, round and round like a spinning top, diligently scouring Joy's shoulders, back, and legs.

There was none of the decadent finery shown in the erotic Ingres paintings in this functional bathhouse, and no signs of the insouciant women of Lady Montagu's letters. Joy certainly couldn't imagine anyone being comfortable enough to smile under the pitiless loofah, but once this cleansing part was over and the attendant began to knead her back and shoulders with lavender-scented oil, she felt her face and body go slack and imagined her own expression turning as indolent and wanton as the faces of those women in the paintings.

As the attendant massaged her fingers, pulling the joints of each, Joy pictured Roxelana, a foreigner like herself, bathing like this for the first time, a frightened captured "heathen" girl from Russia submitting to the rigors of a thorough Oriental washing before being presented to Sultan Suleyman. The young slave could not have foreseen her glorious future then or known that she would one day elevate herself to sultana and have her very own spectacular hammam built near the Hagia Sofia, the one still called "Roxelana's Hammam." Joy and Richard had passed the aged structure several times, now a hall for selling carpets.

Carpets. Again came the jab in her gut at Richard's having gone off with those men, but she forced herself to shut out this worry and luxuriate in the delicate perfume of rosewater the attendant was now sprinkling on her.

She jerked back, ticklish, when the woman started to rub the soles of her feet, but the sensitivity subsided with the expert pulling of her toes and the strong knuckles pressing the crevices of flesh she'd forgotten she even had. She started to feel light, as if the very matter of her body were evaporating. Even her breaths grew slower, her eyes gradually closing as if being pulled deeper into her skull. She was so drowsy she could barely respond when she was finally nudged to turn over.

In the vaporous heat, she grew anxious again. She had no idea what had gotten into Richard to go off like that, and with no apparent regard for how she felt about it. She obviously couldn't influence what he did anymore. Had he not been with her, had she been traveling with twenty strangers as she'd originally planned, she wouldn't have had to deal with this preoccupation.

Soon, however, even this wrinkle of unease was smoothed away by the confident fists, pummeling and pulling, working her body as if it were pliant, willing clay. For a moment, she imagined Richard stroking her.

She thought of how he'd expressed a desire to romance her this morning and how she'd rebuffed his advances without even asking herself whether or not she wanted them. Seduce her? Was he serious? And was it true, as he intimated before going off with those men, that she'd forgotten how to enjoy life? Was she now the one who was a drag?

He'd obviously been aroused this morning. Would she have been swept along? Could they go back to intimacy? Despite her muddled questions and emotions, she was surprised to find that she was now yearning for him in the impersonal, yet pleasurable, handling of her body by this total stranger in this unfamiliar bathhouse.

All at once she felt a familiar current make its way up her body, starting at her knees and climbing up her thighs, then higher where it resonated, taking her breath away. She gasped, embarrassed, trying to quiet the trembling in her hips, hoping the attendant hadn't noticed the involuntary shudder of pleasure gripping her.

She came to, shielding her eyes from the sunlight shooting down from the ceiling.

The attendant was gone, and there seemed to be fewer bathers around. Her swimsuit top lay limply on the marble beside her, and she remembered the attendant undoing it to scrub her ribs and breasts.

She swung her legs off the platform, taking deep gulps of the warm air. Clutching her suit top and the dry towel left there for her, she grabbed her purse from the nearby corner where the attendant had placed it and hurried out of the steaming room.

In the hallway, the cool air blasted like an open freezer. She headed for her cubicle and dried off, then briskly rubbed her hair with the towel and ran a comb through it. She glanced down at her stomach and thighs, now tingling and blotched red from the vigorous scrubbing. She remembered the unexpected wave of pleasure she'd felt under the attendant's massaging hands, as though she were lit up from inside.

The earlier lure of the hammam, she began to realize, was more than simply a desire for an exotic experience or getting back at Richard for having deserted her; it was a primal need for human touch and warmth, a yearning to reconnect both with that neglected part of herself and, surprisingly, with Richard.

21

It was past four when she reached the Pensione, the bath having taken nearly two hours. Without waiting for the elevator, she hurried up the stairs to the second floor and knocked at Richard's door. There was no answer.

She continued up more stairs to her own room where she phoned the front desk, hoping to find a message from him, but she was told she hadn't received any messages.

She lay on her bed and picked up the Roxelana book to distract herself; then, sleepy from the bath, she closed her eyes. She thought she heard Richard's knocking at the door and sat up, wondering how much time had passed. It was only five, however, and no one was at the door. She rang Richard's room again, but there was still no answer. Where the hell is he? she wondered.

She searched in her purse for his cell phone number. They'd converted only his phone, thinking they wouldn't need to use more than one since they'd be together most of the time. She found the number and dialed it from the room telephone. It went directly to his voicemail. She left a brief message for him to call her.

Downstairs, the evening concierge was the same blonde woman as earlier in the afternoon. Her green eyes squinted slightly when Joy told her that Richard, the man she was traveling with, had gone off with two strangers around noon to see some carpets and hadn't yet returned.

"Did he go to the bazaar?" the concierge asked.

"No. To a warehouse somewhere."

"There are many carpet shops," the woman said casually.

"They weren't going to a shop. They were going to a place where they store their rugs."

"Yes, the *hans*, the warehouses, near the bazaar. Don't worry."

"But he told me he would call, and he hasn't," Joy explained.

The concierge nodded. "Don't be afraid."

Joy paused, baffled by her nonchalance. Don't be afraid? It's what Richard had insinuated before. What was wrong with everybody?

"I'm not afraid," Joy said, making an effort to sound calm. "I'm simply concerned. He left six hours ago with complete strangers." She tried to slow down. "You remember him? Mr. Amis? My husband."

"Your husband?"

"He used to be," Joy said. "We're divorced."

The young woman's eyes clouded with confusion. "One moment," she said and went into the room behind the reception desk.

She returned with a smartly dressed man who appeared to be even younger than she. He looked Mongolian, with almond-shaped eyes and high cheekbones. The two exchanged words in Turkish before the young man turned to Joy. "Your husband is missing?"

The woman had apparently missed the distinction that Richard was her *former* husband.

"He's been gone all afternoon," Joy said. "I want to call the police."

The man's mouth tugged into a puzzled grin. "The police?"

Joy's throat contracted. She couldn't help feeling that everyone was conspiring not only against *her,* but against a universal code of common sense.

"You said he went to buy carpets," the man said.

"Yes."

"Madam, that takes time."

"Six hours to look at a few carpets in a warehouse?"

The young man smiled, swirling his hand in a sequence of circles. "Seven, eight hours. A whole day. He must bargain."

"But he was only going to *look*," Joy insisted.

She asked to use the concierge's telephone and dialed Richard's cell phone again. Again, he didn't pick up. This time she didn't bother to leave a message.

Both concierges now looked unsettled, although Joy wondered if it was more because they were unsure how to handle an upset tourist than because they suspected foul play on the part of their countrymen. They exchanged a few more words, and the man looked at Joy.

"Please have some tea, madam," he said politely, gesturing toward a sofa. "I will call the police for you."

He went into the back room, and the woman concierge called a porter, who quickly disappeared down the hallway toward the dining room. The boy returned moments later carrying a silver tray with a glass of steaming tea and a plate of cookies.

Joy thanked him and took the small, gold-rimmed glass and sipped. Apparently, to Turks, tea was the precursor and facilitator to problem-solving. The brew was strong and consoling, its murkiness seeming to hold the secret not only to where Richard was but to why she was suddenly so fearful for him. She bit into the cookie, comforted by the way it softly dissolved in her mouth.

She stared out of the hotel's glass doors at the people strolling by: tight-jeaned young women with bright makeup, conservatively robed matrons, teenage boys chatting on cell phones, family men carrying toddlers as their wives held the hands of older children. The women were particularly alluring, the intricately wrapped fabric of their scarves against their faces enriching the milk-white pallor of some while highlighting the dark eyes of others. All reflected the myriad ethnicities of this country: Central Asian, Greek, Russian, Arab.

The male concierge came up to Joy. "The police are coming." She sighed, grateful. "Thank you."

Perhaps from worry, she was suddenly hungry and remembered she hadn't eaten anything substantial since breakfast. The cookie had merely whetted her appetite. She thought of buying a pastry from one of the stalls near the hotel, but she didn't want to miss the police.

She should have reported Richard's absence hours ago, she told herself, or at least she should have insisted that he not go. She wanted to ask the concierges about the police again, but a cluster of hotel guests had just gathered around the front desk.

Frustrated, Joy pushed through the hotel doors to the street, wondering why it seemed to be her fate to set out on reconnaissance expeditions in strange cities at night in search of Richard.

She gazed in the direction of the bazaar that she and Richard had passed in the taxi that morning and wondered which way the carpet warehouses were. The female concierge had said the warehouses were near the bazaar, and so she assumed that, if she kept walking in that direction, she might find them. She might even run right into Richard returning with a rolled-up carpet on his shoulder like the street peddlers.

After crossing several intersections, she reached the sign for the *Kapali Carsi*, the Covered Bazaar. It was getting dark now, and the glaring street lights had come on. She decided against venturing farther to look for the warehouses and instead entered the bazaar's brightly lit main gate.

The vaulted arcade was still crowded with shoppers carrying bags. She walked past the elaborate window displays of jewelry shops stacked with gold bracelets and necklaces and artisans' kiosks with colorful ceramic pottery and tiles.

A shopkeeper called out, "Hello, madam! *Merhaba!* Welcome, if you please."

A window offered gold-printed manuscripts and exquisite miniature paintings of lush gardens and leaping gazelles. She stared at them, marveling at their intricate perfection.

"Would you like to see Ottoman miniatures?" the proprietor asked hopefully, offering her a glittering piece of golden Arabic calligraphy surrounded by tiny painted musicians and smiling girls. Although she would have liked nothing more than to leaf through the stacked pile of delicate sheets, she forced her eyes away from them and asked the man for directions to the carpet shops. The vendor pointed her toward an arcade farther down.

Someone else called out as she passed, "Please, lady, come and see!"

She kept walking.

"It costs nothing to smile," another shopkeeper chided.

Ignoring the remark, she forged ahead, reaching yet another vaulted hallway where carpets hung in full view in the windows. Irrationally, her eyes darted to the displayed rugs—large, room-size ones, smaller silk ones with pastel animals, and even smaller prayer rugs—for a sign of Richard.

He was obviously not there. She escaped down the hallway, glaring up at the cupolas on the ceiling of the hall, angry tears welling in her eyes. Damn it, Richard, she fumed. I'm in the middle of the frigging Grand Bazaar and can't enjoy a thing. If you're trying to seduce me, you're doing a rotten job of it!

She returned in the direction of the main entrance. Some shops were closing up, metal shutters being pulled down and locked shut for the night. She glanced around for a sign for the main gallery from which she'd entered, the name of which she'd already forgotten. She wanted to give up and cry, let the tears drown out her exasperation and fear, but she could only come up with a numb sigh.

She thought to call Richard again, but then remembered her cell phone had no service. Why on earth hadn't she converted it in case they needed to contact each other in an emergency? He had told her they wouldn't have a need for more than one phone, and she had foolishly gone along.

She caught sight of an extraordinary purple in her peripheral vision, and as she turned, her fear and anger gave way before a knee-length purple jacket, boldly embroidered in gold filigree and glimmering under the display lights. It was similar to the red robe they'd seen in the Topkapi museum that had purportedly belonged to Roxelana. She peered closer. It was velvet, painstakingly worked with shiny golden thread around the neck and sleeves in flowering swirls. Tiny gold buttons streamed down the front. She imagined Roxelana wearing it. She'd read that this very bazaar had been a bustling gathering place even in Suleyman's day, and it was said to have been frequented by the heavily escorted women of his harem.

"You like it?" the shopkeeper asked, stepping out of his store and lighting a cigarette.

She turned to him, unable to resist. "How much?"

"For you," he said, his voice as smooth as the velvet, "nine hundred dollars."

She turned away.

"Eight hundred fifty!" he called after her.

It was nearly eight o'clock when she reached the hotel. She was about to go to the concierge's desk and demand to know where the police were, when a shiny green Mercedes pulled up to the curb in front of her. A tall figure emerged from the passenger's seat.

She stared a moment, wondering whether it was really him or whether, out of desperation, she'd conjured him up. "Rich?"

He spun around.

She felt herself surge helplessly toward him. "For God's sake, where have you been?"

"Hey, Joy," he said, looking somewhat dazed. "It took longer than I expected."

Richard and the large-headed young man of this morning hauled out several bulky bundles from the trunk. Richard shook hands with the man, who smiled and bowed heartily to both him and Joy before leaving.

As she watched Richard and the hotel porter carry the bundles through the front doors, she realized she had to tell the concierges that her husband had returned, so there was no longer a need for the police.

This time she referred to Richard simply as "my husband."

"No problem," the young woman said, looking relieved.

The American expression, uttered so naturally by a Turk, sounded funny. It dawned on Joy that the police had possibly never been notified. Perhaps both concierges had decided between themselves that it wasn't necessary. Everyone in Istanbul but her, it seemed, understood that buying a carpet was a time-worn tradition that required many hours, and to assume otherwise was ludicrous.

Richard beckoned to her, and she halfheartedly followed him and the porter into the elevator.

Once inside his room—the porter gone—Richard turned to her, jubilant.

"You should have come with me, Joy. I had a blast!"

Her initial elation at seeing him safe was fading, and she now felt utterly foolish for having been so distressed.

"Joy, those guys took me to their warehouse and unfolded more than fifty carpets," he went on. "More styles, sizes, and colors than you've seen in your life. They poured me about ten glasses of tea and had kebabs and raki brought in. They're brothers from Konya. They insisted we stay at their house if we go to see the whirling dervishes."

She looked at him in disbelief. She'd been scared to death all afternoon, fearing the worst, while he, oblivious, was being happily wined and dined.

"When I finally chose the ones I wanted and bargained down the price—"

She interrupted. "How could you even know what a fair price was when you haven't seen any others?"

He grinned. "I know. I know. The guys probably made out like bandits, but I got them down pretty low."

"Why so many? How on earth are we going to lug them around with us?"

He yanked at the twine around one bundle to loosen it. "I'm shipping them all home tomorrow. And that one I bought for a friend who asked me to get her one."

A friend? She was surprised by what he'd blurted out, but equally surprised by her dismay at the mention of his shopping for someone else.

Obviously unaware that he'd spoken out of line, Richard proceeded to enthusiastically unroll a blue-and-beige carpet. "This is a kilim," he said. "Do you like it?"

The delicate designs on both sides of the handwoven carpet swirled before her. She wasn't sure what to think of this unexpected news of his shopping for another woman. What about last night? And this morning? She was starting to feel like an idiot.

He pulled off the twine securing the smallest bundle. "Look what I found for *you*."

"Me?" She was even more irritated now. "Why did you get me . . . ?"

He looked up at her. "Honey, I wanted to."

Honey? She stared at him coldly. What gave him the right to call her that after just mentioning another woman? Just how many "honeys" did he have?

He tore open the brown wrapping paper, and then shook out the garment.

She brought her hand to her mouth.

It was a burgundy-colored velvet robe with gold embroidered arabesque motifs and tiny gold buttons down the front, like the purple one she'd just seen in the bazaar. Only this one was even more like Roxelana's in the Topkapi museum.

"It took a hell of a long time to bargain them down on this," he said.

She continued to stare at the plush fabric, holding her breath at the richness of the gold against the deep red, resisting the impulse to reach out and caress it. "Rich, that must have cost a fortune."

He smiled.

"I mean, I *know* how much it costs," she said. "It's way too much."

"Nothing's too much for you."

"Don't say that."

"Why not?" He tilted his head. "And all of these rugs are for us."

"What do you mean, for *us*?"

He ignored her question. "And the little rug is for Maureen, at the bank," he added, as if he'd been aware all along of her earlier aggravation.

"Maureen?" She remembered Maureen, one of Richard's secretaries, a woman her mother's age.

Feeling even more foolish now for having jumped to conclusions, she slowly walked over to him and hugged him, too ashamed to say anything.

He turned his head toward her, and this time she let him catch her, welcoming the warm feel of his lips, soft and full and smelling vaguely of raki.

He kissed her again, and she reached up to his face, tracing his eyebrows and cheeks with her fingertips as though deciphering Braille. Her eyes welled up. "Rich, I thought I'd never see you again."

He pulled away slightly. "Honey, why?"

"Why? You drove off with those strangers—and you never called. What was I supposed to think?"

He kissed her tears. "I'm sorry. I had no idea you'd be worried. I just figured I'd get more value from a warehouse than the bazaar. I thought I'd only be gone an hour, but obviously no such thing when buying a carpet here. Time just flew by."

They held each other in silence, and she felt an aching release, realizing for the first time since the start of their trip how dismal it would be to truly lose him.

He inhaled. "You smell wonderful."

"I just had a Turkish bath."

"Mmm," he mumbled, cupping her face in his hands and once more kissing her, long and passionately on her lips. The lingering scent of cologne on his neck sweetly curled around her.

He gently unbuttoned her blouse and slid it off her shoulders, softly kissing her neck, then her breasts through her bra. She closed her eyes, surrendering to his touch as she had earlier in the warm hammam under the hypnotic kneading of the attendant. At each of his strokes, a new sensation bubbled up, and she sensed a coming alive again on some forgotten visceral level, no longer caring about anything but folding into him the way she used to.

22

*I*t *had* been a long time since she'd felt his caresses, felt him inside her. Her body conformed to his again, as if the memory of his shape has been secretly stored in her cells all this time.

It felt strange and scary, bittersweet and fragile, this coming together again; a tender reconciliation that took her back to those early years when meshing their bodies seemed so miraculous. The comfort of this small bed in this hotel room miles from home, her arms around him and his scent filling her, was more reassuring and wonderful than anything she'd experienced in a long time.

She slid her feet against his warm ones, smiling as she remembered how he'd never minded her cold feet. She cupped her hands around his forearms, enjoying their muscular feel. He obviously worked out these days. She smiled again. The new and improved Richard, she thought. And apartment balcony gardening. She thought of his vibrant flower pots that she'd admired on her visit to New York last year. He'd never shown much interest in gardening other than maintaining the lawn when they had the house. She was more and more charmed by these unexpected changes in him.

"You know how the harem girls used to get into the sultan's bed?" he asked, stroking her hair.

"I can't imagine," she said, pretending not to have read this scintillating detail in Roxelana's biography.

"Well, they had to start at the foot of the bed and burrow up under the covers until they reached the sultan's head," he said, lightly trotting his fingers up her thigh until they reached her throat.

"Uh-huh," she said. "And you need a harem girl to do that."

She nestled closer to him, for once not wanting to think of anything she'd read about this place, only of being with him in this moment.

She sensed the edge of the bed behind her. "How come they gave you such a skinny bed?"

"To make sure I slept alone, I guess."

She smiled at the lame joke.

"We can go up to your bed," he suggested.

"Yours is cozier. Rich, remember when we were happiest?"

"Before we were married?"

"When we were *first* married and living in that tiny apartment and had that tiny bed. It was barely bigger than this one. We were always squeezed together. But I didn't appreciate it enough then."

The memory of that first cramped bedroom in the East Village was so clear that she could almost feel the cold air seeping in under the window despite their endless attempts to block it with duct tape and towels. The small bed had forced them to snuggle, and she always slept with her arm around his chest, serene in the knowledge that their whole life together lay before them.

"I thought you liked our king-size bed," he said.

"But I was never as happy in it as in that first one. Sleeping in that tight bed and *dreaming* of a king-size bed made me happiest. It was pure ecstasy to anticipate the future in those days. Maybe it was *not* having it that was exciting." Even as she said this, she knew it made no sense except to her.

"We can buy a small bed," he offered.

"It's not that. It was the looking forward to something that made it exciting."

"Well, let's start looking forward again, honey," he said softly.

She sighed. "Things aren't that simple, Rich."

"They can be."

He tugged at the sheet, pulling it over them like a tent. He held her close. "What do you say? I *want* us to buy a new bed together. I can see you waking up and putting your toes on that soft kilim."

She imagined the silken wool beneath her bare feet. She'd always wanted a fine Oriental carpet at her bedside, but she felt a sinking feeling in her chest and shifted away from him.

"Maybe we can't go back, Rich. Maybe it was stupid to have come here together, to give ourselves false hope."

"Nothing's stupid if we want to be together."

"We have so much baggage, Rich."

"And we'll acquire new baggage," he said with a laugh. "I want us to get married again, Joy."

She didn't respond.

He rose onto his elbow. "Well?"

That particular warmth in his eyes as he gazed at her got her every time, made her melt inside her skin. Yet she knew there would be more than just this moment. There would be misunderstandings and arguments, times when she'd want nothing more than to be beholden only to herself. We need to get real, she thought. Fantasies won't hack it.

"We already had a marriage, Rich, a dysfunctional one. And now, for a few days, we've had a dysfunctional post-marital relationship. What else is there for us?"

"A functional post-*post*-marital relationship?"

"I'm not joking," she said.

"I'm not either. I never stopped loving you.

"You should have thought of that before."

"Before?"

"Before you and that—"

"Joy, why do you keep bringing it up? It's the past. Finished."

There it was again. The total denial of the pain he'd caused. "I didn't just choose to put myself through that, Rich. *You* were the one running around on me."

"Joy—"

"Right?"

"Well, I'm damn sorry. I've regretted it more than I can say. I want to move forward, Joy. I want to make things work between us."

She could barely hold in the torrent of past heartache and fury charging over her. "Nothing will change things."

"Joy, won't you try? Honey, I'll do anything."

His imploring plucked at her heart, but she couldn't bring herself to respond.

Finally, he said, "What about your infatuations over the years?"

"What infatuations?"

"I managed to overlook those colleagues of yours, those so-called professors who ogled you. And not just once."

"Those were silly, platonic fantasies. I never let them get in the way."

"But they *did* get in the way. Months on end you'd be distant and unresponsive. Don't tell me some of those guys didn't want to jump into your pants. I had my share of suffering, too, Joy." He took a sharp breath. "I had an affair. But it's over and done with. Forgotten."

"Forgotten?" Her voice carved the air in disgust.

"Yes. Forgotten." He rolled onto his back and stared at the ceiling. "You always saw yourself as the one bored with our marriage. It felt like you even blamed me for Stephen's death."

"I never did that," she snapped.

"Well, it seemed like you did. I couldn't do anything to help you or ease your pain. I could never be what you wanted, whatever that was. Then, when I drifted, you were unforgiving. You never seemed to understand why it might have happened in the first place."

"*Drifted?* You think you can just push your little fling into the corner and bury it like a bone? What you did was heartless."

He was silent. Then, looking genuinely remorseful, he said, "It was."

His admission only increased her anger. "You totally forgot about me."

"I never forgot about you, Joy. Ever."

"Sure."

He sighed, running his hand through his hair. "All that testing we did so you could get pregnant. I felt like I'd lost something. You wanted a baby, and that was it. I wasn't enough anymore. I was never going to be enough after that."

She drew in her breath. "Oh, God, Rich! Don't you think I had enough on my mind without having to also prove my love for you all the time? Couldn't you let me grieve for my baby? Couldn't you give me space to withdraw until I was ready to be myself again?"

Despite her words, she knew that what he said was at least partly true. She'd been devastated by the awful loss of Stephen, and then she'd been consumed by her desire for another child. She'd been yanked into the riptide of her own sorrow and emptiness for some time. Maybe until it *was* too late.

They were both silent for a while, pain a stubborn boulder between them.

"It wasn't any good, Joy," he said softly. "You were too far away. I couldn't reach you. Losing Stephen was unbearable for me. I suffered, too. Maybe I suffered differently, but I suffered as much as you did."

His voice cracked as he moved slightly away. They always called Stephen by his name, as if they'd known him, as if he'd been a full-term child and an active part of their lives.

"At the time I felt another woman would . . . I didn't know how else to save myself. It may sound stupid, but I needed to be loved. God, I know I hurt you, Joy. I hate myself for it. But you've punished me enough."

She turned away. "Go to hell."

After a few moments, he said, "At least I didn't give up on us."

"Now you're saying it was my fault?" she said. "Your heart was sucked in by some bimbo you barely knew. No wonder you seemed to recover from it all far sooner than I did. What a convenient little escapade."

She wiped her eyes now, but it was too late even for tears. Nothing would bring their Stephen back, nor their life before. *Nothing.* She knew Richard was sorry, but all she could hold on to was the past. No matter what he said, it *was* too late. She could never be the way she was then, vulnerable and trusting.

She inched away from him. "I just wanted my baby back."

He reached out and touched her shoulder. "Me too, honey. I wanted him back, too. And I want you back, Joy. I want *you.* We can't have him back, but we're still here. We can have each other."

She sighed deeply. "I can't just forget. I don't know how to."

He was silent for a while, then squeezed her shoulder lightly. "I hope you'll try, Joy."

She lay still, wanting to say something but finding no words. This was all so confusing. She had grown used to not trusting him. Now, he was asking her to put herself in his hands again.

"I never stopped loving you, Joy. Please—come home."

The gulp in his voice as he said this let her know he meant it. But was she ready to make a change, ready to make a fresh start with him?

She glanced to where the robe he had bought her was draped over a chair. A few years ago, he might not have thought to get her something so extravagant just because she'd admired it. She imagined herself wearing it with nothing underneath, imagined him undoing those infinite buttons and making love to her all over again as if she were Roxelana. Not the helpless slave girl, but the all-powerful consort in charge of her life, her love.

She was about to tell him that maybe they could give their relationship another shot when he said, "First, I have something to tell you. It won't be easy for you, but I need you to hear me out."

Surprised, she turned to him.

She was suddenly springing from the bed, grabbing the sheet, and pulling it around her. Her insides turned to ice.

"A child?"

He sat up as if stunned himself by what he'd just said.

"From *her?*"

He slowly nodded.

She stared at him, trying to find the words in her mouth. "Where are they?"

"In North Africa. Tunisia."

"How . . . how do you even know it's yours?"

He lowered his head. "She says I was the only one, then."

She stiffened at the resolve in his voice that the woman's claims were true. "And you believe her? Just like that?"

"She's not the kind to lie about that stuff."

She glared at him. "When did you find out?"

"A month ago."

"A *month* ago?" she said incredulous. "You mean you weren't aware of it all this time?"

"No."

"What does she want? Is she blackmailing you?"

He took a deep breath. "She's dying."

"Liar," she said.

He shook his head and said softly, "She has cancer."

She wondered whether she'd heard him correctly.

"Joy," he said, "she wants us to have the child."

"*Us?*" She stared at him.

"She thinks we're still married. She wants us to raise the girl. Her—my daughter."

The words slashed her: *my daughter.*

"She wants a mother for her—"

"No!" Joy vigorously shook her head as if to fling his words right back at him. "*You* did what you did. None of this concerns me."

"Joy—"

"How dare you even—you're on your own, Richard."

She made a move toward the door despite still being naked underneath the sheet.

He reached out as if to touch her, but his hand halted mid-air. "Don't go, Joy. Please."

She pulled back farther. "Don't expect me to get involved in this."

She needed to escape the acute shock in her gut, to get out of there, to go anywhere, but he looked so pathetic that she simply stood where she was.

"Joy. I don't know what to do. I'm sorry," he said. "God, I'm so sorry."

She stared at the ceiling, her eyes starting to well up. "I just don't know what I ever did to deserve this."

"You don't deserve any of it. It's my problem. I don't know where else to turn. All I can think of is you and our life together and how I want it to be that same way again."

"The same? Nothing will ever be the same again," she said. "First, you tell me it's all over and forgotten, and now you tell me this. It's *never* going to be forgotten, Rich. Never!"

He exhaled. "All I can do now is move forward, Joy, and do what's right."

"Do what's right for whom? For you? This certainly isn't what's right for me!"

She grabbed her underwear and slacks from the floor and yanked them on, then slipped on her blouse that an hour ago she'd been only too ecstatic to have him remove. Fool! She felt utterly betrayed. What a fool she'd been! She needed to get back to her own room to burst into tears, explode, anything to rid her of this nightmare.

Richard's hand moved to touch her.

"Don't!" She pulled her arm away, trying to quell her sudden dizziness.

Had his romantic talk these past several days, his lovemaking moments ago, been all a charade? Those feelings he'd so deftly been planting in her since they got here, convincing her that love could sprout anew, had it merely been part of a scheme to draw her into his predicament?

Well, this changed everything. All that she'd created in her mind about a new life with him was now totally wiped away.

"This shit was supposed to be out of my life for good," she said, bitterly. "Now *this*. To haunt me forever."

"I'm sorry," he said, bringing his hands to his face.

After a few minutes, she managed to gain control of herself and cleared her throat. "How long?"

"How long?" he echoed.

"How long does she have?"

"I don't know."

Instead of jealousy or a chafing at how pained Richard must be by this news, she felt nothing. Just an indifferent emptiness.

"Why the hell does she want me in this child's life?"

"I told her about you, how motherhood meant a lot to you. Maybe she thinks you'd be the best one to take care—"

She felt a renewed seething. "How dare you discuss intimate details of our life with that woman?"

He was silent.

"You're really something, Rich. Is nothing sacred to you?"

He stared at the floor.

"She doesn't know we're divorced?"

"No," he said.

"Well, at least you kept that to yourself."

He stood. "I know that, to her, now, you're even more important than I am."

"Don't be ridiculous. You're the damn father. You don't need me. Just go to Africa and meet your damn daughter."

He nodded absently, as if trying to convince himself. "Joy, I can't do it without you. I just don't know what to do with a little girl. I've never seen her and know nothing about her. I can't do this alone. I can't."

She turned away from him and buttoned her blouse. What she really wanted was to shred the air to bits, to destroy all that she'd just heard.

"Life is fucking complicated," he said softly.

She glanced at him. "You're fucking right about that," she said. "It fucking sure is."

In the dark, she heard his breathing. His arm moved next

to her, but she didn't react. When his hand rested on her waist, she wanted to fling it away, but her energy was gone and she had neither the urge nor the will to remove it.

"How on earth do you expect us to go on together after this?" was all she said.

A part of her knew she should walk out of this room right now before being sucked into a vortex of untold complications, that she should go back to her factual, quantifiable life in Virginia, back to her girls and their teenage struggles to find themselves. Oh, God, how benign their adolescent dramas seemed in light of what Richard had just dumped on her.

She didn't move to escape his touch, though, didn't do anything to get away from him. As livid as she was, she found no ability to express it.

Instead, she sat down beside him. For the first time tonight, she actually felt sorry for him.

They lay silent next to each other for what seemed like hours, but she knew it was perhaps only twenty minutes. She stared at the ceiling, barely feeling the pillow beneath her head. Richard had fallen asleep beside her. She wasn't sure whether the fact that he could sleep in the face of what he'd just revealed troubled her or gave her hope. If he could sleep after such a confession, maybe it wasn't all so bleak.

How had he put it? "I didn't know how else to save myself." Is that what had driven him into that woman's arms? The need to save himself from a grief that she'd had to endure just as much? He had to do it to survive? Each had a strategy to keep going. He claimed he needed to be loved. Well, she'd needed love, too, but she knew deep down that she hadn't been receptive to his love at that point. She still didn't understand what exactly had caused her to lose her feelings for him, but she couldn't deny her coldness at the time.

She breathed in and exhaled, trying to flush out all she'd just been told. If she just kept breathing, she thought, she might lull herself to sleep, or at least into a stupor in which she would feel nothing. She'd be able to survive, just one breath after another.

She closed her eyes, continuing to breathe in and out until she felt weightless as she listened to Richard's steady snoring. She was envious that he could fall asleep so easily. She tried to match the rhythm of his breath to maybe achieve the same result, and with each breath she tried to imagine herself slowly lifting off, floating above her body and beyond the bed. She opened her eyes and stared at the robe on the chair again, glanced toward the window where a light from the street flickered off the yellow crystals of the lampshade. The crystals looked like tiny stars, each with its own mysterious galaxy, each beckoning to her.

Then, through the shock and anger, she saw herself wrench something out of the pit of her stomach and throw it into a body of surging blue water. The briny smell of the water was intense, stinging her nostrils.

Was she starting to dream? She did it again, bundled the thing up and hurled it into the waves, then watched the mysterious lump drift away in the endless stream. Had she just hurled a human into the water like a Topkapi assassin? Or had it been something else that she threw away, an inchoate thing symbolic of some paralyzing fear? What *was* she afraid of?

When they'd lost Stephen, she seemed to have lost her reason to be with Richard. Without her baby, she'd simply walked away as if a gate had opened through which she had to exit. The real reason for their divorce, perhaps, had been her inability to see her life any other way than the way she'd once fashioned it in her head: she and Richard *and* their baby. Without the baby, she had seen no reason for reconciling her differences with Richard. She'd thought cutting him out of her life would enable her to set a new course for herself, as if none of the painful past had ever happened.

The nagging question dug into her again. Can love, once lost, ever truly be reborn? Richard claimed that it could, but he'd always been able to compartmentalize, to set his mind to think, accomplish, or feel whatever he wanted to. Whereas she was riddled with bullets of questions and doubts until she finally made up her mind about something, he simply forged on. Was she willing to suspend her skepticism and take the chance he was asking of her? Was she even up to raising this child of his other woman, able to take on that responsibility with an open heart, as if it was something totally normal? She flinched, as though recoiling even from herself, a sharp pull inside that started in her belly and moved up to her lungs, snuffing out her breath. Her eyes began to water, and she felt the warm tears slide down the sides of her face.

Then, slowly, like something emerging through a fog, she saw the child.

Hammamet

RICHARD

❦

23

"We've only been here two days, but something must be wrong. Should we try and contact her office—ex-office? Surely somebody there knows where she lives."

He shook his head, shielding his eyes from the sun as he surveyed the panorama of glittering sea and white domes below them. "She knows we're here."

Joy turned to him. "Do you think she changed her mind?"

"No," he said, although he'd been afflicted the whole morning with this very fear. Had Belinda gotten cold feet? Decided she couldn't part with the child after all? Surely, she would have at least let them know, especially about something so vitally important to her. However, with Belinda, one could never tell if she might merely pick up and leave, he reminded himself.

He focused his lens. "Move a little more to the right so I can get the minaret in," he said to Joy, wanting a picture of the angular tower with elaborate brickwork.

She moved to reveal the four or five little white domes behind her. The backdrop was typical of Tunisia, especially of this renowned seaside town, Hammamet, with its whitewashed domes and bright turquoise doors decoratively studded with black nails.

She tilted her head, obviously more concerned about a flattering shot of her face.

He smiled at Joy's preoccupation with her looks. He clicked the picture. "Do you want one of the rooftops, too?"

"Yes, please," she said, changing her angle.

"Then move to the left," he instructed.

He nodded to their Tunisian guide. "Why don't you stand next to her for this one?"

The young man somewhat reluctantly shuffled over to Joy and stood stiff as a toy soldier beside her. A slight scowl clipped his bronze North African features next to Joy's pink grin.

"It's hot," Joy said, gingerly patting the stone platform next to her. It was one of four identical half pillars set side by side, supposedly the remains of chairs belonging to the four wives of Ismet Pasha, ruler of Hammamet some two hundred years ago. It was the guide who had encouraged Joy to have her picture taken sitting on a pillar, posing as one of those wives.

This flat rooftop of a spice shop, its ceiling-less walls still adorned with blazing arabesque tiles, were the remains of the pasha's grand sitting room. It overlooked the whitewashed town with its signature turquoise windowpanes and nutmeg seaside *casbah*, or fort, Hammamet's one-time stronghold against attacking marauders.

Hammamet's old town, the *medina*, had produced the most aggressive shopkeepers of any market they'd been to, obviously regarding tourists as fecund gold mines. When the young mustached man had come up to Richard earlier near the old town gate with his offer to be their guide and fend off the insistent vendors, Richard had gratefully agreed.

Even with an escort, however, it was hard to dodge the

hawkers thrusting beaded necklaces, kaftans, or men's fezzes at them every few feet, but the guide had sternly waved them off, all the while promising his American clients a worthwhile surprise ahead.

The man wasn't an official guide. He was a waiter at their hotel, he'd told them, reminding Richard that he'd served them breakfast yesterday. He'd insisted on bringing them up to this roof after the long walk through the maze of the *medina* where, for over an hour, he pointed out important landmarks and offered bits of local lore; and he hadn't let them down. This rooftop relic of a former palace enchanted Joy, its walls still brandishing mosaics of hunting scenes and vibrant geometrics in azure, turquoise, and yellow.

"Oriental carpets frozen into stone," she said, dragging her fingertips across the chipped colorful wall of the once-elegant salon.

It *was* a great vantage point, and they'd taken good pictures, but now Richard was fatigued and hungry. Even their peppy guide looked tired. Richard handed Joy the guidebook and pulled out three twenty-dollar bills from his wallet, assuming that US dollars or euros were coveted in turbulent times. At first the young man put up a polite fuss, but when Richard insisted, he graciously accepted the money.

"Is there a good place for lunch?" Richard asked him.

"There." The guide pointed to another rooftop terrace across the street with tables and seating under umbrellas. "Good couscous. I take you?"

Richard shook his head. "Thanks, but we'll sit here a minute. Great tour."

The guide smiled, pocketing the bills with renewed energy, then walked away and disappeared down the steps leading back into the shop they'd come from.

"I'm glad we found him," Joy said. "Those pesky peddlers were unrelenting, wanting us to buy everything."

"It's the unemployment. You can tell from all the loiterers."

"They're supposed to have a relatively high level of education here," she said.

"There also used to be a high level of government corruption. A revolution doesn't change things overnight. When people still can't find jobs and tourism isn't enough to sustain the economy, it'll all blow up again."

She looked surprised. "Things seem pretty calm."

"Just because there are no mullah brigades in the streets doesn't mean things are stable, yet."

Although Richard hadn't wanted to frighten Joy, he'd felt uneasy since arriving in Tunisia, sensing the palpable seething of a place trying to pull back from the brink of disaster. The glut of Roman and Islamic antiquities and the powdery beaches that lured European vacationers barely camouflaged the sullen undercurrent of political instability. The frayed vestiges of government control were, to him, blatantly evident.

It had been a surprisingly short rebellion, the first of a series across the Middle East soon coined the "Arab Spring." Less than three weeks of public protests, sparked by a young vendor setting himself on fire to protest government corruption, had driven Tunisia's head of state out of the country. The moderate Islamist government subsequently voted into power had managed to maintain peace in the streets so far, which was remarkable considering the destruction other Arab nations were facing after a regime was overthrown.

So far, this new leadership hadn't banned the wineries or threatened to exchange the secular laws for Islamic, Sharia law. Still, he had a gnawing feeling that if the economy didn't improve fast, it would only be a matter of time before the country was yanked apart.

"I felt these same vibes in Central Asia before it exploded. I don't want to be around when it happens here," he said.

"Hopefully, we won't still be here, then," Joy replied.

So far, the political upheaval hadn't seemed to extend to the tourism industry, and Richard assumed that all efforts would be made to ensure that tourism flowed smoothly. The taxi drivers and hotel staff had all been courteous, and the vendors, while overly pushy, were welcoming. But that could change in a heartbeat.

"I just can't understand why she hasn't called us, not even left a message," he said.

"We should give her a few more days. She may be having a tough time of it," Joy said.

He sighed. "Yeah."

Richard and Joy had been nearly three years divorced when, breaking her nearly four-year silence, Belinda had sent him a letter.

She was brief, asking how he was, telling him that, although still in Africa, she'd moved from Senegal north to Tunisia. She now worked as a journalist for an English radio show, putting together a weekly feature interviewing local women entrepreneurs. Her letter had offered a further surprise, the picture of a little girl, her daughter, Karma, now three years old.

Once he'd gotten over the shock that Belinda had a child, the next sentence gored him. The little girl, Belinda wrote, was his.

He could still feel the sick spasm of that day upon reading those words. A daughter? *His* daughter? At first, his mind raced to imagine the kind of trouble Belinda must be in, the possible reasons driving her to this weird fabrication. Was she in some sort of bind, in need of money? He'd sunk down on a chair and gone over the letter numerous times. It couldn't be. It had been almost four years since they'd been together.

Yet slowly, in a corner of his brain, sprouted the thudding, growing awareness of the possibility of her claim. The dates fit. All at once, an alarming new reality appeared to replace his old one. He was, apparently, a complete stranger now even to himself, someone he would not have recognized in the mirror only moments ago. He was the father of a three-year-old girl.

The reason she had so abruptly left New York, she wrote, was that she'd become pregnant with his child. She'd already known it the last time she'd seen him, but she hadn't told him for fear it might spur him to make some rash decision that would destroy his life and inflict immeasurable pain on his wife. So, she'd decided she had to leave, had to go to Africa.

He tried to recall their last encounter, the particular hotel room, and how Belinda was not her usual self. He remembered her mention of the Peace Corps guy and his rush of jealousy. She'd already known she was pregnant? Heading to Africa was directly linked to *that?* All he'd known then was that she was gone, and he had imagined the reason to be the man she mentioned. She'd simply disappeared and wouldn't return his calls.

Although at the time he'd hated the thought of not seeing her, the hardest part had been that he couldn't even contact her.

He'd been right. According to the letter, Belinda *had* gone off with the Peace Corps guy, but she left *him* several months before her baby's birth. She'd still resisted informing Richard for fear that he would pressure her to return to New York. Instead, she had moved to Tunisia, found a job at a radio station, and was raising the child there on her own. She said that she was managing well, that Tunisia was a friendly place, and childcare was plentiful. There were good beaches and pretty towns, and the place was a magnet for European tourists and retirees. She informed him she had learned some Arabic but got by on her French, the country's other main language. She loved being a mother, she wrote. Motherhood had quelled the restless nomad in her, and she didn't even miss traveling.

Her reason for contacting him now, she went on, was that she did need his help, although not in the way he might think. First, she was adamant that he not feel any need to provide financial assistance for the child, since she herself had a secure job. There was a more urgent reason for this letter. Although he'd intuitively braced himself for another bombshell, he couldn't have predicted what followed.

A few months ago, she wrote, she'd begun having severe headaches, then some slurring of her speech. Her concerned co-workers had insisted on taking her to the hospital where, after a battery of tests, it was discovered that she had a brain tumor. From a biopsy and further tests, it was found to be malignant.

Fearing the cancer would spread faster if operated on, the doctors were treating her with new medications. The tumor had already shrunk a bit, and her doctors were cautiously optimistic. If the medications worked, she could possibly lick this illness and live a normal life. But her doctors were also realistic. If the cancer had already spread, they told her, she might only have a few months to a year.

Cancer? A few months to a year? His breath had stopped. What the hell? He had read on.

"As you can imagine, I am devastated and frightened," she had written. "But I have to accept it."

She would remain in Tunisia where her life was now so rooted and where she was familiar with the doctors and confident in their latest technology, she wrote. She didn't believe she'd get better medical treatment anywhere else, not in France or even in the US. Her main concern now was for her daughter. She needed a family for Karma if . . . when . . .

She couldn't bear the idea that her daughter would end up in an orphanage. She wanted Karma to be raised by her own flesh and blood, and Belinda's parents, her only relatives, were too elderly. That left Richard. More than anything, though, she wanted her child to also have a mother. She knew that Joy would be perfect. If he and Joy accepted this offer, and the responsibility, Karma would be theirs.

His hand had started to shake. He'd sat down and reread the letter again. He stared dumbfounded at the picture of the girl, studied her cheerful smile with the full lips, her small nose and wide brow. He thought he recognized bits of Belinda, even of himself, in her features, but he mostly saw the precocious face of a dark-haired child, a perfect beauty.

Belinda had ended the letter on an absurdly jolly note, sending loving wishes from sunny Tunisia along with assurances that she would write again soon with an update. Her last line was emphatically underlined: "Live, Richard! Live and don't hold back."

That's when it had hit him. "Fuck! She's dying!" he'd said aloud.

Before he knew it, he was shaking again, crying silent furious sobs. Although he hadn't seen her in four years, he'd known she was alive somewhere, living, laughing—and painful as it was to admit, screwing. He'd pictured her in front of a microphone in a tiny recording room, gamely interviewing women about their business ventures, drawing them out in that convivial way of hers. He'd imagined her alongside her small daughter, teaching her the things she'd taught at her preschool in Paramus. Although she hadn't been where he could actually see or interact with her, he knew she existed. That was enough. But hell! That might soon change, he realized.

He had no idea now how long he'd sat crying, his heart hammering, and then how long he'd sat staring at the wall, practically comatose. She wanted him to take her child, *their* child. She wanted to give the girl to him and Joy.

"Shit!" he'd muttered, dumbfounded. He wasn't even with Joy anymore.

He hadn't been sure how to react or what to do, whether to write Belinda back and tell her Joy had left him, send her money, demand to see her, as well as his daughter—all things she'd instructed him not to do. His gut had contracted every few seconds at the idea of her dreadful disease, and at the same time he had been seized by an urgent pull to the photograph. He wanted to see the child in person, hug her, acknowledge her existence, comfort both her and her mother.

He had slowly realized, however, that he could do none of this. At least, not yet.

It was only after a day or two that he'd been able to get some perspective. If the dismal prediction of Belinda's doctors came to pass, he needed to make sure that the child was safe with him. He had no idea how he was going to manage to take on the role of a parent, but he would do it. But he needed Joy, too, of that he was sure. He had no idea how to raise a girl. Joy had never parented, either, but as a woman she would intuitively know a little girl's needs far better than he. Prior to this new complication, he had wanted Joy back in his life, but now he desperately needed her. He had to find a way to tell her.

He had, in fact, wanted Joy back since their divorce three years before and had taxed his brain for ways to woo her again, to atone for his infidelity, to beg her to come back. Previously, he had been planning to try, but this news made approaching her both harder and yet more imperative. He needed to see Joy, to ask her to consider reconciling—and sooner rather than later. Although this new scenario had presented a complication, he'd realized that it might also have just handed him the perfect excuse, albeit a terrible one, for her to take him back.

A few days later, he'd learned from a woman in the English department at Hunter and with whom Joy was still in touch that Joy was planning a trip to Turkey. He'd had no time to lose. He had to go to Turkey with her.

Mercifully, she'd agreed to travel with him.

For several weeks after he'd disclosed his predicament, Joy had still been on the fence about taking him back, understandably cautious about committing herself to sharing this unforeseen situation. Yet her heart had been larger than he'd ever imagined, and incredibly enough, she'd agreed.

Meanwhile he'd held on to the hope that nothing more would become of Belinda's illness. By a stroke of luck, like a meteor veering off its deadly course, the cancer would miss its mark and she would recover and resume her former life. He would still insist on meeting the child, of course, and lending support. He had contacted Belinda and said as much. Even Joy would want that, ultimately. He could be, if not a father, a sort of uncle to the child. "Whatever you want, Belinda," he had told her. Deep down, however, he suspected that Belinda's recovery was a far-fetched fantasy. When she had sent word some eight months later that her condition had worsened and that he should come to Tunisia for the child, he'd realized that he'd been preparing himself despite his denial.

"What do you feel like eating?" Joy asked now, browsing through the guidebook as if she hadn't heard the guide's earlier recommendation for couscous across the street.

He didn't answer as he sat next to her on an adjacent pedestal chair for the pasha's wives. He closed his eyes and angled his face up to the sun. The flat heat on his skin felt good. He opened and shut his mouth several times, trying to ease the mild pain in his jaw that he'd had since waking up that morning.

Joy's voice pierced his drift. "There's a nice place on the water just a ten-minute walk from here."

"He said the place across the street has good couscous," he reminded her.

"It's so much prettier on the water," she said, having obviously made up her mind.

He sensed her leaning over him, peering down at his face and closing off the sun. Her breath swept across his cheek, coating him with a sweet balm of lipstick and peppermint.

"Rich?" she said softly.

He forced open his eyes, wanting to hold in her smell and the comforting feeling it brought, a feeling from the long-ago day when he'd first kissed her. Her pale eyes look worried despite the hint of a smile playing about her mouth.

Her behavior these past few days had been erratic. She fluctuated, at times looking sad and almost regretful, then in the blink of an eye looking irrationally cheerful and solicitous, as though trying to cheer him up. Maybe, he thought, her moodiness was all his imagination, brought on by his own angst. He couldn't stop thinking how his past actions had now come full circle, how something that should have been relegated to the safety of the past had resurfaced and forced Joy to confront her pain all over again, head-on. She was being made to accept a situation that was none of her doing, to open her heart and life to a child she would obviously prefer didn't exist. It whittled away at him inside that she'd been dealing with this pain, although she'd been extraordinary at concealing any upset from him, her features shrouded in a veil of calm. She'd held up like a bulwark so far, and so she was entitled to plummet now and then, he had decided. Still, this new wistfulness he was witnessing right now felt different.

"I don't want to wander, Joy. Why can't we just go across the street?"

"But it's too nice a day to miss the water."

He forced himself up. "Let's go then."

She turned, and he followed her across the roof and down the steps, through the spice shop and out to the street. To the amused bewilderment of the spice vendor, she'd earlier taken dozens of photographs of the hefty burlap bags, their powdery contents stacked into tall, shimmering cones of ground scarlet pepper, powdery cinnamon, and jade oregano. Back home, she'd enhance these photographs with paint and paper, creating handsome collages for their walls.

She paused now to examine some large sacks of dried herbs in the street.

"No more pictures," he said gruffly. "I'm hungry."

She turned and looked at him, again that fleeting look of concern in her eyes. "Sure. Let's go. It's on the main boulevard. It won't take long."

"I must not have had enough for breakfast," he said.

"Well, I'm famished, too. I'd love a *salade Niçoise*. I can't get enough of their tuna."

"He said the other place has good couscous," Richard repeated, more in the mood for the earthy local specialty of grain-like pasta smothered in stewed vegetables and meat than for a salad or a seaside grill.

She smiled and started walking again. "We can have couscous tonight."

He followed grudgingly, aware that despite her earlier claims, walking to the seaside boulevard took at least twenty minutes.

However, ambiance was everything to Joy, and Richard wanted to give her the sea view, especially because of all he was putting her through.

He had to admit that dining by the water was refreshing. Last night they'd strolled along the lively seaside boulevard to throbbing Arabic music blaring from loudspeakers, the aroma of candy-roasted peanuts and jasmine in the air. In a waterfront cafe, they had drunk hot mint tea garnished with pine nuts from small, gold-rimmed glasses. Enticed by the smell of freshly fried pastry, they had each bought a *brik a l'oeuf* from a stall, finding that the square pastry held a delicious surprise inside: a soft egg yolk that seeped out when they bit into the warm dough. The vendor had smiled at their shock, handing out several more napkins to wipe their mouths and hands.

The jasmine vendors, elderly elfin men in red fezzes, had held out sweet-smelling necklaces and posies made from fresh blossoms. Richard had bought a jasmine necklace for Joy and a posy to tuck behind his own ear, copying the vendor. The old guy had winked slyly and warned Richard that a flower behind a man's ear was an invitation for romance to passing females.

"What the heck," Richard had said, and he'd kept the jasmine sprig behind his ear for all to see.

24

*B*ack in their hotel room after lunch, Richard felt better, the ache in his jaw gone. Tension, he thought. For their mission, but also because he knew that the office problems he'd left behind weren't going to simply disappear. This personal challenge couldn't have come at a worse time for his work.

He'd been wanting to resign from the bank for several years. For some time, he'd sensed a conspiracy afoot in top management. Younger, less-experienced vice presidents were being promoted over him, guys without his knowledge or contacts, "yes" men willing to toe the line for lower pay. Or else they were part of the Princeton frat club. In the end, the Irish Princetonians always won out in that bank. After everything Richard had done for them over the years, it all boiled down to politics; kids came along who thought nothing of putting anybody over forty-five out to pasture.

He'd held on to the hope that the opportunity to resign would present itself before too long. He'd long toyed with the idea of running an exporting operation: food, machine parts, computer software. Russia was gulping down American products in an effort to modernize factories and dilapidated machinery; and just like there was a demand for computers and software throughout the Middle East and Africa, Russia was an insatiable market for American wheat, corn, and meat.

His work at the bank had introduced him to several over-seas importers as well as American suppliers and shippers. He was confident he could get representational agreements. He wouldn't have much overhead, and he wouldn't need but an assistant and a secretary at first. He was aware, however, that the stress would be tremendous, worse than what he experienced as a bank officer. Working solo, he'd have only pigheaded determination to sustain him.

Joy had been shocked when he told her of his thoughts of resigning, however. Although she was back at Hunter, safely ensconced as an associate professor in the English department, she'd never expected him to resign. After they left Turkey, she'd made plans to end her contract in Virginia at the end of the school year in June. A month later they'd moved back in together, and she'd started back at Hunter in August. When he'd explained his bank problems to her and told her that they might be a blessing in disguise, freeing him to move on to do what he'd always wanted to do, which was to start up his own import-export company, she was adamant that now was not the time. They still faced an uncertain and possibly rocky path ahead, she'd stressed, not only in starting a new life together, but also in opening up their lives to the presence and needs of a small child.

So he'd agreed to put his dreams on hold for now. He had to admit that Joy's practical approach to their immediate future was the right one.

The air conditioner breathed wafts of cool air onto the bed, like angels teasing him with tender puffs. The bed was comfortable, despite being a single mattress on a simple wooden frame. It seemed a challenge to get real luxury in Hammamet, anyway, which appeared to cater to modestly priced British and German tour groups content with basic amenities. But as long as it was cool and clean, Richard thought, it was fine.

There was a time when a cheap hotel room would actually drive him wild, when he purposely sought them out for those feverish interludes with her. Belinda. He only occasionally said her name to himself these days. Although it seemed like yesterday, it had been five years since those moments had started to fill his life. His eyes shut at her memory, that most lively of saviors during the hellish period filled with enough loss and despair to bury him alive.

He glanced over at Joy, now, and was jolted by a shudder of remorse at the pain he'd caused her. She'd always been the love of his life, and yet, aside from his sorrow for having hurt her so, he couldn't bring himself to regret his time with Belinda. How could he have forgone that nirvana? His biggest regret was that he hadn't achieved that nirvana with Joy.

The uncanny irony was that the very person who had enticed him away from his marriage to begin with had been the one to draw him back in.

These past months he and Joy had spent back together had been quite wonderful for the most part, and yet, despite both their efforts to instill a new spark into the marriage, at times it did feel more like a resigned partnership than one of passion.

While tentative about moving back to New York at first, Joy seemed to settle into his apartment and cohabitation as if she'd never left. Like a pet reclaiming its favorite chair, she'd taken possession of his kitchen, inspired to create for him some of the recipes she'd discovered since she'd gone to Virginia. Then she streamlined the living room of his gadgets and what she deemed "a mess," which she replaced with cheerful ceramics and paintings.

Although she'd invaded half of his study, filling one bookshelf with endless stacks of student papers, he had to admit that she had turned his sloppy bachelor abode back into a tasteful, cozy home. She'd left only his terrace intact, admiring the planters he'd filled with flowers, his experiment in balcony horticulture.

Amused but guarded, he'd shifted from one side of the apartment to the other, ceding territory as he tried to both lovingly welcome her and at the same time preserve some vestige of the independence he'd come to value after the shock of divorce. He realized he had become a different man in her absence. The search to redefine just who he was and who he wanted to be in this new arrangement for the foreseeable future became a struggle in those first months of their new life together.

If Joy was going through something similar to his confusion, she never let on.

Then there was the sex. That mysterious and delicate and yet most vital bond. Both floundered in the beginning, alternately baffled and aroused by each other's feel and rhythms after so long. Joy had grown both fuller and leaner over the past three years, more muscular in her thighs and arms, probably because of her passion for rock-climbing. She was almost a different woman to him. This newness was undeniably exciting, the way her body seemed taut yet tender, giving yet withholding, and he delighted in observing her anew: her skin's supple radiance in a certain light, her hair's silkiness.

While she still mesmerized him, however, he wasn't sure how she perceived him after their time apart. Had she grown new feelings for him, like new cells? He didn't know and didn't dare ask.

Although he knew it was unrealistic to expect to resurrect the same amorous feelings of their earlier years, he was touched at how solicitous she now seemed of him, asking how he slept, more curious than she'd ever been about his work at the bank and the internal pressures he rarely talked about. She seemed to want to be near him a lot more than she had before, laying her head in his lap when they watched television, threading her fingers through his when they were out walking or driving. She was, however, unpredictable in bed, at times eager for his advances, at others drawing back, as she had the other night.

"Is something wrong?" he'd asked.

After a pause she'd said, almost reluctantly, "Rich, do you mind if we skip the foreplay?"

He was taken aback. "Honey, if you're not in the mood, we don't have to—"

"I am in the mood, but I'd prefer it not take so long."

He'd stared at her a moment, then backed off, lying beside her. She'd never been so blunt before.

"I do want to make love," she'd said softly. "Just, not all the other part."

"It's all part of making love, honey," he'd said simply.

"I know it is, but I'm not up for it these days."

He'd waited a few minutes. "You still enjoy sex with me?"

"I do. . . ."

"Then?"

She sighed. "I enjoy the closeness more. The cuddling and affection."

She mostly wanted communion rather than physical love, it seemed, and it saddened him. He'd also sensed that she was less focused on her own physical release, as if orgasms were no longer important. Although he felt guilty enjoying his own orgasms with her, he knew he couldn't make her want something she didn't. The ignition key to spark that volcano beneath Joy's cool surface often seemed just out of his reach, and he suspected that on some level she was holding back as a way of punishing him for the past. After a few frustrating attempts at mutual pleasure, he realized that for the time being it was best to simply enjoy the amiable encounters between them, at least until she was ready for something more. It seemed that in this aspect, too, there was no fairytale ending for them yet.

Joy now had the guidebook propped up on her raised knees in bed, her reading glasses resting midway down her nose. She met his gaze from above her glasses. "Have a nice nap?"

He smiled. "I was just thinking you look like the Big Bad Wolf with your glasses like that."

"The Red Riding Hood wolf?" she said.

"A sexy wolf," he said, and he whistled, his erection grounding him as the sleep lifted from the rest of his body.

She smiled distractedly.

"What time is it?" he asked.

"Four-thirty."

He yawned. "I'm still exhausted."

"You're just restless, honey. Try to relax."

He sighed. "I just can't process this whole thing. It's like it's happening to somebody else, and I'm just an observer. Only I'm not." He sighed again, trying to free his lungs from the relentlessly oppressive anxiety. "I just need for things to fall into place. Right now, I feel like such a hypocrite."

She looked surprised. "Why would you feel that?"

"For what I've caused you to go through. I don't feel good about myself. I'd have ridiculed someone else in my shoes."

She looked at him. "Well, don't do that to yourself, Rich. We're all hypocrites to some extent. None of us lives our truths fully." She smiled gently. "Maybe that's why people write, so they can get it right at least on paper." She paused. "And don't worry about me. I'm fine."

When they were first living together again, Joy had made it clear that she'd be able to handle the situation of raising the child, but by the time the news came from Belinda, he'd sensed that she was growing anxious despite her assertions to the contrary. They'd been through this before, talked at length about undertaking the life-changing task of raising an unknown child, albeit his own, and assuming parenthood in such an abnormal situation. He'd told himself to be patient, to allow himself to adjust one step at a time. Just as Joy kept telling him to do. After all, once she'd agreed to get back into the relationship and be a mother to his child, she'd never once complained about the challenge ahead, although he assumed that she was worried sick at times. He was more grateful for her support than anything.

He found her hand now and squeezed it, but her claims of feeling fine did little to reassure him. He wished he could truly make all of this up to her somehow.

He also promised himself that he would be calm about Belinda and her failure to reach out to them since they had arrived here. He couldn't do anything until she contacted them, he told himself, and so, difficult as it was, Joy had the right idea in suggesting they should distract themselves with some sightseeing.

He grew aware now that he'd been observing her, watching her chest rise and drop as she read, noting the minute twitches in her face as her eyes progressed down the page. She seemed fascinated by what she was reading, and she looked more youthful than he'd seen her in a while.

How had he reached his forties so fast? What had been going on in those intervening years between young adulthood and now? He failed to remember the details. Those years were more a jumble of montages—business travel, commutes to the office, trips with Joy—than tangible images. He could scarcely remember specifics except for the terrible loss of Stephen, his dizzying time with Belinda, and the wrenching divorce.

His own mortality had been weighing on him for a while, and he wondered whether it was a midlife crisis or something else. Belinda's illness suddenly made him feel more vulnerable than ever. He'd had a death dream a few nights ago. He didn't remember the details, only how it turned out—with him dead. Now that he was going to be a father to a very young child, he worried he might not last to see the job done, that his dream had been a portent that he was nearing the end.

He still couldn't believe that someone as plucky and alive as Belinda could ever get sick. Sickness and death were for others. He wanted to pull that damn tumor right out of her and fling it to hell, but he couldn't do a damn thing. He couldn't even show his deep sadness and horror at the possibility—now, apparently, the inevitability—of her death. He couldn't hurt Joy any more than he already had. Although she'd pretend to understand and sympathize, she'd be pained beyond belief to see the extent of his grief; so he kept his feelings for Belinda private, mourned the cruel cutting-short of her life in silence.

Although both were waiting frantically for Belinda to contact them, for a while he *had* managed to keep his mind detached long enough to appreciate the sights of this North African town where the cerulean windows and doors of the whitewashed houses rivaled the blue of the sea. But then it had all come rushing back like a tidal wave crashing down on him, filling his head and lungs with a torrent strong enough to suffocate him. Especially this morning. He'd woken up feeling depressed and sluggish, as if a huge tarpaulin had been slung over him during the night and he needed to claw his way out for air.

"Rich!" Joy abruptly squealed.

He jerked up from under the covers.

"I can't believe this! Look."

"Honey, don't yell like that."

"Well," she said. "See for yourself." She took off her glasses and handed him the guidebook.

The print was small, and he had to hold it farther back to bring it into focus.

"It says right there. Rich, he was fooling us."

"Who?"

"That guide—our waiter—or whatever he was."

After reading a few lines he understood. Son of a bitch! It was a common ruse in the bazaar, apparently, to approach tourists and claim to be the waiter at their hotel to gain their trust, then trail them through the bazaar and make a commission on anything they bought.

"And we *tipped* him," she said, bursting into laughter.

He continued to read. The rooftop terrace depicted in the warning was the very spot they'd photographed from, and it was a fake, a recent addition to the store below that was often used to deceive gullible foreigners into thinking it was once the extravagant residence of a local notable. He stared at the picture. Those were the very columns he and Joy had sat on, the so-called chairs of the four wives of the Pasha of Hammamet. Damn fakes.

He handed her back the book. "Fuck the bastard."

She shook her head, smiling. "You'd think we could spot a con, by now. I did think it strange that a pasha's wife would sit on a backless seat, and I don't really *remember* the man ever having served us breakfast. Do you?"

"No."

"But I don't pay attention in the morning. He could have."

"He didn't," Richard said.

"Are you sure?"

"Forget it. We'll be more careful from now on. No wonder he didn't want his picture taken."

She giggled, snuggling closer to him under the sheet as if their shared ignorance delighted her, made them accomplices in their own duping.

He closed his eyes, unable to see the humor in it. How stupid could he get? He could normally pick up on a con job, and it was out of character for him to accept that sort of offer. He'd been too preoccupied with Belinda for his normally sensitive antennae to be operating at peak form, he told himself, but he should have been more careful about succumbing to out-of-work predators. Despite the sights, he was beginning to want to get out of here.

"I guess we can't blame him for trying to make a buck," Joy said.

She scooted even closer to him and started to stroke his back as though to soften the blow, then reached around his belly. He thought he heard her giggle again and felt her breasts against his back.

"I thought you hated being swindled," he said, although he felt his anger subsiding. Whereas prior to this she might have worried herself sick about being cheated, she seemed to not be offended by it now.

She continued to chuckle. "I just can't believe we were so taken in."

"It's not that funny."

Obviously sensing his irritation, she asked, "Are you okay?"

"I will be if you keep rubbing my back like that."

To his delight, her arm ventured out again and encircled his waist, and this time he caught her hand and guided it back to where it had started to go before he'd frightened it away. Being swindled together had apparently excited Joy, and he wasn't about to let this opportunity slip by. He would not make *two* mistakes in one day.

The pain in his jaw was finally gone. He started to hum "Sexual Healing." Marvin Gaye sure had it right.

He looked at his watch. Time to get some dinner. He glanced over at Joy, who was now huddled under the covers. She tended to do this after sex, even in the heat, to shut out the world and withdraw into her cocoon to fall asleep. Although he couldn't hear her breaths, he could detect the rise and fall of her shoulders in the darkened room.

He'd been confounded by how radiant she'd been since the start of the trip, though he knew that she too must be tied in infinite knots by Belinda's silence and what lay ahead.

They'd discussed it endlessly, even seen a therapist to make certain that, should the need arise, Joy was ready to take on the responsibility of raising his child from another woman. He wanted to make sure that she wasn't doing this solely for him, that there would be no lingering grudges that would poison them all. Would she forever see Belinda in the child and harbor some latent ill will toward her? Surely there had been times in the past months when Joy must have doubted her ability to do this, but she never let on. Ultimately, he had to take her word that she knew herself well enough to actually be able to handle something when she said she could.

Perhaps, despite the ambivalence, the anticipation of approaching "motherhood" was the cause of her current glow. He wanted to believe that, but he couldn't help wondering whether it was something else. Perhaps being back at Hunter and in the company of all those professors had prompted some secret attraction to someone else. It was an irrational thought, but he couldn't help it. He'd seen those expressions before, brief but definitely there, but this time he had no patience for her floating away.

25

*T*he stooped old German beamed his eager smile as he patrolled the hotel's beach, diligently scooping up the stringy cylindrical jellyfish in a wire kitchen strainer.

The jellyfish were bobbing like a swarm of corks along the sparkling shore this morning, coming a full two months early this year, according to the concierge. These weren't the variety of jellyfish they'd encountered in Mexico once, the malicious pink spheres with translucent tentacles that lashed at their limbs and left welts that burned for days. These resembled harmless scraps of brown seaweed, and their touch irritated only slightly more than a mosquito bite. Still, they were a nuisance, spurring swimmers to the concessions stand for pats of soothing ammonia. After being stung a few times, Richard avoided the water, enjoying the beach from the safe shade of the umbrella.

"I haven't been bitten once," Joy said, obviously baffled that he could resist such glorious water because of something as trifling as *these* jellyfish.

"So you keep telling me."

"Isn't that old man gallant to fish them out? He's been busy all morning trying to make swimming pleasant for everybody."

Richard glanced up from his book. He'd seen the man but was less impressed by the old-timer's chivalry. "It's a ploy to attract women. See them gather around him to look at his catch?"

"Well, if it's a ploy, it's a nice one."

"What choice does he have? He's not exactly Don Juan anymore."

Joy dismissed this with a wave of her hand. "He just keeps depositing them on shore and going back in, over and over. I haven't seen him actually swim at all. And he has such a sweet smile."

"He must not have anything else to worry about."

She shrugged. "We can't worry about what we can't control. We agreed to give her a few more days, so we just have to be patient. Meanwhile, enjoy the view."

He nodded. She was right. They had to sit tight. This was Belinda's call, and they had to let her do things at her own pace.

At least there was a serenity to the beach that was absent in the frantic mood of the street where the anxious hustlers were bent on flogging their wares. He and Joy had avoided the *medina* since that first day. Since vendors were barred from the hotel's beach, there were, thankfully, none trekking here in search of tourists.

He observed the German again as the frail fellow held out his strainer to the scrutiny of two middle-aged women pausing in their walk. Both women peered at his catch and nodded approvingly. They appeared to be German, too, with their cropped light hair and sunny demeanors. One had a square face that reminded Richard of his mother, who'd died two years earlier.

He'd been to Los Angeles to visit his mother after her stroke, and once she recovered, he had helped move her back into her assisted living facility. Two weeks later, after he got home, she'd passed in her sleep. No warning. Nothing. It was, according to all, the best way to go, but he'd agonized for months that he'd spent so much of his life away from her.

His younger brother, Carl, had died several years earlier from melanoma. Barely forty, Carl had never married and had struggled to make it as a movie producer, like countless others in LA. He'd gone to live near their mother and gotten to know her better than Richard ever had. Richard hadn't been there for Carl much either in those later years. Although they'd both been absorbed in work and personal lives, it was something he still hadn't forgiven himself for.

"Why do you think we marry the people we do?" Joy asked abruptly. She'd just come from the water and was rubbing her wet hair with the beach towel.

"Ouch! Honey, you're getting sand everywhere with that towel."

She continued rubbing her hair, giving no sign that she'd heard him.

"Joy!" He shut his eyes.

She stopped drying her hair and spread the towel back on the sand as he dusted off his book.

She lay belly-down on her towel and unhooked the back of her swimsuit top. "Can you put some sunscreen on my back?"

He unscrewed the tube she handed him and rubbed her back, down to the top of her swimsuit bottom. Her skin was already warm from the sun, and he marveled at the pretty curve of her back that he'd always liked, the way it dipped in and then out like a pear and displayed those two little dimples.

"I asked, why people marry—"

"I heard you," he said, still gazing at her back.

"Well?"

"Different reasons. How should I know?" He blinked and rubbed his eyelid to dislodge sand crystals.

"I've been looking around the beach," she said. "The couples seem to be the weirdest mix. There's a funny-looking short man over there with a gorgeous young woman."

"Doesn't mean they're married."

"She's carrying a baby and he has his arm around her. He looks twice her age. It's just odd."

Richard sat upright. "Where?"

"Wading in the water."

He spotted a slender woman with a blond ponytail as she handed a short, older man an infant before carefully sliding into an approaching wave, holding her head high to avoid wetting her hair. Although he didn't get a clear look at the woman, she appeared to be young and pretty. The man could be mistaken for her father, but they certainly acted married.

"Maybe he's got money," Richard offered. "Maybe he's a Russian oligarch. Maybe he's brilliant. Or maybe he's just a nice guy."

Joy continued to watch them, looking amused but unconvinced.

"Why do *you* think?" he asked, deciding to let her take this where she wanted.

She shrugged. "She's so lovely. She could obviously have someone more dashing. It's just surprising."

He felt compelled to come to the maligned husband's defense. "Not really. Some women like older men."

"Security."

"What?"

"She wants stability and security for her child."

He watched the man, who was now trudging up the sand with the child snuggled in his arms. The man went to the umbrella, placed the baby in a bassinet in the shade, and carefully spread mosquito netting over it.

Richard felt a twinge of jealousy at the satisfaction that being a loving father must yield. A fading memory of Stephen flowed through him, followed by a vision of Belinda and her daughter. What kind of father would he have been to Stephen? What kind would he be to the girl? To Karma. Would he find his true calling in being a parent as Belinda said she had? What about Joy? Would she secretly resent Belinda's child although she'd assured him she was totally free of any ill feelings?

Joy interrupted his contemplations. "Women in childbearing years are blind to all but security, financial and emotional."

He caught his breath. Belinda had once called him dependable, but he'd assumed it was an added quality in him she liked, not the main reason for her attraction to him. Was Joy saying these things now to dispel any notion he might have that Belinda had truly loved—or might still love—him? Might she be wondering whether he still harbored feelings for Belinda?

"For most young women, security's a downright aphrodisiac," Joy continued. "It overshadows everything else."

He glanced at her, again wondering whether she was insinuating that this was the main reason Belinda had been attracted to him. "If you say so," he said.

She smiled. "You've never been a woman. We may *dream* of Che Guevara on his motorcycle, but we *marry* Gerald Ford."

He started to laugh.

She nodded knowingly. "Most women will settle for Plain Joe when looking for a mate."

Plain Joe? He looked back at the man settling into a beach chair under the umbrella, beside the baby's cot. Okay, *he* was a Plain Joe.

"And how about us men? How do *we* choose our mates?" he asked.

She smiled. "Well, you dream of screwing Marilyn Monroe, but most of you marry your mothers."

He glanced at her, eyebrows raised.

"You need the Virgin Mary," she explained.

He grinned. "I married a very sexy Madonna."

She shrugged this off. "Men, in general. It's that same longing for security. You may want great, raw sex—"

"Ah, Marilyn Monroe," he said, unable to push the thought of Belinda aside now, her ebony hair, olive skin, those steamy afternoons and evenings. . . . He stopped himself. He could have chosen that, could have followed her to the far reaches of Africa, but he hadn't. He had chosen to stay, chosen Joy. He, too, had picked security in a sense.

"—but you're terrified the nympho will leave you," Joy went on, "and so you settle for the nurturer. Few men take on a challenge in marriage. You don't have the stomach for it."

He was starting to get exasperated. At one time, she would have criticized *him* for making such generalizations. If anything, he felt he was the opposite from the men she described.

"So, where does that leave *us?*" he asked.

She looked as though she'd been waiting for this question. "I think I married the first time in large part for emotional security."

He raised his eyebrows. "And now?"

"Now I'm with you for love."

"Whoa, I'm flattered," he said, although he wasn't sure whether to be relieved or disappointed at those missed years before.

She reached over and patted his slight paunch as though to temper his sarcasm. She used to be on him whenever he gained weight. Now, she seemed not to mind. Or perhaps she'd given up, Richard thought. Perhaps she'd decided to leave his health issues to him. Maybe she had married him for love this time and was blind to whatever had bothered her the first time. He wished to hell he could believe that.

"Joy?"

"Hmm?"

He wanted to ask if she really loved him, but instead he asked, "What kind of parents will we make?"

She looked at him. "Good parents."

"I mean, will we be permissive or strict, hyper-protective, overbearing—"

"We'll be good, loving parents. The rest doesn't matter."

"She's almost four. I have so much to learn." He looked at her. "I honestly don't know what I'd do without you, Joy."

She smiled. "You'd do fine."

"Maybe we should move out of Manhattan, move back to Westchester or to Connecticut for the schools."

She sighed. "Let's not worry about that, now."

He sat in silence, staring out to sea. He knew he had to start making some serious decisions soon. Whether Joy admitted it or not, their lives *would* change, and dramatically.

Joy said matter-of-factly, "You, on the other hand, married your mother both times."

"What?" He looked at her then, realizing she was back to their earlier discussion, he feigned shock. "Never Marilyn Monroe?"

"Nope."

"Not even on the second round?"

"Uh-uh," she said without the slightest doubt in her voice. "But that's good. That's why you're happy."

"Who says I'm happy?" he said, enjoying the uneasy arch this put in her brow.

"At least you're content, aren't you?"

He tilted his head as though unsure then smiled, indicating with a nod the fellow peacefully reading his book. "So, that schmuck with the baby married Marilyn Monroe, and I didn't?"

She glanced at the man under the tree. "Oh, he married his mother, too."

"And just how do you figure that?"

"She's a nurturer. Not just because of the baby, but because of her stance, the way she stood with him earlier, almost cradling him like *he* was the baby."

"You've been reading too many novels," he said.

She paused, thoughtful for a moment, and then smiled back at him as she picked up her book. "It comes with the job. It's what literature is all about. Sorting out life's absurdity."

26

$\mathcal{T}$he sea shimmered like blue topaz—the color of Joy's eyes— in the afternoon sun. They'd come to the archaeological site of ancient Carthage, and she was standing at one corner of a large square next to a headless marble torso of a youth with coils of hair touching the shoulders. Richard stared at the sensuousness of the Roman statue's musculature, the tight torso brazenly erotic, the piece in remarkably intact condition except for the missing head and penis.

They still hadn't heard from Belinda. To their surprise, a woman did finally contact their room two evenings ago and told Joy, who had answered the phone, that Belinda had been hospitalized. It was for some routine testing, she said, and Belinda would send word within a few days. She wouldn't give Joy any more information or a telephone number, only insisted that Belinda would soon call them herself.

Although it was a great relief to receive even this morsel of news, neither he nor Joy had been able to sleep after that. It was all he could do to keep from demanding that the hotel have the call traced, but Joy had convinced him to wait a few more days as the woman had instructed.

He now followed Joy across some wild grasses through an elaborate ruined archway, an obvious later Roman addition to the earlier and simpler worn-down Phoenician—Punic—Carthaginian structures. He remembered studying about the Punic wars in high school, battles fought between Rome and Carthage, most famous for the campaigns of Hannibal, the Carthaginian general who crossed Spain and France, hiking the Alps with his army and elephants to attack Rome.

"These ruins are from later, from Roman Carthage, which was rebuilt by Julius Caesar in 46 BC," Joy said, sounding disappointed.

"Yep. Hannibal's Carthage was destroyed by Rome in vengeance after his defeat. The Romans killed and scattered the population to make sure they never raised an army again, then sowed the fields with salt to make sure they couldn't grow food."

"Ugh," she said, with a shudder.

"Warfare hasn't changed. Destroy or be destroyed."

"Look at—honey, what's wrong?"

He realized he must have been grimacing again from the throbbing in his jaw. "Nothing."

"You don't look good at all," she said.

"It's that filling. I've got to change dentists."

He didn't want to concern Joy, but he'd had this pain on and off since they got here, especially when he was stressed. But he was sure it was just tension. Maybe he was clenching his jaw in his sleep. At any rate, he didn't want her to worry.

She looked at him a minute longer as if straining to see him clearly, then seemingly satisfied by his explanation, returned to her initial focus. "Look at this floor," she said, pointing to the faded tiles at her feet. "The partridge over here, and that gazelle, and fruit. This might have been a dining room. I can see why these are considered some of the best Roman mosaics in the world."

He gazed across the ancient site that was obviously a valued tourist attraction. Great care had been taken in its preservation despite the apparent political upheavals in the rest of the country. They were lucky in that, except for a watchman, they were the only ones here.

His thoughts drifted back to Manhattan, to the office turbulence, but he roped them back in with the reasoning that someday, none of his work problems would be important. They, too, would pass, like this once-great empire beneath their feet. All that were left of these ancient mercantile honchos of Phoenician Carthage were some commemorative headstones in museums and the urns in the pits down the hill once used to store the ashes of first-born infants sacrificed to the gods in times of national crises.

He glanced about him at the entire panorama of Phoenician and Roman ruins. There had clearly been more to this once-thriving metropolis than ritual sacrifice and destruction. Successive epochs had spawned brilliant architecture, luxurious leisure facilities, art; but ironically, what lingered to glare back through the centuries was barbaric child sacrifice.

"Pray you don't reincarnate as a Punic infant," he said.

She shuddered. "How could they kill their own children?"

"The gods were pretty demanding in their day," he said, although this was equally unimaginable to him. Particularly painful because of Stephen. In a way, they'd already had to sacrifice their firstborn.

Richard stood perfectly still for a moment, as if he were suddenly hollow and could disintegrate without a trace. He was struck again by how time marched on, slipping by out of control, indifferent to the desires, loves, pains, or joys of the living. It wouldn't be long before he and Joy and their lives would also pass into oblivion like the lives of those who'd built these structures—pass into the indifference and obscurity of history.

His entire life flashed by him in an orb of incomprehensibility. What would he leave the world to remember him by? So far, a less than gratifying career, a crippled marriage, a child out of wedlock.

He reached out and took Joy's hand.

"Although I don't like to live in the past, I can't help wishing I could create my life over again, do it all differently," he said.

Joy shrugged. "We all wish for that at some time or other. We just have to accept our choices. We learn as we go along."

His mind raced to his daughter. He had to do right by her, make *her* world matter. He vowed to give her all the love, powers, and skills she'd need to grow into a happy and healthy woman and create the life she wanted. *His daughter.* It occurred to him now that it was through her that he would continue to live on. She was his one connection to the future, drawing him along into the next generations like a line on a fishing pole.

How could Belinda have kept this to herself for so long, kept him away from someone who should have been his main focus and source of happiness? He knew she had been protecting them all in a way, and yet she had forced him in the process to give up his only child. In exchange for Joy and his life as he knew it, as he—wanted it. Perhaps Belinda knew him, even then, better than he knew himself.

At what point, he wondered, as he had so many times since receiving her first letter, had she gotten pregnant? She said she'd been on the pill, and so he wondered what had happened. She'd also once told him she'd had an abortion in college. He assumed she would have had another. *If*, that is, she had *not* wanted a child.

"Richard?"

Joy's voice roused him. She was posing behind another headless statue, this one of a woman in a clinging tunic. He was startled for a moment. Her head fit the sculpture's voluptuously draped body perfectly, and she looked like some specter from another time. He stared at her, trying to smile through his conflicting thoughts.

"Take a picture!" she urged playfully.

He raised his camera, focused, and clicked.

"Please!" The watchman called out, beckoning to them.

Richard lowered the camera, thinking he might be objecting to Joy resting her head on the statue's broken neck. When they reached him, however, the watchman sprinkled water from the spout of a watering can onto yet another mosaic floor.

"Oh," Joy gasped.

Moistened by the water droplets, the mosaics began to emerge and sparkle: a dove's eye turning mauve, a feather glimmering green. Grapes and vines breathed in the wetness. The watchman splattered more droplets and brought to life a banquet of figs, plums, apricots, and olives.

Joy bent for a closer look at the floor mosaics. "Unbelievable!" she said. "All this beauty—it's a miracle it survived. These are as good as those at the Bardo." She chuckled. "I can just see Julia Child, even Martha Stewart, applauding."

Richard nodded.

"Imagine growing up with all this history in your backyard. I like these mosaics a lot better than those burnt children's coffins."

"Yeah, me too," he agreed.

At the mention of children again, the earlier question that had been plaguing him for some time returned. Had Belinda *planned* to get pregnant?

JOY

∽✽∾

27

*J*oy looked around for a doorbell, but couldn't find one, or any name posted to indicate the house's owner. Above the arched doorway, there was only the address, 24 Rue Koubba, which she had been told to give the driver.

She peered through one of the double wooden doors left ajar. The doors of this white villa were painted a bright yellow rather than the usual turquoise, and they were ornamented with the customary black nails studded in delicate, arabesque patterns. One of the doors had a large, iron-ringed handle.

She thumped the heavy handle against the door. "Hello?" she called.

She waited a few moments. When nobody answered, Joy stepped through the open door into a small foyer.

The white vaulted ceiling curved above a tall rubber tree that arched up against it. On the black-and-white tile floor were two wooden chairs inlaid with luminous mother-of-pearl, like some she had admired in the *medina* market. Behind them, glass doors opened out to an interior courtyard with red-flowering bushes. There was no indication that the home was occupied by an American expat rather than a local family.

Joy's chest caught. Thief! She couldn't help thinking she was one, standing inside the home of a woman whose child she would soon take.

She knew it was absurd to think this. The girl *was* also Richard's child, but Joy couldn't help feeling that she was stealing, through another woman's death, something she'd always wanted for herself.

She sucked in her breath, wishing things could have been different. Different for her and Richard, different for the woman, different for the child.

"Come at two," the voice had said over the phone. Joy knew it to be Belinda's from its sensual low timbre that had struck her when she'd met the woman several years before, unsuspecting back then. She still couldn't believe she'd overlooked the possibility at the time that Richard had something going on with the woman, what with the way she was overly friendly with both of them and the slight discomfort Richard had shown in her presence.

She'd marveled that this same voice could now belong to such a sick woman. "And please," the voice had continued firmly, "come alone. Just you."

"Hello?" Joy called again, now catching a sweet, full-bodied aroma like baking bread coming from farther inside the house. Although she'd clearly been told to come at two o'clock, Joy had the uneasy feeling now that she was intruding on lunch.

From a side hallway came shuffling footsteps. An elderly woman appeared, wearing a long gray robe and a white scarf loosely draped around her head.

"Hello," Joy said, somewhat embarrassed to have let herself in.

The woman looked surprised to see her as she wiped her hand on a rag and mumbled something. The fair, wrinkled skin of the woman's chin and forehead was dotted with what appeared to be small blue tattoos.

"Belinda?" Joy asked. "Is Belinda here?"

The woman continued to wipe her hand, then turning away slightly, called out shrilly, "Sitty!"

Joy thought she heard a child's voice. Her spine stiffened in an involuntary jerk, and she wished she'd disregarded the instructions to come alone. She could have asked that they meet in some public space, in a cafe or at the hotel. She could have at least insisted that Richard accompany her, but she was also relieved that he was not here. As wary as she was, she knew she needed to have this first meeting alone.

The elderly woman turned back to her and gestured for her to follow.

Joy walked behind her down a hall past a kitchen, where the homey scent of cooking grew stronger, and then up a narrow staircase. They climbed up two flights to a sunny, flat rooftop with rooms on one side. A warm breeze rifled through Joy's blouse, drying some of her nervous sweat.

The elderly woman walked over to the open door of one of the rooms and called in, softly this time, "Sitty?"

A woman's voice instantly responded in English, "Come in."

Joy started at the sound of the cadenced voice, knowing that it was addressing her. She slowly walked to the open door and, bracing herself, glanced inside.

Like the rest of the villa, the walls of the room were stark white, but sheer indigo curtains billowed at the open windows, casting a cool blue pallor over everything. Two white sofas were set across from one another with a scattering of colorful cushions on each. A low coffee table, like a floating island, sat between the sofas. Out a window, a silken streak of aqua sea lit up the horizon.

On one sofa reclined a striking, youngish woman dressed in a long purple robe, her head wrapped in a vibrant yellow-print scarf tied to one side of her face.

"Joy," the woman said cheerfully, lifting her hand as though to wave her in.

The very air of the room seemed to grow dense, as though taking on a suffocating shape. Joy had expected to find Belinda more gaunt and sickly, but there was an animated glow to her face despite the notable absence of the black hair and eyebrows that had so defined her at their one meeting in New York. Also, she looked plumper than Joy remembered, with a rosy complexion that made her look almost angelic. When she'd met Belinda that previous time, Joy had been acutely aware of her vibrant youth. The same inadvertent feeling of being old by comparison returned to her now.

She took in the whimsical room and this woman on whom she'd fixated for so long, one moment demonizing her as a Jezebel and the next elevating her to the sacred status of the terminally ill. The woman before her now seemed to be neither. She was simply an attractive woman whose missing eyebrows and drained expression were the only signs of illness.

"I'm so happy to see you at last," Belinda said with a smile and in that rich, earthy voice.

The vivid fantasies again invaded Joy's head like lightning: this woman and Richard together, their bodies heaving in passion. *How dare you!* she wanted to scream, but she swallowed her breath and glanced away, out the window to the sunshine and sea.

"Please, sit down," Belinda said weakly, gesturing with her outstretched arm.

Joy hesitated, wondering whether she could endure staying in the same room and retain her composure. She sat on the sofa across from her, the buffer of the table between them.

"I wanted to call you sooner, but I've just returned from the hospital," Belinda said matter-of-factly. "My stays there are getting routine now. They give me blood, and I bounce back for a week, and then I slide downhill again."

Joy continued to fight the urge to get up and run out of there, never to see the woman again or deal with any of this. She resented, more than ever, having to pick up the pieces of Richard's affair. Then she thought of the little girl about to lose her mother, a child with nobody to replace the only parent she knew. Like a book she felt compelled to finish reading, even when she didn't enjoy it, Joy knew she would have to plod on with this for all of their sakes.

Clearing her throat, she forced herself to ask, "How are you feeling?"

"Not as bad as I must look," Belinda said with an apologetic chuckle. "I'm thankful I'm still able to dress myself and help care for Karma." She glanced at her watch. "She'll be home soon. They let them out at two."

A quiver of anxiety ran through Joy at the mention of Richard's child, the child she couldn't give him. Would the girl look like him? Would she have the shape of his eyes or mouth? From the one photo he was sent, Joy knew she had her mother's dark hair and eyes.

Belinda went on. "It's a long school day for a little one, but she's happy there. She fusses when she's at home, especially now that I've lost my energy. I'm not fun to be with anymore."

"It must be hard," Joy said, nodding, an inadvertent rush of sympathy washing through her. A natural compassion for this sick mother was almost as quickly squelched by the overwhelming awareness that she was facing her one-time rival.

Belinda sighed. "Kids gravitate toward life. It's their nature. She knows something's wrong with me, but the pull of the healthy world outside is overwhelming."

"I'm sorry." Although Joy wanted to offer words of comfort, she also needed to keep this meeting strictly business. They were only in this together for the sake of the child.

She now sat forward and said, "You asked to see me, but isn't it Richard you should be talking to?"

Belinda met her gaze, and Joy, absurdly, suddenly felt like *she* was "the other woman." If not for her, this woman and Richard could have been a family with their daughter. If *she*, Joy, had been the one to get sick rather than Belinda, if *she* were to die, Richard could simply have brought them both back to New York to live with him. Happily ever after. She wondered how often Belinda must have had these thoughts herself, wishing that Joy were out of the picture. She suspected that Belinda did not want Richard to come along today for fear of betraying the love she still had for him—or that he might reveal his feelings for her.

"I don't need to see him," Belinda said simply.

Joy was surprised, even annoyed, by this pretense at indifference to Richard. It was she, after all, who had wanted him back in her child's life. "What if he needs to see you?" she asked, wanting to get it all out in the open.

Belinda wrinkled her brow. Perhaps she wasn't expecting Joy to acknowledge that Richard might want to see her. "I only mean that I already know him and know the kind of father he'll be." She paused. "But I needed to see the woman who'll be my child's mother—"

"You don't have much of a choice at this point," Joy interrupted, anger rising in her at her qualifications as a suitable mother being questioned by someone who was practically forcing her child on her. She curled her fingers into the sofa, and then released her grip, willing herself to simmer down.

"I know you'll be kind and loving—"

"You *don't* know that," Joy said, resentment rearing again at this assumption about her.

"I think I do know," Belinda said calmly. "I knew even before I had Karma that you'd be a wonderful mother."

Joy stared at her. "What on earth are you talking about? Why would you have even thought of me?"

"Because having this child involved you."

There was a brusque noise at the doorway, and both of them turned to where the woman who'd brought Joy upstairs had reappeared, carrying a tray with a silver teapot and glasses.

The woman padded barefoot into the room and set the tray on the table between the sofas. The current threatening to ignite the air a moment ago dissipated with the elder woman's quiet presence. The woman lifted the ornate, round silver pot high from its handle and, holding two small glasses low in her other hand, poured the steaming liquid into each glass in a precise arc. The scent of the fresh mint punctured the air as the familiar little pine nuts floated to the surface of the tea. She replaced the pot on the tray next to a brown cake on a china platter and a bowl of white candied almonds. Using silver tongs, she plucked a sugar cube from a silver bowl and glanced at Joy.

"No sugar, thank you," Joy said.

The woman looked at her questioningly but handed her the glass. She then placed two cubes into the other glass, stirred it, and handed it to Belinda.

"I've given up resisting," Belinda said. "Tea without sugar is practically unheard of here. It's bad for me, even bad for the cancer, they say. But one of the advantages of having been colonized by the French is that Tunisian pastries are as good as in Paris." She smiled. "They're to die for."

Joy was struck by the irony of the idiom that now seemed patently sinister: *to die for*. She tried not to show her renewed shock at the stark reality of Belinda's illness.

Belinda started to sip her tea, making little slurping sounds, then she looked at Joy. "I'm sorry. My manners have deteriorated, too. We slurp all hot drinks here. It's not considered rude."

"It's not rude," Joy said, although it always grated on her when Richard slurped his coffee. Had he learned from *her*?

Belinda pushed herself up off the sofa with effort, leaned over the coffee table, and sliced a thick piece of the dark cake. She put it on a plate and offered it to Joy. "It's date cake. Aysha just baked it." She glanced affectionately at the older woman standing slightly away from the table.

The woman, Aysha, now immediately clucked her tongue and rushed to take over, gesturing for Belinda to retake her seat on the sofa. She said a few words in Arabic, and Belinda sighed as she settled back and allowed herself to be served.

"Aysha doesn't realize that moving does me good," she explained. "She also doesn't know that I'm never getting better. She just concocts her village herbal drinks for me as if I have a cold and need a few days of rest."

"It's good that she takes such good care of you," Joy said, almost envying the way the older woman hovered protectively above her charge.

"It sure is. *Alhamdullilah*."

Joy recognized the words. Thanks to God. Everyone here seemed to say it.

Joy took a bite of the cake, sweet and dense and unexpectedly scented with cardamom. "It's delicious," she said, nodding first at Belinda, then at Aysha.

"Thank you," Belinda said. She touched the yellow scarf on her head. "I don't usually wear a scarf. But I've lost most of my hair now, and the scarf is a lot more comfortable than a scratchy wig."

"The yellow is pretty," Joy said.

Belinda smiled wearily. "I never imagined myself without hair. Scarves help." She took a few more slurps of her tea, then added, "I was saying that I knew even before having Karma that you'd be a great mother."

Joy bridled again. "Richard had no right to discuss me with you."

Belinda went on as though she hadn't heard her. "If I didn't believe you'd be a great mother, I wouldn't have had the baby for you."

Joy blinked at her. "What?"

Avoiding direct eye contact, Belinda said, "I wanted you and Richard to have a child."

Joy wondered whether she'd heard her correctly.

Belinda sat up straighter, as though she had rehearsed her next words. "I know how much you wanted one."

Joy stared at her in horror. "And just how did you know that?"

Belinda seemed to be struggling to keep her gaze level. "I knew your inability to have a baby had strained your marriage."

"Strained my marriage? My life was none of your business!"

"I wanted to help—"

"Help?" Joy blurted out in disbelief. "Is that how you were going to help? After destroying our marriage? The minute you took that first step into our lives our marriage was over."

Belinda lowered her eyes and bit her lip. After a moment, still looking down, she said, "I wish you could forgive me. I'm so sorry for—for the pain I must have caused you. I never knew if he'd told you about me, but I assumed you eventually knew."

Joy continued to stare at her. "You're sorry?"

Belinda was silent.

"Too late for being sorry."

Belinda sucked in her breath.

Joy glanced at the ceiling. She'd planned to stay unemotional. She looked outside the window to the swath of blue sea and imagined Richard sitting on the beach right now. A sourness frothed inside her. Damn him!

She looked back at Belinda. "Whoever said I wanted a child that much?"

"It seemed to be what drove you apart," Belinda said, her voice low.

"Is that what he told you?"

Belinda emphatically shook her head. "No."

Joy exhaled. "You don't know anything about it. It was much more than that. It doesn't matter now."

Belinda looked away. "I'm sorry."

"It wasn't just not being able to have a baby," Joy said flatly. She briefly closed her eyes, as if she could make everything before her just disappear, make the entire past evaporate. Why was she even here?

When she opened her eyes, she looked straight at Belinda. "I did get pregnant. I suppose he told you about that, too? We had a son, a stillbirth. We couldn't have another. Being told you can't have . . ." She stopped, and then went on, her voice shaking, "The pain is there forever, but eventually it fades to the point that you can stand it."

"But you deserved a child," Belinda said softly. "You went through so much."

"Yes, I did deserve a child. But I wanted my *own* child!"

Belinda winced.

Although Joy instantly regretted her outburst, she was fed up with pleasantries. She owed it to herself to say what she felt: I don't want your child!

She glared at Belinda. "Did Richard want you to have his baby?"

Belinda vigorously shook her head. "He didn't know. It was me. I thought I could be—like a surrogate."

"A *surrogate?*" Joy exclaimed in disbelief. "We never wanted a surrogate. And in case you don't know, surrogates don't fuck the husband!"

There it was. She'd wanted to remain cool and above it all, but the old rage surged up and out of her like a shark.

Belinda shrank back into the sofa.

Joy shook her head in disbelief. "It's completely nuts! You had a baby for *us?* So you could—could get rid of your own guilt maybe?" She started to laugh at the craziness of it. "Just what, exactly, did you have in mind? A *ménage a trois*, all of us living together?"

Belinda looked away again. She looked exhausted.

Though still in shock, the piercing inside Joy dulled somewhat. She shook her head slowly. "You just don't decide to do something like this. It's downright crazy."

"I know that, now," Belinda said.

"And you came all the way out here? Why not just stay in New York?"

"I—I saw that I couldn't have the baby there. Richard might have misunderstood and felt obligated to help me out of some sense of duty—"

"That would have been just dandy," Joy cut in.

"No! I never wanted that. I had to leave. I couldn't tell him."

Joy flinched at the insinuation that Richard might have left her if he'd found out about Belinda's pregnancy. She brought her hands up to her face. They were cold, despite the heat. She had no idea what to make of this odd *naïf* who'd just informed her that she'd had a baby for her—to save her marriage.

"But," Belinda went on, her voice low, "I also saw that I hadn't been truthful, not with myself. I realized I couldn't give my baby up. Not even to him. Once I felt her growing inside me, everything changed." Her face turned pale as a sheet of paper. "I couldn't do it."

"Maybe it was Richard you didn't want to give up," Joy said coldly. "Keeping his baby was like keeping him."

"No," Belinda said hoarsely.

Joy felt she was like a spectator viewing somebody else's illogical, tragic life play out. She glanced out the window from which now drifted the faint sound of the call to prayer from a mosque. Outside, the world was going about its business, going to pray, to offices, to schools, everyone unaware of the madness infesting this room.

⚬

She looked at Belinda. "Do you still love him?" The words hung on her tongue like a barb.

"I wanted the baby for both of *you*," Belinda said.

"Do you still love him?" Joy repeated, coldly.

There was a pause. "Not in that way."

Although she didn't believe her, Joy let this go. "Did you ever stop to consider what it would actually be like to give up your child, consider the impact it would have on *her* life? On *our* lives?" She exhaled in exasperation. "Don't you see what you're imposing on us? You're asking me to relive this—this horrible part of my life over and over again . . ."

"I wanted to help out."

"God! Do you really think you were helping? What about your child? Do you think she'd have chosen to be separated from her own mother?"

"I didn't think of it that way. I didn't think of it as a separation.

The baby would always be a part of me even if she was with you. But when I began to feel her moving and I started to have emotions I never could have imagined, I was terrified. I couldn't give her up. Not then."

Joy looked for some clue that Belinda might be lying or making up this entire story. What sort of woman planned something like this and then chose to believe she wasn't actually abandoning her child? What *crap*. But Belinda looked utterly serious, her face betraying no hint of deception.

Joy thought she saw what must have so enticed Richard, that look of defiance accompanied by a strangely sweet sincerity. It wasn't hard to fill in the blanks, to see how the combination could be the lure of a siren. But she'd be damned if she was going to be taken in.

She leaned forward and rested her forehead on her fists, and then looked at Belinda over her still-clenched hands. "I don't know what to say to you. I don't know whether you expect me to sympathize, to tell you everything is okay. I don't even know how I feel about Richard, right now. Your bizarre ideas may excuse you, but they don't excuse him."

"Please don't blame him," Belinda said quickly. "He would never have agreed to become a father this way."

Joy glared at her, resenting her coming to Richard's defense. "At that point, our marriage was over. We were headed for divorce. You might as well have dragged him off with you."

Belinda emphatically shook her head. "He wouldn't have left you."

"I don't know about that."

"I do," Belinda said. "I saw how much he loved you."

Joy was too upset to take satisfaction in the suggestion that Richard would have chosen to stay with her over Belinda and their unborn child.

She thought of Richard, now. She'd always assumed they'd have this meeting with Belinda together. She now felt stupid that she'd left him to come here, honoring the request to come alone by telling him she was going to photograph some things close by. Finally, she asked, "Don't you want to see him at all?"

"No," Belinda said, her voice almost brutal.

"What if he wants to see you?" Joy asked, surprised to find herself more disappointed than relieved by this response. "Doesn't what he wants matter?"

Belinda's features suddenly looked distorted as if they didn't know where to settle on her face. "It's better that he doesn't see me. He won't understand."

For the first time this afternoon, Joy thought, what this woman had just said made sense. "Nobody would understand," she said flatly.

Yet Joy knew that she wanted Richard to see Belinda, see her in this new reality, see the woman she was rather than some glorified image he might still have enshrined in his mind. Whatever emotional price she herself had to pay, he had to close the book.

Belinda looked at her and said quietly, "There's just one thing. You must take her next week."

"Next week?" Joy knew this was a stupid question, but she also couldn't actually believe that they would finalize this process in a mere few days. She wasn't prepared. Belinda looked okay, after all. Maybe in a few more months. Maybe they could go home and come back to take the girl, then. Maybe Belinda would improve, and they wouldn't have to take the child at all. It was possible that the doctors were wrong.

"Yes," Belinda said. "Next week."

"Why so soon?"

Belinda didn't answer but reached for something behind her on the sofa and pulled out a small manila envelope that she placed on the coffee table. "Her birth certificate and her passport," she said. "The passport is new. She's never needed one before. She's never traveled out of the country. Richard is listed as the father on the birth certificate. Everything is in order."

Joy stared at her, desperately groping for some way to respond. She found herself resenting Richard being listed as the father, and yet that's what he was. How else to do what they were heading so inevitably toward doing?

She took a deep breath and paused for a moment. When she spoke, she heard her voice as if it were coming from outside of herself. "Then I must ask you for a favor. Richard needs to see you. I won't come with him, but you need to see the father of your child."

Belinda sighed, slow and deep. Her eyes were misty now, her cheeks seemingly more sunken. She nodded, slowly. "I'll see him. Only Karma mustn't be here when I go. I'm—I'm struggling each day. I don't have long but I can't let her see me—"

Joy broke in, "But it may not come to that."

Belinda closed her eyes. "It will come to that." She stayed quiet for a bit. Then she said, without opening her eyes but with a faint smile, "There's no such thing as death. It's an illusion."

There was the abrupt sound of a door opening downstairs and a shrill yelp. This time it was the unmistakable voice of a child.

Belinda's eyes shone. "She's home."

Joy froze. She wasn't ready. Too much had just been thrown at her. She'd give anything to be sucked out of this room into oblivion, but it was too late.

There was the sound of a child's protesting whine downstairs and a muffled response from Aysha.

Belinda started to chuckle as if none of their previous

conversation had taken place. "Aysha makes her drink a glass of warm milk as soon as she gets home from school and before having any sweets. I'm way too lenient in that regard."

Joy barely heard Belinda because her heart was pumping so fast. She'd imagined this moment countless times: how it would be to see Richard's daughter for the first time, how she, Joy, would welcome the child into their lives. As much as she'd tried to prepare herself, she was now practically crumpling at the thought of the girl.

"I'm not sure . . ." she stammered. "I'm not sure I can do this. I'm sorry. I'm just . . ."

Belinda had gotten up and was now standing beside her, taking her hand which had started to tremble.

Joy pushed herself up from the sofa. Next to her, Belinda seemed small and fragile, but Joy felt she was the one who would topple over if Belinda let go.

Belinda placed her other hand over Joy's. "She's only a child," she said gently. "And she already loves you. You are Mama Joy to her. I've talked to her about you. I've told her that you'll take her to some special places, the skyscrapers in New York and the rides at Disneyland. That's why she's arguing with Aysha downstairs. She wants to come right up to see you."

Joy felt utterly inept as she hung on to the hand of this frail woman who was practically pleading with her, bequeathing her most cherished love to her. What did she, Joy, know about motherhood? Not a damn thing. She fought back tears, trying to look strong and standing as straight and rigid as she could to support the sick mother.

"How?" Joy stammered. "How can you just give her up like this?"

Belinda's eyes reddened. "I don't have a choice," she whispered. Underneath that serene smile that Joy found so confounding was finally the devastating truth.

"I feel we're stealing her from you—"

"No," Belinda cut her off. "You are her parents. She only came through me."

Joy stared at her. Was she actually supposed to believe this? Did Belinda believe this?

"There's no such thing as separation or even death," Belinda said calmly. "It's an illusion. I'm not leaving her. I'll always be with her—just differently." She sighed aloud as if unable to contain her sadness. "It's the end for me but a new beginning for you." She smiled weakly. "I hope you'll find it in your heart to love her. Only, will you make sure she doesn't forget me?"

Joy's tears were streaming freely now. She stifled a sob. She thought of her anger a moment ago and of the past few years, how she'd have gladly strangled her husband's former lover with her own hands when Richard had first confessed their relationship. Now, she'd give anything to reverse Belinda's trajectory, to breathe life into her as she'd breathed it into the dummy years ago in a CPR class. Now, all she could do was shake her head. "We'll never let her forget you," she said. "Never."

The door burst open and a small body with a mass of black curls bounded noisily across the room and into Belinda's open arms. Joy watched as the mother and daughter held each other a few moments and giggled as if at some hilarious, private joke.

After hugs and kisses, Belinda slowly straightened up. She wiped her eyes and gently cupped the child's dainty chin in her palm. Looking into the small ruddy face adoringly, she asked, "My love, Karma, do you know who this nice lady is?"

The child stared up at her mother a long moment, then nodded shyly and, with no further prompting or any sign of surprise to find her mother and a stranger both in tears, she turned to Joy and flung her arms around her hips. "Mama Joy!"

Amazed, Joy hugged the child back, caressing her tight curls. She could hardly believe this was happening, that she was actually feeling the live child in her arms. The small warm head, smelling of the heat outside, pressed against her thighs as Joy's heart raced again; but this time she held the child close in her arms, bending to kiss the top of her head as if she'd always done so. She gulped back a sob.

When she glanced back up, she saw that, behind Belinda's tears, was now what seemed to be a grateful radiance, as if she'd just completed a mission, as if this were the way it was meant to be, the way she'd always dreamed it would be.

Joy felt herself mouth the words "I love you" into the child's hair. "I love you," she mouthed again, knowing that she meant these words even more for the courageous woman standing beside her.

Kairouan

RICHARD

28

They were in a taxi on their way to Kairouan, Tunisia's holy city.

It had grown noticeably hotter these past few days, so it seemed absurd to be heading inland, away from the cooling breeze of the sea. Richard was going along with Joy's wish to visit Kairouan today because it was just two hours away and had two notable mosques she wanted to see.

It did feel good to get beyond the commercial hubbub of Hammamet and into a more pristine countryside of olive and citrus groves bordered by thick cactuses. Farm women sat on the side of the road in the shade of small swaths of cloth draped over poles, their baskets of fruit for sale next to them. As the taxi passed one of these makeshift stands, the driver pulled up to the vendor and bought several freshly peeled cactus fruits, which he offered Joy and Richard. Although Joy seemed to enjoy the knobby texture of the reddish lumps, Richard found the hard seeds too numerous to spit out and yet uncomfortable to swallow. His jaw was better this morning, but he didn't want to risk biting down on anything hard.

"'Kairouan was founded in 670 AD,'" Joy read from the guidebook. "'It's considered so holy that seven trips here equal a pilgrimage to Mecca.'"

Richard nodded. "I have an odd feeling that I'm on a pilgrimage of my own."

These past few days, some kernel had sprouted within him, a recognition that his life was changing for something entirely new. He felt as though he'd previously been submerged under water and was now resurfacing as a vitally different person. He'd never quite felt that way before and was quite exhilarated by this new awareness.

Although it was only mid-morning, the heat was stifling, and the car's air-conditioning barely reached the back seat. His feet inside his shoes were hot, and his perspiration was starting to seep through his shirt. "We should have come last week when it was cooler," he said, rolling down his window.

"Well, mosques are always breezy," Joy said, clearly not minding the heat.

"When you're sensitive to something—" he began.

"Honey, you worry about heat like you do traffic. It's never as bad as you anticipate."

He left this alone. Joy always made this correlation with his intolerance of traffic, but despite what she said, the traffic was usually every bit as bad as he predicted. But she was right about his paranoia. He dreaded traffic jams long before he saw them. They just happened not to bother *her*. She could sit in traffic indefinitely, listening to music, idly thinking of her students' papers or some article she was writing, impervious to the delays that drove him rabid. He wished some of her blind optimism would rub off on him.

He closed his eyes, sporadically dozing for the remainder of the warm ride. He dreamed briefly of Joy strolling down a scorching beach with a man who looked oddly familiar. He felt a brief wave of panic.

It's what had been puzzling him these past few days—her recent aloofness. Maybe that distance was her way of dealing with all the waiting, but it seemed she suddenly just wanted to be on her own. Just yesterday afternoon, she told him she wanted to go shopping on the street next to the hotel and needed to go alone. She wanted to wander around and not worry about whether he was bored, she had told him. She just wanted to look at stuff and take a few pictures.

At first, he objected to her going, but she assured him she wasn't going to the *medina*, only to the tourist shops nearby. He didn't particularly want to browse in the shops while she zeroed in on whatever minutiae she found fascinating to photograph, but he did think it odd that she didn't want him to join her, as if she intentionally wanted to escape him. He wanted to remind her to be careful, but he knew she'd say he was making too much of his sense of the unsettled political atmosphere. He'd spent the afternoon in the room, reading and somewhat worried, relaxing only when she finally came back several hours later looking tired but settled, briefly showing him some of her shots. Nothing more was said of the afternoon, but it still surprised him that she'd wanted some time away from him.

They arrived in Kairouan shortly past noon and were let off at the town's historic Great Mosque. The recent change of government had obviously taken a toll on tourism. As in Carthage, except for some schoolboys and their male teacher, he and Joy were the only visitors in the spacious courtyard.

Although Joy was appropriately draped in the scarf, long sleeves, and long skirt required for women entering Muslim holy sites, the guard at the door emphatically told them they couldn't enter this sanctuary. Its importance meant it was designated for

Muslims only. They could glance in through the open doorways, the guard said, but go no farther.

"Why didn't they tell us back at the hotel?" Richard said, fanning himself with the guidebook.

Joy seemed unperturbed. "Honey, never mind. Come here and see this."

He walked to where she was standing and peered in through the massive doors. Rather than the vibrant carpets richly coating the floors of most mosques they had visited, the vast floor of this one was covered by simple straw mats, giving the immense chamber an ambiance of bare, subdued calm.

Even more unusual, the ancient structure was supported by a virtual forest of tall, mismatched marble columns, some Corinthian, some Roman, and others like the starker Punic ones they'd seen in Carthage.

"The columns are all different," he remarked.

Joy nodded. "They supposedly used looted ones of different pagan eras from all over."

He studied the columns' non-uniformity and felt unexpectedly uplifted. Although the columns' disunity was evident, the room radiated a profound cohesiveness and harmony, proof that differences could mesh. So why shouldn't they? The three of them—he, Joy, and the child?

After they were done looking, they were driven a few minutes away to the smaller mosque of *Sidi Sahb,* Friend of the Prophet. This mosque was pretty and airy, and light years away in mood and style from the lofty austerity of the first one. Unlike the larger mosque, this shrine to a seventh-century holy man was open to all, and there were already plenty of locals praying or milling about as well as a small group of tourists taking a tour.

Joy was glancing up at the ornamented ceiling of the main prayer hall. "It's like being inside a wedding cake."

He gazed up at the lacy white plaster molding that resembled edible curls of white frosting, as did so much of the plasterwork of Tunisia's historic buildings.

By contrast, the walls of the hallways and of the outer courtyard were done in colorful flower-motif tiles. As Joy had predicted, the corridors were cool, and they found a bench facing the central courtyard and sat down.

Despite the bustling worshipers, there was a gentle peacefulness about the place that gripped him. He'd been needing this kind of solace these past few days. For the first time he was beginning to understand Joy's fascination with temples. It wasn't the sanctuary, as she'd once explained, but the stillness within oneself that the sanctuary brought about. He reached over and touched her hand, not wanting to disturb her reverie, yet somehow wanting to atone for his own dumb lack of appreciation all these years. It had taken nearly a lifetime for awareness to sink in.

She glanced at him and smiled, although she soon seemed to be journeying to some other place in her head.

In the courtyard garden before them, a young mother in a long robe and headscarf was washing a toddler from a spigot in the center fountain used for prayer ablutions. The child seemed at home in the mosque, and his mother didn't seem concerned when he wandered off to explore the hallways, the safety of unattended children perhaps not such a worry here. Richard pictured Belinda bathing her daughter like that, tenderly rinsing the child's face.

He inhaled abruptly. "You realize we're on the Dark Continent?"

Joy smiled. "That refers to sub-Saharan Africa, Rich."

"It's still Africa." He added, "I don't feel so good today."

She turned to him. "Why?"

He shook his head.

"Physically?"

"Everything."

"Still that toothache?" she asked.

"Damn it, honey! Just listen a minute."

She stared at him, a ripple of alarm in her eyes at the sharp edge in his voice.

His snapping at her surprised even him. "I'm sorry. I just wish things could be different between us. I'm so freaking tired." He looked back at the courtyard where the young mother was now wrapping a diaper around the child, who squirmed on the grass for the changing. "I just want . . . Joy, I just feel you're hiding something from me."

She looked surprised.

"I do," he said.

She half glanced at him as though to avoid any accusation he might be about to hurl at her.

"Rich, we've been making the best of things just like we agreed. What's wrong?"

"You. *You*." His voice rose in agitation. "Don't think I don't see it."

The young mother, now holding her child again, glanced over at them, probably wondering what vacationing tourists could have to argue about. He almost envied the man *she* was married to. She seemed so firmly anchored to her baby, to an accepted reality that seemed to elude Joy, who remained so often buried in her literature and fantasy.

Then an image of Belinda flashed before him. She was laughing as she embraced her daughter. *Their* daughter.

"See what?" Joy said, looking confused.

He returned to her. "Well, for one thing, what you said the other day on the beach about Gerald Ford, about women wanting excitement but settling for security. You were thinking of me."

"No, I wasn't, Rich. I was generalizing."

"You meant *us*, though."

"It was a flippant thing to say. Don't let it bother you."

He patted her knee. "Look. It just makes me think. You must feel you've wasted your life with me. I'm not adventurous, not a thrill-seeker. Remember how you used to call me a stick-in-the-mud? Well, maybe I am. You must feel bored out of your mind half the time."

She looked at him with an odd expression. "Of course not. Don't be silly."

"I know you always wished I was some other way."

"I don't know what you're talking about."

"You're right about my being uncomfortable taking risks. You could have ended up with—"

"Richard, you're wrong. I chose to be with you. And I'm happy we're back together."

"Are you?"

"I wouldn't be here if I weren't happy with you."

He exhaled. "Shit! Is it so impossible to understand each other after so many years? I've been trying my best to deepen my relationship with you, make it more meaningful—to both of us. What the hell is love, anyway? A commitment to stick it out together year in and year out despite obvious incompatibility? You're always yearning for adventure, and I automatically seek safety. I know you're disappointed." He sighed. "I just don't know how to fix things between us. I'm sorry."

She was looking off to the side now, but he thought he saw her eyes moisten. She touched his arm. "Rich, I have no idea what's riling you, but please stop. Just think how fortunate we are and how beautiful this place is. I *am* happy with you, and we *are* compatible. You *are* what I need."

"What you *need?* What does that mean, for Christ's sake?"

She looked uneasy. "Honey, whatever you are, it's what makes me feel good about life, about myself. Why would you even think that I want to be with somebody else?"

Her words gave him a moment of calm, but the rocky waters surged again. He didn't know why he was suddenly so confused and afraid.

"I want to be who you love, Joy. I want to bring out your *passion.*"

"You do bring out my passion."

"How?"

"Well," her eyebrows rose as if to pull invisible answers from the crown of her head, "I like to travel with you, and we enjoy the same foods."

He shook his head. "I'm not talking about the damn trips or food. I'm not talking about the pseudo-life of hopping from hotel to hotel. We're in this for the long haul, Joy. I want to see your eyes light up, and I want you to be drawn to me like you used to be."

"I *am* drawn to you."

"I don't feel it. It just seems like we fuck without feeling much of the time. I can't reach you. I can't get past the damn fucking to whoever you really are."

"Shh!" she whispered, looking mortified.

He could see that she was distressed by his sudden mood and by his language in this place of worship. He heaved a sigh. What the hell difference did it make where he said it, but then, where better to be honest than in a place of worship?

"Well," she said quickly, as if afraid he might erupt again, "I don't know, Rich. I didn't know you felt that way. You've changed. I've changed. Sometimes we change too much. We lose some of the chemistry, I guess." She paused, obviously trying to choose her words carefully. "We've had a lot to cope with recently. We're charting a new course. Sometimes that takes time, Rich. But we're adjusting, and we're moving forward. Just be patient. Things will work out."

She seemed unflappable, that wistful look that was about to give her away only moments ago evaporating. Again, he thought, she was in total damn control.

"I feel lost," he said quietly.

She said nothing, only stared ahead.

"You might have naturally chosen somebody else if you hadn't come back to me, Joy," he pushed on. "Maybe I limit you. Maybe with somebody else you could do more of what you really want. You asked me yourself the other day why we choose the mates we end up with. Well, I can't help feeling you could have had some-body else, somebody who could give you what you want and not put you through what I have."

She stared at him, plainly annoyed. "Rich, why are you so down on yourself today? And what on earth are you suggesting?"

He sighed. He honestly didn't know why he felt so crappy; and what, indeed, was he suggesting? That she leave him? Now?

"I'm just hit with these big questions," he said.

She sighed. "Well, there are no big answers, Rich. We just have to live each day and do the best we can. Be grateful and happy for it all."

He was starting to get irritated by her stoic tone. She was starting to sound like Belinda, living in the moment rather than securing a future. Maybe it was a female trait. "I am grateful, Joy, but it doesn't stop me from questioning."

"Rich," she said, turning to look directly into his eyes, "most things are just a matter of perception and aren't real unless we make them so. We have enough drama going on at the moment without adding to it. Just decide to be happy and forget the rest."

He stared at her. "Well, some things *are* a matter of perception, but other things are real. I can't pretend they're not, Joy. I'm not making things up. You've been acting funny, lately."

She shook her head. "It's all in how you choose to see it."

He exhaled noisily, practically throwing his hands in the air in exasperation. That was the kind of inscrutable answer that drove him crazy, but the last thing he wanted here, he decided, was a quarrel or even a heart-to-heart—or her telling him to relax or to see a shrink. "It's the heat," he said. "Let's zip through this place, then have lunch so we can get back."

"The thing is, Rich . . ." She stopped herself.

He waited a few seconds. "Yeah?"

"It's just something that occurs to me sometimes. About us. About you, mainly."

"Tell me."

"You seem uncomfortable in your own skin. You seem to feel that the world is out to get you. I never feel that way."

He didn't answer her. It sounded ridiculous, and yet somehow it might just be the most accurate thing she'd said to him. He couldn't stand feeling disconnected, and he was often not as emotionally self-sufficient as she. And he did tend toward pessimism.

"And . . ." She hesitated a moment.

"Yes?"

"Maybe it's just not possible to have a partner who fulfills us in all ways. Maybe we should just find happiness where we can instead of obsessing about what's missing."

He could see sadness in her eyes. His heart skipped as he braced himself for what might come next.

"In a way, Rich . . . we're all just trying to grow up in life," she said. "Don't take things so seriously."

He stared at her. "Joy, I can't help taking things seriously. That's who I *am*. Otherwise, I'd give up."

"Give up what?"

He wasn't sure whether she was genuinely curious or playing with him. "Give up on *us*."

"Why on earth would you give up on us, honey?" she asked. "Why can't you just be kinder to yourself? Why not just recognize that we're not perfect, not as people or as a couple, and just accept that? You're way too hard on yourself these days, and it makes things harder on both of us."

He sighed. "I'm obviously anxious. And I dread getting old, especially now."

She laughed. "You're not old. Anyway, isn't that the point? To live into old age?"

He shrugged. "I worry about getting infirm."

"Well, you're not going to get infirm if you keep active."

"Well, there'll come a time when—I need to stay strong for the child. Damn, Joy, our entire lives are about to change. I'm having these existential struggles, fears for my health I never had before. I even read the obituaries in the paper, which I never used to do. I can't believe you're so calm about all this."

She took a deep breath. "Rich, we'll just face it like we do other things. This is going to be new for both of us. I'm anxious, too, but embrace the change. Become a better man for it. Embrace this new life we've been given."

They sat in silence a few minutes, then Joy said, "Look at it this way. We constantly discard our old selves and give birth to the new people we become each day. Just think that you're being reborn every day into a stronger, better you."

He continued to stare at her, intrigued. He wasn't used to hearing her expound so philosophically, and again he thought he heard traces of Belinda. He sure the hell hoped she wasn't veering in that direction. Right now, he needed solidity, not airy whimsies.

She must have read his thoughts because she smiled. "Look, Rich. Let's just focus on the good stuff. Let's be kind to ourselves and to each other. If we don't reach out and help each other, and help others in the process, our lives won't mean a thing in the long run. Let's try to be more content and less harsh."

"Am I being harsh?"

"Oh, God," she said with a laugh.

"I'm serious."

"There you go again," she said. "Drop the serious part and just *be* for a while. Enjoy all this."

She spread her arms as though to embrace the vibrant garden and courtyard and the mosque's jewel-like walls around them. "Just *be*, Rich. Close your eyes and *enjoy* this perfect moment while we have it." She shut her own eyes and lifted her chin, a soft smile meandering across her lips. Like a succulent sponge, she seemed to be soaking in every ounce of their surroundings. He started to wish he'd taken her advice years ago and taken up yoga as she had, something to get him out of his damn head all the time.

"What if," she continued softly, "there is no meaning to any of life other than sustaining our existence through kindness and love? I've spent my career trying to find meaning through stories, and I've concluded that we create stories to make the mystery of life less frightening." She looked at him closely. "Remember, we're going to be just fine. No matter what."

Although what he really wanted to do now was lean over and kiss her moist lips in gratitude, he took a deep breath and tried to do as she said, to think of nothing, to let go and just *be*. He closed his eyes and listened to the echoes of the hallways, to the murmurings of those strolling and praying. He repeated Joy's mantra to himself: We're going to be just fine.

He remained totally still and tried to ride that warm breeze of contentment that seemed to float just below Joy's body and carry her off.

He was aware of his feet on the ground but tried to concentrate on his breath instead, as she seemed to be doing. He steered himself to thoughts of how lucky he was to have her, to have an established, workable life. He thought of how lucky he was to have found love with her, imperfect though it might be, and also to have had his brief, intoxicating time with Belinda. How lucky he was to have a child he would soon get to see and hold and take into his life. It all seemed like a maddening dream to him, but Joy seemed to be accepting it much more readily.

Maybe that was it. Maybe love was simply about embracing the imperfect. To just *be*, as she said. Maybe life was just a series of gains and losses, like business, and you lost one account but got another. They'd lost one child but were gaining another. They'd lost one love but were now building another. Couldn't he have faith that they were all going to be just fine at the end of the day? Wasn't life, as Joy intimated, more about being content than achieving objectives?

He glanced at her, a tender ache welling in him at how her lower lip jutted out in a slightly pensive pout.

"Sweetheart, you're damn sexy when you're preaching," he whispered, the desire to kiss her now overwhelming.

She opened her eyes wide and stifled a giggle. "We're in a mosque, Rich!"

"Damn it all, you turn me on," he whispered, fighting off the urge to slide his hand up her leg and under her loose skirt.

A coy smile played on her lips. "Later," she said.

"I'm not sure I can wait," he said, but he forced himself back into the quiet of her gentle assurances, soothed by her hint of excitement to come.

Then, as if in a dream, Joy's voice came to him. "I've seen her, Rich."

At first, he didn't comprehend what she meant, and then he turned to look straight at her.

She nodded.

"Belinda?" he stared at her in disbelief.

She nodded again.

He felt his chest tighten. "When?"

She took a breath. "That woman who called our hotel a few nights ago to tell us Belinda would be in touch soon? Well, she did call. You were in the shower."

"Belinda called?"

"She told me she wanted to see me. She was emphatic I not tell you."

"Why the hell not?"

She ignored his question. "It was yesterday when I said I was going to the market. I went to her home, instead. She'd just come back from the hospital. She goes in every few weeks for blood transfusions."

"Joy, why the hell didn't you tell me?"

"I wanted to, but it wasn't my decision."

Belinda's face, smeared in blood, flashed before him. He ran his hand through his hair, pushing the image away. "Well? How is she?"

"She's . . ." she said, staring at him as if searching for his feelings in his eyes.

"Yes?"

"She's very sick."

"Can't I see her? I mean, I just want to reassure her that we'll take good care of her child." He still couldn't bear to say "our child" in front of Joy.

Her eyes clouded. "She wasn't so sure—but I insisted—"

"I have to see her!"

Joy was silent, as if she'd been struck.

His pulse started to race. What if Belinda had changed her mind as they'd feared? "And the—child?" he asked.

She nodded.

"She'll let us have her?"

"Yes."

He sighed and closed his eyes, relieved that at least that hadn't changed.

"You know what she said?" Joy's voice now cracked.

He opened his eyes.

"She said she had the baby for us, for you and me. She wanted us to have a child."

His mouth opened but no words would come out.

"Rich, she said she'd gotten pregnant for *us*. She'd always meant for us to have Karma and to raise her." Joy's words gushed quickly as if she was afraid she wouldn't be able to complete what she wanted to say. "She said she was afraid you might leave me, and so she went away."

He continued to stare at her, trying to make sense of her words.

"I was shocked and angry," Joy said. "I thought she was some kind of lunatic. But I couldn't stay mad for long. She wanted us to have a baby."

He exhaled in disbelief. Belinda had a baby for them? He felt a searing in his core. What on earth had she been thinking?

"And, Rich?" Joy said, her voice trembling.

He fought back his shock. "Yes?"

She swallowed. "She's put all her faith in us. I never expected to feel how I did. I felt myself changing in that room. I was beside myself with rage and confusion, and I couldn't imagine anybody doing this just out of the blue, but she was totally sincere. And then when I saw Karma and realized what Belinda must be feeling at the thought of leaving her, I just broke down. I just hope

I—we—can live up to this." She wiped away her tears. She shook her head and then whispered, "And Karma—Karma is beautiful."

Richard took a deep breath, almost choking on his own shock.

They sat in silence as though the very memory of how to speak had left them both. He desperately wanted to reach out and hold Joy tight, to keep her close and safe, but he knew he must wait until they left the mosque.

It was Joy who placed her hand on his knee. "We should go."

29

The taxi driver pulled up to a familiar, low building on the outskirts of Kairouan that they'd passed that morning as they entered the town. Richard remembered it from the baskets of garish plastic flowers flanking the entrance. Now, two huge tour buses were parked in front, the first they'd seen all day.

"No, no," he abruptly told the driver, in no mood to be crammed into a hall with a gaggle of tourists. "We want a quiet restaurant. Tunisian."

"This Tunisian," the driver said, looking to him and then to Joy for approval.

Richard shook his head. "No shows, please. Just food."

"Best couscous here," the driver replied stubbornly.

"He probably knows what he's talking about," Joy intervened, obviously aware that Richard's irritation at the driver had more to do with his anxiety about her recent revelation.

"It's a tourist trap," Richard protested. "Just look at the buses."

"There may not be anything better around," she said patiently. "It'll take us a while to get back to Hammamet."

He followed her out of the car, sending a warning frown the driver's way. If it were up to him, they'd go straight back to Hammamet. In all the upheaval of the past hour, food was the last thing on his mind, anyway. He couldn't bear the idea of sitting still long enough to finish a meal. He just wanted to find a way to call Belinda and then go to her home, whether she wanted to talk to him or not. He had never had a proper goodbye and had not been able to ask her about the child, or why she had run rather than tell him she was pregnant. Although he was happy with Joy now, he needed to hear Belinda's voice. He wanted to hold her, to feel her warmth, her life, in his arms, to hold on to their past wild joy together one last time before she was gone forever.

Inside, a large room was set up with tables placed in a wide semi-circle. To one side was a group already being served. Germans most likely, he thought, to judge by the plentiful bottles of beer.

A waiter ushered the two of them to an empty table on a quieter side of the room. Colorful arabesque lanterns flooded patterns of blue and red onto white tablecloths. Richard managed to loosen up somewhat. The place was better than he had expected.

They each ordered a glass of Tunisian red wine and the special on the menu, *salade Niçoise* and couscous.

"Not bad," Joy said, in that way of hers that meant, although she wasn't gloating, that she had been right to insist they come in.

She went to the restroom to freshen up, and he closed his eyes, sinking into his chair and stretching his legs.

Karma. Belinda. He sighed. Could all this be happening to him? Joy and Belinda actually meeting? It was once what he had guiltily fantasized about, what he'd secretly wanted in a perverse way when he'd been torn between the two of them. Now things had changed. His obscene wish was being oddly played out in a quite unforeseeable and heartbreaking way.

Now that Joy had seen Belinda and was obviously smitten by Karma, it was as if, for the first time since learning of his daughter's existence, he'd been given permission to feel his love for her, a father's love for his child. My daughter, he thought.

His chest lurched. He couldn't wait to see her, his arms already feeling her softness as he imagined giving her a tender embrace. Even more, he wanted to see Belinda, wanted to reassure her of how good a father he'd be, assure her that all would be taken care of. Although he was still stupefied by her motivations for having the child, and at times almost wished he had never set eyes on her in the first place, he also wanted to thank her for this colossal, incomprehensible gift.

A man dressed in a traditional *jellaba* robe, a burgundy fez on his head, strode to the center of the dining room. He informed the guests in German, then in English, that there would be entertainment.

"What'd I tell you?" Richard said as Joy returned and sat back down. "A tourist trap."

"Relax, honey," Joy said, chuckling. Her face was fresh and glowing, and she smelled of the jasmine perfume she'd bought in the market that first day.

He folded his arms. "I hope this doesn't take all night."

The waiter brought their salads, and shortly thereafter more waiters emerged from a doorway carrying a huge tray with a large earthenware urn balanced on it. The waiters stood with the tray in the center of the room. The man in the fez, who Richard gathered was the master of ceremonies, began to announce something in German to the beer-drinking crowd, who laughed and clapped loudly.

"They're so damned happy all the time," Richard said. "Obviously overjoyed to get away from the cloudy Rhineland."

Joy smiled. "At least they have a sense of humor. We can all use—"

A loud crash interrupted her.

Kairouan

Richard lunged forward to protect her and scanned the room, his first instinct being that it had been a gunshot or bomb, that the country had imploded as he'd feared it would. He'd watched footage on CNN that morning of extremists bursting into a shopping mall in Cairo. He could imagine this room being overrun by gunmen. As Americans, they might be targets.

Then he saw that it was the master of ceremonies who'd just swung down a wooden cane to smash the urn on the tray held by the waiters. A large crack in the pot was oozing something red. The German audience emitted a gasp of appreciation at the culinary explosion.

Growing impatient with the theatrics, Richard thought he saw the old German from their hotel beach sitting at one of the tables. It had to be him—the bald head and hunched shoulders, the foolish grin.

Presently, the waiters brought Richard and Joy each a plate of couscous along with bowls of a vegetable stew in a tomato sauce from the cracked pot. The enticing aroma of cumin pierced his nostrils, but having finished half of his salad, Richard felt full.

He looked at Joy, whose eyes were feasting on both couscous and the stew. He regarded his own dish of couscous without touching it.

Another young man, this one looking like a dervish in long hair, baggy trousers, and a belted tunic, now joined the master of ceremonies in the center of the room and immediately pulled something out of a bag tied to his waist. Although Richard couldn't see what it was, he guessed it was something live from the way the man began to tilt his arm as if the thing were crawling on his skin.

"Oh," Joy said, halting a spoonful of couscous before it reached her mouth. "It's a scorpion, for God's sake."

Richard strained to see what the young man, who had his

back to them, was doing. The Germans had the full view of whatever he was showing, and they seemed fascinated.

Richard, suddenly nauseated by the sight of food, pushed away his plate.

Joy looked surprised. "You don't like it?"

"I can't eat."

"But you barely tasted—"

"I can't."

She stared at him as she deposited her own spoonful of couscous into her mouth. "You've got to try this. It's just delicious," she said, a look of rapture on her face.

He took a breath but said nothing.

Then her demeanor changed, and she said, "Rich, what did you mean earlier when you said you wished things were different between us?"

He stared at her but didn't answer. Although he heard her, he was feeling too uncomfortable to embark on their saga right now. He leaned back in his chair, trying to relieve the pressure in his gut. He felt stuffed. Maybe something in the salad had been bad.

"Are you okay?" she asked, looking concerned.

He nodded, although he was aware that he was starting to sweat. He tried to stand to relieve the discomfort, but he slumped back down into his chair.

She gasped, scrambling to get to him. "Honey!"

He could hear noises coming from the other side of the room. He looked at the master of ceremonies, then at the man in the baggy clothes, dangling something into his mouth. *"Jesus,"* he muttered.

She was by his side now, her lips pale with panic. "Honey, what's wrong?"

He tried to catch his breath. "Did he just eat that scorpion?"

"Honey, look at me," she pleaded, grabbing his face and turning it toward her.

He glanced at her, obeying. His Joy. His Madonna. Or was she Marilyn Monroe?

"You know," he heard himself say, and then he tried to take a slow, shallow breath but felt the pain squeeze his belly and his jaw. "I think I'm having a heart attack, Joy."

"Oh, God! Rich, don't!"

"Joy," he said, taking another shallow breath. Rather than pain, an excruciating rush of love for her surged through him this time.

"Aspirin!" she cried out. "Honey, do you have any aspirin?" She was looking about frantically. "Does anyone have an aspirin?"

Her voice was coming from far away although he could see her right beside him. Her eyes flew about like crazed bees as she tried to get someone's attention. She turned back to him. "Rich, don't leave me here!"

He took another breath, "Joy—call—"

He didn't know how long it was before faces began to hover over him and he heard loud shouting in Arabic. Joy was repeating his name. She was cradling his head in her arms as more faces peered down at him and more voices shouted in loud, guttural spurts, a jumble of tones he couldn't comprehend.

Joy was drying the sweat from his brow with a napkin. He looked up at her, surprised by her frightened scowl, and reached up to touch her cheek. He shut his eyes and felt time tick by in a sharp blade of panic.

"Joy," he whispered.

"Hold on, Rich, honey," she pleaded. "They're getting an ambulance. Just hold on!"

He nodded, wanting to obey her, but it was so comfortable to simply close his eyes and let himself be enveloped in her jasmine-scented lap, her soft thighs that seemed to cradle him and gently coax his fear out of him.

"Joy?"

"Honey?" She frantically stroked his cheek, her hand trembling.

He reached up and tried to lift the hair off her neck. "Am I Gerald Ford?"

She looked confused. "What?"

"Ford. Plain Joe."

"No, never! Oh, honey, don't talk now. Just breathe slow and deep. Just rest easy."

"Joy?"

"Yes?" she practically wailed.

"I'll always love you."

She fastened her eyes on him as if to keep him from slipping away. "I love you, too, Rich."

Through the pain in his chest, Richard felt himself smile. "Joy, life's a hotel. You know that?"

Joy nodded absently, still looking frantic.

Isn't that what Belinda had once said? *It's all just temporary. We're all waiting in this hotel, waiting for our lives to start, waiting to be with the one we love, waiting for our children to be born. Life is meaningless. A game to play.*

Nothing is real unless we make it real. That was Joy just a while ago. God, these women knew everything! They'd worked their magic on him.

He felt his sweat under her cool fingers. "Joy, we're all here for just a while. Just staying in this damn hotel. One big fucking hotel."

He realized more than ever just how true this was. No wonder Joy loved to travel. This was the real truth of life, fluttering from place to place like birds, exploring, in constant search of sustenance, of love, of *value* to their short, flimsy lives.

But Joy only stared at him as if not comprehending what he said, or else in total denial of it. "I don't know what you mean, Rich. Now, just look at me, honey. That's it. Help is coming."

"A hotel," he said again. "Life's all—" he stopped a second from the pressure in his chest, "temporary."

She stared into his eyes, narrowing her gaze. Then she shook her head. "No, Rich, no it's not temporary. Listen. Life is for a long time. You're going to be here for a long time. Remember what you said? We're in this together for the long haul. Isn't that what we're planning? Our little family? But I can't do it alone, honey. You have to help me."

He closed his eyes.

"Oh, God!" Joy stroked his head. "Rich . . . we're going to get you to a doctor."

The pain shot through him again. *Life is all temporary,* Belinda once said. *Nothing to get too serious about.*

Suddenly, another name thundered in his ears. *Karma. Karma! Damn!* What was going to happen now?

The child's face from the photograph planted itself more forcefully in his mind. Damn! Joy was right. For Karma, life wasn't short or temporary. Her entire life lay ahead of her, and he would be a major part of it—Joy, too. They had to get damn serious, and right away. They had to find a school, a bigger home . . . they had so much to learn.

He tried to lift his head. "Joy, we have to—need to do something about the girl. We need to tell Belinda."

Joy put her fingers gently on his lips. "Honey," she said, her lips quivering, "we'll take her next week."

He stared up at her.

She nodded rapidly. "You've got to hang in here. For me. For your daughter."

"Joy."

He shut his eyes. What was she saying? *How are we going to take the child if I—*

A dull ache throbbed above his stomach. He wanted to ask Joy more, but somehow he couldn't think. He tried instead to feel the space between her thighs under his head, a place so soft he never wanted to move.

"Come on, Rich," she whimpered. "Don't do this, now. Don't do this to me, honey. I need you. *We* need you. Where are they? Oh God, hurry!"

He tried to smile up at her through the tightening grip on his gut. He wanted her not to worry. He wasn't going to leave her. Ever. How could he? He couldn't imagine not being with her, couldn't now imagine all three of them *not* together.

He opened his mouth and took a breath, barely able to stand the pain. This was love. It had to be. They were in this together. For the long haul. We are going to be just fine, he thought.

Other faces were around him now, other voices shouting again.

"Joy, our passports—"

"Shh," she whispered through her tears. "They're in my purse. Don't talk."

Now a man was peering into his face, an old man. Richard stared up at him. He said something Richard didn't understand, something that sounded like German. Cool fingers intruded into Richard's mouth, forcing something under his tongue.

He heard Joy start to protest, then change her mind. "Thank you! Oh, thank you," she sobbed.

"Joy, is that the German—" he managed to say.

Joy placed her palm over his mouth. "Keep it under your tongue, honey! It's medicine from this nice man."

He craned his neck to see who she was looking at.

Words were flying above him again, giving advice, giving directions. French? German? Arabic?

He stared up at Joy, not wanting to lose sight of her face in the commotion.

A dense, marshmallow calm began to cascade over him, cradling each part of his body as gently as if he were a newborn. He shut his eyes. Through the numbness in his face he sensed her patting his cheek, repeating his name as though to keep him awake.

He opened his eyes. Several men in blue coats were bending over him, placing their hands under his armpits and knees.

"Honey," Joy said anxiously. "Let them lift you. We're on our way."

"Joy," he mumbled.

"Just keep the medicine under your tongue," she implored.

There were loud orders by the men in blue coats to one another. Cool hands were opening his shirt, pressing his chest. More orders.

He tried to surrender to the gentle contentment enveloping him. There was nothing but this warm flow ministering to him with such care, this current of bliss washing over him. He remembered that he was in the holy city, although he couldn't think of its name.

"I'm going to be okay?" he asked.

A hotel. It had taken him half his life to realize just how fleeting life was.

First and foremost, they had to arrange to see Belinda and pick up Karma. After that, they'd figure out the other details.

Where was Joy? He had to get out of this place! There was no time to lose.

The bleeping of the machine above him startled him. He vaguely remembered the voices talking loudly above him, reviving him from the sleep he'd so craved and was beginning to enjoy, his head in Joy's lap. There had been the clamoring of the paramedics moving him onto something cold and hard and transporting him. Even before that, the slipping of the tablet under his tongue had freed his chest of the awful pain that had gripped him just after he'd eaten. The next thing he knew he was fully alert and looking up into Joy's eyes as she spoke his name.

"You've had a heart attack, Rich," she'd said, sounding reassured now that they were surrounded by experts. "But you're going to be all right. The doctors here in the hospital used those pads on your chest to revive you. You're in the intensive care unit. They've put you on medication and an IV, so you need to sleep, now. I have to wait outside in the waiting room."

He looked at her, saw the relief in her eyes, and whispered, "Don't go. I love you."

She squeezed his hand. "I love you, too. I'll be right here. Just let them take care of you. I'll check in on you soon."

"Really?" he asked her. "You'll be here?" He had the feeling that time had stopped, that he was in a dream and when he woke up she would have faded, none of this real at all.

She looked at him strangely, and then smiled. "Yes, I'll be here. Always."

Now, finally, he heard her steps, hesitant and treading softly, but clearly hers. He saw her face in the doorway, and he knew they were going to be just fine.

END

Epilogue

This was the first night Karma had slept straight through without waking up from the hacking cough she had caught in preschool. It was normal for kids to pass it around, their pediatrician had assured them, especially at the start of winter.

Richard and Joy had tried to take heart at it not being unusual for children to sound as if they were coughing up their lungs at night, but every time they heard her, they couldn't help tiptoeing into her room to adjust her blanket, switch the direction of the humidifier to bring more moist air her way, or bend down and listen to her breathing. Joy had rubbed Vicks into Karma's chest, and Richard had suggested they put a warm washcloth on top for added steam, something his mother had done for him when he was a child and suffering from a cough. Although Joy was skeptical it would help, she had gone ahead and done it, probably more to ease Richard's worry than anything else.

"I'll take the next shift," she said to him. "I don't have an early class tomorrow. You need to sleep."

"Yeah," he said, "but wake me up if you need me or if she gets worse."

"She won't. The cough just flares up at night. You can tell it's almost gone because she's not wheezing now."

"You're the best," he said, leaning over to kiss her cheek. "You sure have a knack."

"It's just common sense."

"Mother's intuition," he said. "I like that." He dragged the cover

over his shoulder and fluffed up the pillow on either side of his head. She'd been teasing him these past few nights that his habit of sleeping with the pillow blocking out sound was a man's natural instinct of tuning out a baby's cries. But she was wrong. He wanted to hear every cry the child made.

He glanced at her, "We're doing good?"

She smiled and tilted her head in either direction as if to say so-so. "We're learning. Now, go to sleep."

He turned over a few times, but his natural habit of falling asleep as soon as his head hit the pillow now seemed to be a thing of the past. "Joy, I can't thank you enough."

"For what?"

"For doing this. For taking care of Karma—"

"She's our child," she quietly cut in.

He nodded. "Yes, she is."

"I don't think of her any other way."

"I know you don't," he said, "and that's why you're so special."

"I promised her mother, and I intend to keep that promise. She's an amazing kid. And I love her."

He nodded. Joy was incredible.

"And you enabled me to do something I wasn't sure would be possible," he said.

"What's that?"

He paused. "To tell her mother goodbye."

She was silent for a moment. "You needed it, and she did, too. And I needed it. We all did."

"Yeah," he said, remembering his half-hour meeting alone with Belinda in her home that Joy had arranged after he got out of the hospital, how he had held in his initial shock at Belinda's paleness and frailty, their brief time together with Karma when she had come in to meet him, leaving him both breathless and speechless, and then Belinda's insistence that he and Joy come back the following day to take

Epilogue

Karma. She wouldn't see them off tomorrow, she said, but Aysha, her caretaker, would be with Karma.

There had been a bittersweet moment when he instinctively stepped forward and embraced her, not as a lover, but as an incredible, elusive presence and memory he never wanted to lose. She felt unbearably light, like an empty casing, and for a moment he forgot himself and held her tighter as if he could will her to materialize into the woman he had held in those hotel rooms in New York. She seemed uncomfortable in his arms, however. She stiffened, as if to keep from hugging him back or allowing him to say anything more, and softly asked that he leave. Then, as he stepped away, she seemed to think better of it and smiled, almost becoming her old self. "Be happy," she said. "Life is meaningless without being happy. Make a happy life for all three of you, and that will make me happy."

He had nodded, aware that his lips were quivering from the emotion he was trying not to show.

"And please take care of yourself," she had said. "Get stronger. Karma needs you."

He had left in the taxi waiting outside.

When he and Joy had arrived the next morning, they were told that Belinda had been taken to the hospital. Karma was with Aysha, who gave them her suitcase. The old woman had drawn her shawl over her mouth to hide her distress as the three of them had left, the child sitting quietly between Joy and him in the taxi, looking happy enough to go with them.

In the three months they had been in New York, Karma had surprised them by adapting extremely well to her new school and environment. They had visited Disney World in Florida as Belinda had told Karma they would. She'd made friends at school and seemed to take to Joy as naturally as if she had always known her. Although she had asked several times about her other "mama," she didn't seem worried when they told her that Belinda was with Aysha in her other home far away.

He would see Belinda's bright sparkle in Karma's eyes whenever the child laughed, and he would feel his gut contract. Then he would remember Belinda's last words to him: Be happy.

"Be happy," Richard mumbled now, as he drifted into sleep.

"I am happy," Joy said, her hand resting softly on his shoulder.

Acknowledgments

I owe a ton of gratitude to all my excellent readers, editors, friends, and family who have helped me hone this manuscript from its first inception to its final form. Without you this book would not have been possible.

Thanks to my beloved 'Group' who have encouraged and helped me over the years and who read the manuscript along the way. Your friendship means the world. A particular thanks to Barbara Esstman and Ginnie Hartman for their invaluable input.

Thank you to Toni Werbell, Ann Patty, Margaret Herdeck, Caroline Upcher, Sandi Gelles-Cole, Steve Parolini, Michael McIrvin, Beth Bruno, and Sarah Aschenback who each helped steer this book forward.

A special thanks to Mary Claire Mahaney for her keen eye, invaluable input, and wonderful friendship. Your faith in this book bolstered me at a much needed time.

A warm thanks to Brooke Warner, Lauren Wise, and everyone at SWP for doing all that you do and for enabling this book to come to light. It has been a joy to work with you.

As always, my amazing family has been there to inspire me and offer their love and support over the years. You are special and amazing.